Praise for Bob

"A deeply moving, even event in American histo hardly bear to read on, yet could not put it down. J. M. Hochstetler and Bob Hostetler have brought the pathos and beauty of the American frontier to the page with rare authenticity and depth, crafting a story from their family legacy that will stay with you long after you finish. This historical novel is among the finest I have ever read."

—Laura Frantz, Christy Award finalist and author of
The Frontiersman's Daughter and *Love's Reckoning*

"There are few better ways to learn history than through the well-told story. *Northkill* is one such incredible story of my family torn asunder by massacre and kidnapping, barely patched back together by faith, fortitude, and sheer luck. Read this book if you love suspense and survival against the odds. Read this book to learn about the settling and unsettling of America at the time of the French and Indian War. Read this book to discover how one family's commitment to peace was tested beyond measure, whose legacy lives on in a trail of descendants who still ponder what the cost of such peaceful convictions mean for us today. Read this book!"

—James Hostetler Brenneman, President, Goshen College

"A riveting tale based closely on the life of the authors' eighteenth-century Amish ancestors during the French and Indian war, *Northkill* kept me up nights unable to stop reading. The terror, grief, and peril faced by Jakob Hochstetler and his extended family and community are unflinchingly portrayed. Some cling to the hope that even through the most tragic and bewildering of circumstances a loving God has not abandoned them. Others struggle with doubt. Every character's journey rings with authenticity. I look forward to the conclusion of this thrilling and absorbing story with great anticipation."

—Lori Benton, author of *Burning Sky*

"I am pleased that the authors of *Northkill* have preserved a sense of the ancestral struggles experienced by settlers of the early American Peace Church tradition. Their story drew me in by its vivid imagery and fluid writing style."

—Perry White, President, Bethel College

"*Northkill* is a thoroughly riveting tale all the more powerful because it's factually based on a real-life family drawn into actual events in American history. Once I began reading about the Hochstetler family's successful endeavors in taming a wild, unforgiving land, I couldn't put the story down. Their descent into tragedy through no fault of their own kept me reading, as well as aching for their suffering. When I finished the story, I longed for to know more about this remarkable, peace-loving family.

—Louise M. Gouge, award-winning author

"*Northkill* by Bob Hostetler and J. M. Hochstetler is a beautifully poignant tale as deep and varied as the frontier upon which it's set. Remarkable characters facing extraordinary tests of courage and faith make this story a *must* read!"

—Elizabeth Ludwig, author of *No Safe Harbor*

"J. M. Hochstetler and Bob Hostetler have created a story and a world that took hold of my imagination and interest. To know that this involves their own family history was compelling and heartbreaking. The research that has gone into this is astounding and will be a true delight for those who enjoy historical fiction."

—Rene Gutteridge, author of *Misery Loves Company*

"A masterpiece. *Northkill* stole my breath and my heart. With expert skill, the authors blend nail-biting suspense, blood-pumping drama and heartbreaking history into a tale that will both haunt and inspire. A book this rich and multi-dimensional deserves to be read more than once. The second book in the series can't come quickly enough for me!"

—Jocelyn Green, award-winning author
of the Heroines Behind the Lines Civil War Series

Northkill

Northkill

NORTHKILL ⬤ AMISH
BOOK ONE

BOB HOSTETLER

J. M. HOCHSTETLER

Elkhart, Indiana 46514

Northkill
Copyright © 2014 by J. M. Hochstetler and Bob Hostetler

Please address requests for information to:

Joan M. Shoup
Editorial Director
Sheaf House Publishers
1703 Atlantic Avenue
Elkhart, IN 46514
jmshoup@gmail.com

Library of Congress Control Number: 2013956175

ISBN: 978-1-936438-35-8 (softcover)

All scripture quotations in German are from Die Bibel nach der deutschen Übersetzung D. Martin Luthers. Quotations in English are from the King James Version of the Bible. The Lord's Prayer is taken from Matthew 6:9-13. Quotation on page 301 is 1 Peter 4: 12-13*a*.

Cover design and interior template by Marisa Jackson.

Cover image from iStockphoto.

Map by Jim Brown of Jim Brown Illustration.

14 15 16 17 18 19 20 21 22 23 — 10 9 8 7 6 5 4 3 2 1

PRINTED IN THE UNITED STATES OF AMERICA.

The Story

NORTHKILL IS A FICTIONAL ACCOUNT closely based on what is known of the true story of our ancestors. Jacob Hochstetler, his wife, and two young children immigrated to this country from the Alsace region between France and Germany in 1738. They sought sanctuary from religious persecution and the freedom to live and worship according to their Anabaptist beliefs. Sailing aboard the ship *Charming Nancy,* they arrived in Philadelphia on November 9. By early 1739 they had settled with other members of their church in the Northkill Amish Mennonite community at the base of the Blue Mountains, near what is today Shartlesville, Pennsylvania.

During the French and Indian War, early on the morning of September 20, 1757, their lives were forever changed when their home was attacked by a band of Indians. Jakob's wife and two children were killed, and he and his two younger sons, Joseph and Christian, were carried away into captivity.

Jacob managed to escape in April 1758, and after a harrowing journey arrived home by the end of May. He immediately began efforts to find his sons, and Joseph and Christian were finally returned to the Northkill community after the war's end. Both struggled to assimilate into a culture they barely remembered. The account of this family's trial and triumph is both wrenching and deeply inspiring.

This our legacy. And this is our ancestors' story, as we envision it.

—*Bob Hostetler and J. M. Hochstetler*

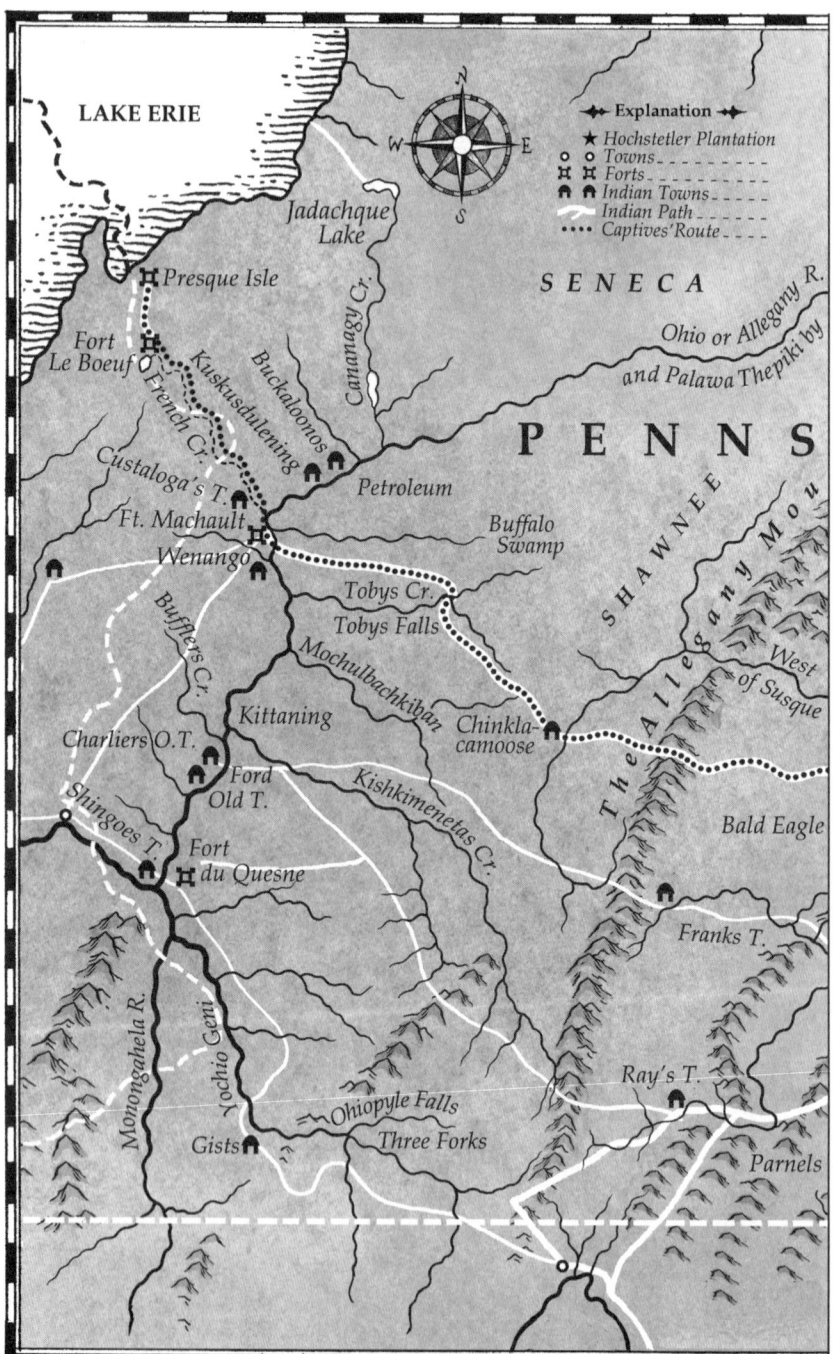

LAKE ERIE

Jadachque
Lake

SENECA

Ohio or Allegany R.
and Palawa Thepiki by

PENNS

★→ Explanation →★
★ Hochstetler Plantation
○ o Towns ----------
✕ ✕ Forts ----------
⌂ ⌂ Indian Towns ----------
~ Indian Path ----------
•••• Captives' Route ----------

Presque Isle

Fort
Le Boeuf

Kuskusdulening

French Cr.

Custaloga's T.

Ft. Machault

Wenango

Buckaloonos

Cananagy Cr.

Petroleum

Buffalo
Swamp

SHAWNEE

The Allegany Mou

West
of Susque

Tobys Cr.

Tobys Falls

Mochulbachkiban

Chinkla-
camoose

Bufflers Cr.

Kittaning

Charliers O.T.

Ford
Old T.

Kishkimenetas Cr.

Bald Eagle

Shingoes T.

Fort
du Quesne

Franks T.

Monongahela R.

Yochio Geni

Ohiopyle Falls

Three Forks

Ray's T.

Parnels

Gists

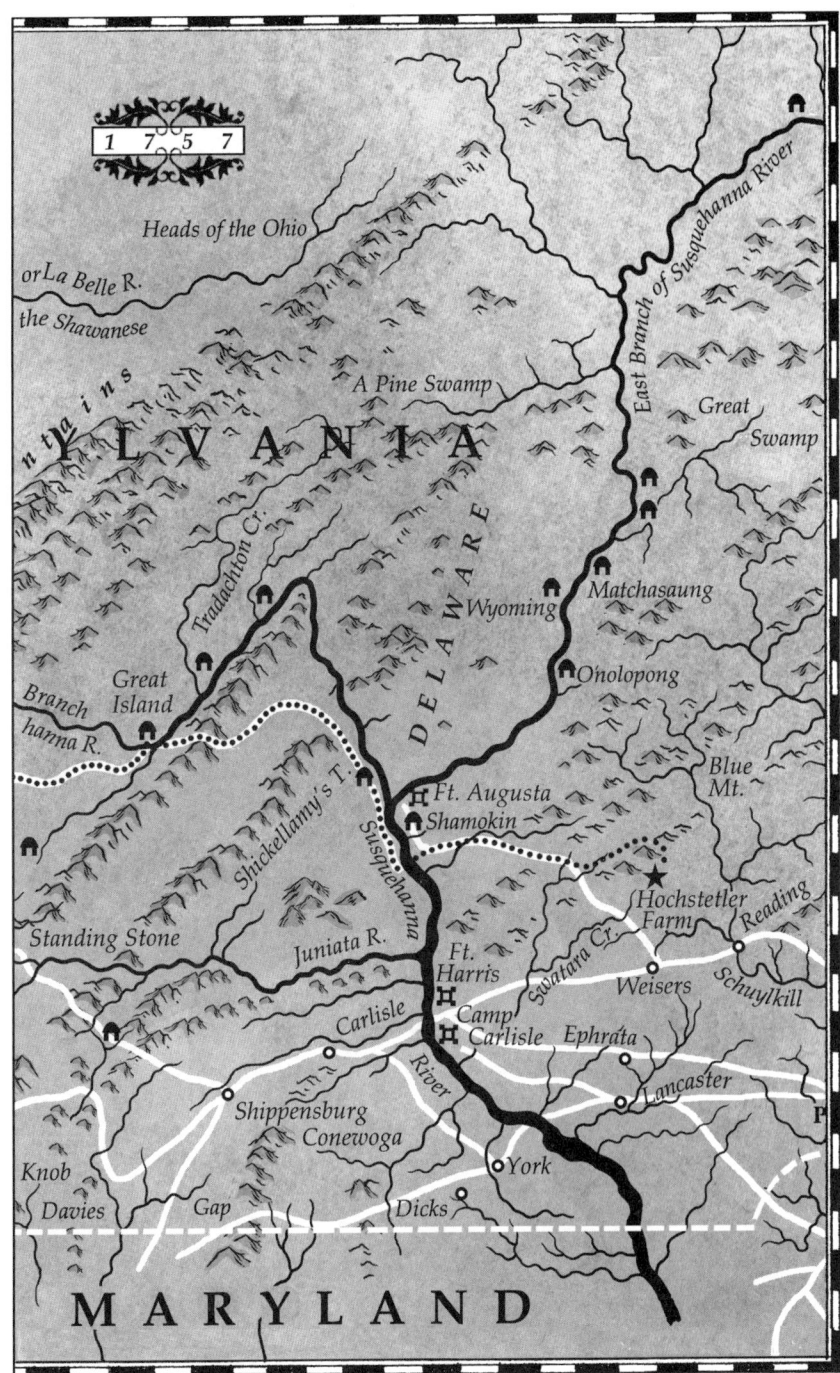

"Jesus answered, 'My kingdom is not of this world: if my kingdom were of this world, then would my servants fight.' "

—John 18:36 (KJV)

Chapter One

Friday, September 22, 1752

"CHRISTIAN!" Stiffening, seventeen-year-old Barbara Hochstetler came to an abrupt halt on the stone threshold of the log house.

Out in the yard, her little brother, sky-blue eyes wide, reached up to touch the silver baubles that hung from the neck and ears of the Indian warrior who bent over him. While Barbara watched in breathless terror, the man returned the boy's smile and trailed claw-like fingers along the soft curve of the child's cheek, speaking in a melodious language she could not understand.

The sight of the wide bands of black and red paint slashed across the warrior's lean, pockmarked face, caused Barbara's heart to contract so painfully she felt lightheaded. "Maam!" she gasped, frantically searching the farmyard for her mother's ample form.

On the near side of the barn by the chicken house, she saw her mother, Anna, swing around at her cry, the pan of crushed corn she had been scattering for the hens dropping on the ground. Barefoot, Maam ran back toward the house with astonishing speed for one so plump, her full petticoats bunched in her clenched fists, the wide brim of her flat straw hat bouncing with every step.

"*Christli, ins Haus! Schnell!*" In the house! Quickly!

Christian jerked around at her scream, his expression registering confusion and fear. A flurry of squawking, flapping fowl scattered out of Maam's path as she crossed the dusty yard to pull Christian away from the warrior.

Biting her lip hard, Barbara focused on the man's face, which darkened into a frown. Eyes narrowed, he straightened to his full height and spoke again as he reached for Christian. This time the menace in his voice and gesture was all too clear.

Maam shoved the boy in Barbara's direction and, hands on hips, planted herself protectively between her children and the warrior. Her stance reminded Barbara of an angry hen guarding her clutch of eggs

If she had not been so frightened, she would have laughed. Instead, she sucked in another sharp breath as five more warriors, painted and armed like the first, emerged from the woods behind the springhouse.

Before she could cry out a warning, Christian collided with her so hard he almost knocked her to the ground. She staggered, then regained her balance and caught the six-year-old in her arms. Sobbing, he pressed hard against her legs, burying his tear-streaked face in her petticoats. She was shaking as much as he was.

To her astonishment, her mother did not shrink back at this new threat. Instead, she kept her narrowed eyes on the man in front of her, whom Barbara took to be the roving band's leader.

He was angry, that was clear. But Maam held her ground, even when the other warriors advanced.

They all carried muskets, with a tomahawk hanging from their belt, and a hunting knife dangling from a rawhide thong against their chest. The weapons glittered in the sunshine. Barbara pressed her clenched fist against her mouth and breathed a fervent plea for God's protection. She tried to think where the rest of her family would be at that hour.

By now ten-year-old Joseph should be driving the cows up from the pasture for the evening milking. Today, as usual, he lagged in performing his chores, and she added a prayer for his safety.

Early that morning, twelve-year-old Jake had gone with their father to Christian Stutzman's plantation a mile away. The men of their Amish Mennonite community were completing the roof of the new house Crist was hurrying to finish in time for his and Barbara's wedding in October, only a few weeks away. Daat and Jake should be on their way home along with her oldest brother, Johannes, who lived with his wife, Katie, on the adjoining plantation.

She wanted to go to Maam but dared not leave Christian alone. He clung to her so tightly that she was afraid he would panic if she pulled away. If the worst happened, she and Christian might have time to escape through the house and out the side *Stube* door, intercept Joseph on the path to the barn, and make it to Johannes's home. But their seeking sanctuary with Johannes might lead the Indians to her brother and sister-in-law and their new baby. She felt sick at the thought.

Daat, come quick! she pled.

The warriors had made no further move toward her mother or the house, and for an instant Barbara dared to hope they might yet leave peaceably. But then a sneer twisted the leader's face. He spoke in rapid, unintelligible syllables, while waving one muscular, dark-skinned arm in the direction of the fat, golden loaves of bread cooling on the trestle table beside the outdoor bake oven.

Maam shook her head in stubborn refusal, the muscles of her jaw clenching. Barbara's stomach churned.

She had been only three when her family settled in the tight-knit Amish Mennonite community sprawled along swift-flowing Northkill Creek in Berks County, Pennsylvania. While encounters with roving bands of Delaware who lived in the region had been common as long as she could remember, most of the time the natives simply asked for food or offered handmade goods for trade before continuing on their way.

Recently, however, the community had been alarmed by rumors that the French were once again stirring up the tribes in an attempt to halt the spread of English settlers, soldiers, and forts that continued to creep over the boundary of the Allegheny Mountains into the continent's fertile interior—territory claimed by France. And now, as Barbara studied these warriors more closely, she concluded that they were most likely members of the warlike Shawnee from beyond the Blue Mountains, whose hazy bulk formed her family's western horizon.

Suddenly she heard a dog baying, followed by a cry that caused her to swing around, her hand pressed to her bosom.

"I'm coming!"

It was Joseph. Barbara's heart sank when saw her brother race toward them from the direction of the pasture, their dog, Blitz, a white streak several yards in advance.

"Go back in the house, Maami!" Joseph shouted. "I'll drive them off!"

❖┄┄┄❖

JAKOB SHOOK THE REINS over the rumps of his matched black Belgian horses, his sturdy forty-year-old frame ramrod straight on the wagon bench. Squinting, he tilted his head to assess the angle of the pale gold sunlight that slanted low through the dense trees and underbrush bordering the path.

"It's getting late. The milking should yet be half done."

"Joseph will have the cows up from the pasture and in the barn—you'll see." Jakob's namesake flashed a confident smile.

The wagon wheels jerked across the ruts in the dirt road, jolting both of them hard enough to rattle their bones. Even after the long day's labor, he noted, Jake clung effortlessly to the wooden seat with no sign of weariness. The boy already worked like a grown man.

Jakob's fingers tightened over the reins as he urged the Belgians to a faster pace along the narrow lane that connected his homestead with Johannes's place, where they had dropped off his oldest son. The team leaned into the harness, their huge hooves kicking up plumes of dust on the dry track.

"I can't count on him the way I do on you and Johannes. He has yet to learn responsibility."

"He's only ten. Neither was I so responsible at his age."

The boy always rushed to defend his brothers, Jakob reflected, and his stern visage softened. He couldn't help wishing his younger boys were more like Jake.

"*Ya*, but you're one to take things more seriously. Ten is old enough to get chores done on time—and not go running off on some foolishness like chasing that fox that's been after the chickens."

"Joseph wouldn't do that. Not after you told him not to anyway."

Jakob raked calloused fingers through the untrimmed beard that fringed his face. Rubbing a bead of sweat off his shaven upper lip, he glanced in his son's direction.

"I'll get the fox the next time he comes around. Joseph would only waste time and gunpowder. He's not a good shot yet, nor does he track so well as you do."

Noting the late afternoon chill and the flame and russet that burnished the leaves of the taller trees overhead, he pushed back the broad-brimmed black felt hat clamped over his curly black hair. "It took longer to top off Crist's roof than I expected. He's building a good home for our Barbara, *ya?*"

"*Ya*, Daati. And we worked hard today for sure."

Jake pulled off his own hat, revealing damp, dark brown hair plastered against his forehead. Taking his kerchief out of the shallow crown, he wiped perspiration from his brow and fanned his flushed face before replacing the kerchief, and then the hat.

"Now that we have the house under roof, Crist only needs to put in the windows and move in furniture."

"With the wedding coming up right after we harvest the corn, it's good we kept at it till we finished. But it'll be dark by the time we get the milking done. Your Maami won't be happy to keep supper waiting so long." Jakob gave a sly smile. "She may just skin us." Jake grinned. "She might catch you, but I run too fast."

The wagon rolled out of the woods into cleared land, where rolling pasture alternated with cultivated fields. Jakob's smile vanished as his gaze took in the rangy red cow emerging from the rows of cornstalks at the edge of the field up ahead, her udder heavy with milk. Acknowledging them with a twitch of her ears, the animal continued to chew contentedly on the corn leaves hanging from her mouth.

"*Vass iss des?*" What is this?

Jakob drew hard on the reins. With a jingle of harness, the Belgians snorted and came to an abrupt halt, tossing their heads and sending his heavy wooden carpenter's toolbox sliding the length of the wagon bed.

Another cow wandered into sight. Shaking long, curved horns, she lowed softly while trampling the pumpkin and squash vines that twined through the hills of corn. Jakob could hear still others thrashing among the drying stalks. Hastily he set the brake and wound the reins around the handle.

Jake jumped off the wagon and headed for the wide opening where fence rails lay scattered on the ground. "I'll drive them out and get them up to the barn."

Jakob began to climb down from the wagon but arrested at the sound of Blitz's furious snarls, followed by a deep-throated howl that raised the hairs on the back of his neck.

The commotion came from the direction of the house, blocked from their view by the large bank barn directly ahead. Hearing loud, angry voices, he froze.

Jake turned sharply to look at him, alarm written on his face.

"It's Maami!"

Jakob had already recognized Anna's voice. The men spoke in one of the native tongues, their tone threatening. Indians. Probably members of the Delaware tribe, or Lenape.

He dropped from the wagon's step and raced up the path past the orchard. Behind him he heard Jake's footfalls at his heels.

Their Amish community maintained peaceful relations with their Indian neighbors and carried on a mutually profitable trade with those living in the area. That had not always been the case for the surrounding communities of *die Englishe*. The English, as the Amish referred to outsiders, seemed more interested in taking the Indians' lands for themselves than in living peaceably with them. A number of incidents over the past year had resulted in violence that had spilled over into the English and German communities closely bordering their own in this frontier region. The thought caused Jakob's heart to hammer.

Rounding the barn, he came to a halt so abruptly that Jake collided with him from behind, his hat flying into the dirt. Jakob took in the scene in an instant.

Directly in front of Anna and Joseph, six warriors clustered near the stone bake house, shouting and making threatening gestures with the muskets they clenched in their hands. Blitz paced up and down between the two groups, teeth bared, hackles raised.

"*Vek!*" Anna shouted, motioning violently for the Indians to leave. "*Geh vek!*" Away! Go away!

Jakob took a step in her direction. She started and glanced toward him, her round face flushed and perspiring beneath the plain white linen *Haube* that covered her hair.

"Jakob, make them go!"

She struggled to jerk Joseph behind her as she swung to face the warriors. Joseph appeared equally determined to maintain his position between his mother and the intruders.

Movement in the doorway of their two-story log home caught Jakob's eye, and he saw that Barbara stood there, her face contorted with terror. Christian cowered against her, red faced, eyes squeezed shut, hands pressed tightly over his ears.

"Maami," Joseph pled, "go inside! Please! Let us men handle this."

Before Jakob could stop him, Jake darted around him and ran to plant himself in front of Joseph and Anna. Instantly, every warrior dropped a hand to the tomahawk at his belt, while the leader of the band reached for the boy's arm, waving his musket with his other hand.

Anna shrieked. The dog set up a furious clamor and lunged for the man.

Jakob sprang across the yard, gripped Blitz by the nape of her neck, and yanked her back. "*Nchutièstuk! Nchutièstuk!*" Friend!

It was one of the words in the Lenape language that he had picked up while trading with Delaware families who lived nearby. The warriors glared, and Jakob repeated the word, worried that they were unable to decipher his thick German accent.

He noted telling differences between these tall, muscular men and the Delaware tribesmen he frequently encountered. In spite of the cool weather, they wore only mid-thigh-length fringed leggings, moccasins, and breechclouts. Their hair was entirely plucked off except for a scalp lock at the crown of the head decorated with feathers, tufts of fur, or silver ornaments. Silver medallions hung from their earlobes, and the savage designs tattooed on their shoulders lent them an even more fearsome appearance.

It was the broad slashes of black and red paint across face and torso that constricted Jakob's breath, however. They were painted for war.

Releasing Blitz, he snapped his fingers and pointed down. *"Nieder! Sei schtill!"* Down! Be quiet!

The animal hugged the ground but continued to eye the warriors, teeth bared, ears laid back. Cautiously Jakob straightened and raised his hand, palm outward, in front of his forehead, with his index and second finger pointed to the sky. He prayed that the warriors knew the Delaware sign for friend.

"Nchutièstuk," he repeated, speaking slowly and distinctly.

The band's leader stared at him through narrowed eyes for a long, tense moment. At last, to Jakob's relief, he perceptibly relaxed his stance.

Jakob drew in a shaky breath, struggling to recall the French he had learned growing up in the Alsace, the region that straddled the border between France and the German Palatinate. Most of the tribes were allied with the French, and he knew that many of the native peoples spoke at least some of the language.

"*Paix, amis,*" he offered. Peace, friends.

When he repeated the sign and words, he sensed a distinct change in the war party's manner. Keeping his movements slow and easy, he crossed to the rude table under the overhanging roof of the stone-walled bake house, where a week's worth of fresh bread lay cooling. He took a quick count before motioning to the warriors to help themselves.

"Daati, *nay!*" Joseph protested hotly. "They'll take it all!"

Jakob silenced him with a glare. Softening his expression, he again offered the bread to the warriors. The men exchanged suspicious glances, but after a brief hesitation, they came forward one by one to each claim a loaf.

Jakob nodded and smiled broadly. "*Bon!*" he said. Good.

The warriors' leader fixed him in an unreadable stare. His dark eyes bored into Jakob's, then he glanced at the rope strung between two trees on the far side of the kitchen yard, where Anna was airing her quilts in preparation for the cold months to come. He waved his hand toward the brightly colored rectangles fluttering in the autumn wind.

"*Nay!*" Anna cried. "The bread is enough! Don't give them my quilts, too—not with winter coming on!"

Jakob hesitated. The warrior's steely gaze warned him that his decision would tip the confrontation either toward peace or disaster. At last, closely trailed by Blitz and the warrior, he strode over to the quilts.

Both Jake and Joseph joined their mother's protests now, but Jakob abruptly motioned them to silence. He scanned the quilts quickly, then pulled one off the line and offered it to the warrior.

The man accepted it warily, seeming to weigh it in his hands while he scrutinized the quality of the fabric and the fine stitches that wove an intricate pattern across the colorful quilt blocks. At length he looked up and nodded in approval. His eyes had lost their hardness, and Jakob felt the knot in his chest loosen. Without moving his gaze from the warrior's face, he dropped his hand to pat Blitz's head. "May *Gott* bless you on your journeys."

The warrior inclined his head and uttered several syllables Jakob interpreted as thanks. Then he turned and motioned to his companions. Together they moved to depart.

As the warriors filed off around the end of the house in the direction of the orchard, Christian slipped free from his sister's restraining arm and stepped cautiously out of the doorway onto the broad stone that served as a front step. He wanted to get a better look at the war party, but halted quickly when the band's leader paused to wrap the quilt around his shoulders.

Without warning, he fixed Christian in an unblinking stare. The boy froze. But with a solemn expression the warrior made the same sign Daati had used earlier: *friend.*

Christian smiled shyly and raised his hand to return the sign. As he did so, he caught sight of Maami's frown. He flushed and hastily put his hands behind his back.

It was a move he instantly regretted. The warrior had caught the exchange, and he rounded on Maami, his eyes narrowed. Returning to the bake house, he snatched up a charred stick used to poke the fire, then strode to the end of the house as though he meant to follow his companions. With a single fluid motion, he slashed a strange symbol across the weathered, square logs. Then he tossed the stick disdainfully to the ground and stalked around the corner and out of Christian's sight.

❦⋯❧

THE INSTANT THE WARRIOR disappeared Barbara fled across the yard to Maami's arms, while Christian hurried to squeeze in between them. Joseph watched, scowling, then bent to scoop up a handful of dirt and pebbles from the yard and ran to the house. He had to stand on tiptoe to reach the charcoal streaks, but he vigorously scrubbed at the warrior's mark until all that remained was a grey smudge.

His father's sharp command halted his work. He turned to see Daati facing Maami, his stocky form tense, muscular arms crossed.

"How did all this start?"

Joseph could see Maami's hands shake though they stood several yards apart. She loosed the ties that held her scoop hat in place and pulled it off to fan her flushed face, while with her free hand she straightened the white linen *Haube* that covered her hair.

"Barbara called to me while I was feeding the chickens. That one who marked the house was bending over Christli like he meant to carry him off. I no more than sent him to the house when the rest of them showed up and tried to take our bread."

"I was bringing the cows up from the pasture when I heard shouting, and—"

Jakob transferred his steely gaze from Maami to Joseph. "*Ya,* and now the cows are in the corn, trampling down what they haven't eaten yet."

Joseph could feel the heat climb into his face. He dropped his gaze and wiped his hands on the seat of his brown linen breeches, digging his bare toes into the dirt.

I can never do anything right in Daati's eyes. The bitter taste of resentment welled up in his mouth.

"He was afraid, Jakob," Maami protested.

Barbara flashed Joseph a sympathetic look. "We all were, but he tried to protect us."

Daati swung back to Maami. "Have I not told you time and again never to deny them bread? All you accomplish is to tempt them to harm you and the children."

Joseph glanced at his mother, then quickly away. As far back as he could remember, she had appeared to accept the ceaseless toil of their life without complaint.

She always supported Daati unquestioningly in everything he did. At least in front of him and his sister and brothers.

The death of his baby sister four months earlier, just hours after her birth, had changed things between them, however. Joseph wished desperately that his parents' relationship was as it had been before. But his mother was different since the day they laid little Freni in the ground, while his father seemed unwilling or unable to acknowledge her grief.

Or his own. For Joseph sensed a difference in Daati, too, though his father showed little outward change.

Now, as she had with the Indians, Maami refused to back down. "Should I bake bread and work my fingers to the bone for every savage who passes by? Should I have given them your son too?"

"I think they were Shawnee," Joseph broke in hastily. "From the way they were painted up, it looks like they're on the warpath."

As though catching on to Joseph's attempt to distract them, Jake added, "The French must be stirring up the tribes again. Crist's brother Hans said he heard that there've been more attacks on the English trading posts and settlements on the other side of the mountains."

"*Daß sich* Gott *erbarme!*" God have mercy! Maami threw hands up and lifted her eyes heavenward. "The savages are going to kill us in our beds! Why ever did we come to this forsaken land?"

Daati scanned his children's faces, and his mouth tightened. "Now is not the time to talk of this."

"We'll be ready the next time they come," Joseph vowed. "From now on I'm going to keep my rifle loaded and primed."

"*Nay,* you will not! The Lord God commanded us to do no murder. Christ Jesus said we are to love even our enemies and do good to all men, and we will act as Christ did. We will not lift our hand against any human being."

"The English fight," Jake protested, "and they believe in God too."

Daati regarded the two of them with a look as unyielding as stone. "Words come cheap. How you live proves what you believe. Our example is Christ, not *die Englishe*. What other men do is on their heads. What we do is on ours."

Christian shifted uneasily from one bare foot to the other. The flat finality of his father's words cut off any further discussion, and although he could not understand everything the others were talking about, even he could feel the tension that hung heavy in the air.

He shivered. The sun had sunk out of sight behind the darkly wooded ridge that defined the western boundary of Pennsylvania's Great Valley, sprawling from northeast to southwest two miles west of their plantation. The lengthening shadows cast by the trees and the house held an autumn chill.

Daati motioned toward the barn. "We should have started the chores an hour ago. I'll bring up the wagon. You boys drive the cows out of the field and into the barn."

His stern gaze fastened on Joseph. "By the time we finish milking, it'll be too dark to see how much damage they did. Tomorrow morning early I expect you to go through the field and clean up as much as can be saved."

The two older boys wheeled in unison and took off toward the cornfield, with Blitz bounding ahead of them. Christian moved to follow them.

A heavy hand on his shoulder stopped him before he had gone two paces. "You have chores to take care of."

Christian looked up to meet his father's frown. "But Daati—"

Daati shook his head, cutting off his plea. "Go help your mother and sister."

Christian threw a mournful glance after his brothers. "*Ya,*
Daati.*"

✦ ···· ✦

FOLLOWING JAKE AND JOSEPH with long, easy strides, Jakob
watched them race each other down the path toward the cornfield, exchanging playful taunts, while Blitz danced around them,
barking in excitement. They briefly disappeared from his sight,
but when he rounded the barn, he saw Joseph a short distance
ahead of him.

The boy bent to catch up two objects from the grass beside
the path, one long, the other smaller. Then he hurried on, keeping his hands in front of him. Jakob did not have to see what
Joseph carried to know.

Several quick strides brought him to Joseph's side. He
wrenched the finely crafted, long-barreled Pennsylvania rifle out
of his son's grasp and held out his other hand. Their eyes locked
for a tense moment, then Joseph dropped his gaze and grudgingly surrendered the powder horn.

Jakob bit back his anger and motioned Joseph toward the
cornfield. Without a word or a glance back, the boy strode after
Jake, who waited by the fence, brow furrowed, a look of apprehension on his face.

Chapter Two

"ACH, NOW SUPPER is going to be late."

Maam swung the crane anchored to the side of the fireplace toward her. She hung a kettle filled with vegetables and water on the trammel's lowest hook and pushed it back to hang above the coals that remained from the noonday fire.

Barbara tucked a wayward lock of her dark brown hair back under her white cap and glanced sympathetically at her mother as she started toward the outer door. "I'll bring in the bread. Shall I fetch some pork from the smokehouse for the stew?"

Smiling, Maam reached for the poker. "That sounds real *guud.*"

Just then Christian came through the door, feet dragging, head down. His lower lip stuck out in a pout.

Maam shot him a quick glance. "Barbara, let me fetch the bread and meat while you stir up the fire and start the biscuits. Christli, why don't you come help me, and then we can gather the eggs together, *ya?*"

Christian brightened. Maam squeezed past Barbara with an apologetic look and went to join him at the door.

"It'll do me good to keep busy right now. Sometimes your Daat—" She shrugged her words away.

After they went outside, Barbara crossed the room to the yawning, smoke-blackened stone fireplace that that spanned most of the *Küche's* inner wall between the *Stube,* or parlor, on the right and her parents' *Kammer,* or bedchamber, on the left. Its opening was high enough for an adult to step inside without stooping, and the hearth could accommodate several fires at once. A cozy settle occupied the space between the end of the fireplace and the *Kammer* door.

She grabbed kindling from the wood box built into the stones on the right side of the fireplace. With the ease of long practice, she stirred to life the embers banked in the ashes before laying the small pieces on the glowing coals.

Her hand was suddenly shaking, and she had to make a conscious effort to steady the poker. She struggled to focus on her task, to shake off the fear that kept pushing into her consciousness, but without success. While she layered on smaller split logs and built up the flames until the fire gave off sufficient heat for cooking, her thoughts drifted back to the confrontation with the Indians.

Her family regularly dealt with the natives, though never before under such threatening circumstances. Of course, it was generally the Delaware from nearby villages who stopped by, and her father had always been close at hand to keep encounters friendly. Had he been there when the Indians appeared, such a confrontation would never have happened. Yet at the same time Barbara understood her mother's concerns.

She sighed and tugged the heavy cast-iron Dutch oven onto the hearth. Hearing someone enter the house behind her, she turned to see her mother and little brother carry inside the remaining loaves of bread. Maam gave her a tight smile before bustling back outside, Christian on her heels as she headed in the direction of the smokehouse.

She works so hard taking care of the house, the garden, the chickens, us Kinder—*and everything else. And when Crist and I are married, it will be the same for me.*

The thought of Christian Stutzman prompted a smile. Handsome, with a farmer's sturdy build, the blond-haired, blue-eyed son of Maudlin and Jakob Stutzman had captured her attention as far back as she could remember, and the attraction had been mutual.

Just the previous week the deacon called the *Stecklimann* had ridden over to their plantation to offer gifts to her and her parents and present Crist's proposal of marriage. The time the two of them had been allowed to spend together had by custom been strictly limited to church events, community celebrations, and frolics—always in the company of their parents or friends. But Crist had made his intentions clear, and Barbara had anxiously expected the *Stecklimann's* arrival for weeks.

In spite of the endless labor required by life on the frontier, she welcomed even hardship as long as this man was by her side. And so the date had been set for the announcement to be read before the church congregation. The wedding would follow toward the end of October after the crops had all been harvested and the butchering done, and it could not come soon enough for her.

"Heyah!"

Joseph shoved the cow against the nearest wooden stanchion and sprang away from the yellow stream that splattered to all sides. Plodding behind her, another of the docile beasts lifted her tail and began to drop soft, dark pats onto the barn's dirt floor.

In the cool air, warm steam rose from dung and piss and beast, filling the milking parlor with a mix of pungent odors. Joseph wrinkled his nose and muttered an English swear word.

Hooves sliding in the muck, the four cows filed to their places between the stanchions. Despite their foray into the corn, they immediately buried their moist muzzles in the aromatic hay that filled the feedbox in front of them.

He startled as Jake suddenly appeared at his side. "Don't scare me like that!"

Grinning, Jake set his water bucket down. "Where did you learn that word?"

Joseph glanced warily toward the stalls at the other end of the bank barn's lower level where Daati moved between the partitions, scooping oats into the Belgians' feedboxes. In the light of the lantern hanging from one of the huge beams that supported the upper floor, he threw an enormous shadow that rippled across the barn's walls and floor with his movements.

"Shush! Daati will hear."

"I bet you heard it from John," Jake guessed, referring to their cousin, Uncle Jakob Buerki's youngest son. "He's picked up a lot of words from their English neighbors—and not always nice ones."

Joseph cocked his head, listening to the stamp of the horses' hooves and the muted grinding of their teeth as they fed. Reassured that their father was still safely occupied, he gave a kick that scattered the mewing barn cats that already crowded close to beg for milk.

"You'd be surprised how many English words I know."

"I've learned a few too."

Jake pushed the wooden shovel into Joseph's hands. Pulling free the rag stuffed into the top of his breeches, he wrung it out in the water and stooped under the first cow to wash off her teats.

At their father's approach, Joseph busied himself carrying shovelfuls of muck outside to the dung heap. When he finished and came back inside, Daati was seated on a stool beside one of the cows, rhythmically squeezing milk into a wooden bucket. Joseph avoided looking in his direction, not anxious to learn what the punishment for his latest infraction would be.

"Looks like you did more damage to the corn driving the cows out than they did while they were in the field," Daati growled.

Jake finished washing the last cows' teats and grabbed a milk bucket and stool. "Even Blitz had trouble rounding them up." He pulled a stool up to the cow beside Daati's. "I guess the corn just tasted too *guud*."

Joseph held his tongue and directed a grateful glance at Jake. He could always depend on his brother to intervene on his behalf.

"We can't afford to waste anything," Daati reminded them soberly. "Winter will be here soon enough, and then it'll be months before we can plant, and longer still until harvest. If we don't want to go hungry, we must make sure we have enough stores to carry us through."

"Do you think Maami wants to go back to the Alsace?" Jake asked, referring to the region from which the family had migrated.

Daati gave no indication that he had heard the question. As Joseph carried a bucket past the cow Jake was milking, he caught his brother's eye and gave him a discreet nod of encouragement to keep trying.

Seated on the low stool, Jake leaned into the cow's side and squeezed a stream of foaming milk into his bucket. "Why did you and Maami come all the way across the ocean to live here to Pennsylvania, Daati? Tell us again."

✦┈┈✦

THE DOOR BANGED OPEN, admitting a chilly gust of wind. Maam bustled inside and carried a joint of smoked pork to the table in front of the fireplace. Behind her trailed Christian, his small arms wrapped around a woven basket heavy with eggs.

While he ran to the springhouse to fetch fresh milk and lard and Maam went down to the cellar, Barbara took a large knife from the rack on the wall. In minutes thick chunks of pork joined the vegetables in the kettle, filling the expansive space with a rich aroma that made her mouth water.

Maam returned upstairs, arms loaded with small pots of apple butter and pickles, which she set on the table. As Barbara measured out flour, Christian burst through the door, cradling a small crock in the crook of each arm.

"They've started milking," he announced, adding his crocks to those already on the table. "Jake said the cows made a mess in the cornfield."

Maam raised her eyebrows and glanced at the window, where dusk already darkened the panes. Smiling, she turned back to brush the sweaty hair off his brow.

"Set the table for me, Cristli. They'll be finished in the barn and wanting supper before it's ready yet."

Barbara beat biscuit dough in a wide, shallow wooden bowl, her thoughts again straying to what had happened that afternoon. Beginning at daybreak on that oppressively warm September day, she and Maam had worked to mix, knead, and bake the heavy mounds of dough. Now only five loaves remained of a whole day's hard labor meant to feed their family for a week.

Resentment flared, and she flung spoonfuls of biscuit dough into the Dutch oven. "I can't believe Daat gave away all that bread!"

Tight-lipped, Maam bent over the fire to stir the simmering stew. "Thanks to your Daat none of you children got hurt or carried off. I praise *Gott* for that."

"The English drive the Indians off. If they or their families are threatened, they fight them—even kill them."

The words were no sooner spoken than Barbara shook her head in apology. "Ach, I'm just mad because we did all that work for nothing, and on top of it they took your quilt too. But Daat is right. Christ's teachings are clear. We have to turn the other cheek, even to the Indians."

Maam straightened with a groan, her hand pressed to the small of her back. "Anymore it seems like that's getting harder for me to do. But your Daat always tries to do the right thing. He's a *guud* man."

And a stubborn one too, Barbara thought, remembering how he often told them, *Es iss nett unser vek.* It is not our way. The Amish were plain, and they didn't indulge in the *weltlich* manners and lifestyles of the English.

But are all their ways so bad? Although she suspected Maam at times fell prey to the same rebellious thoughts, Barbara kept her opinions to herself.

She loved her parents dearly and a never doubted that her father loved her mother and each of their children. Still, there were times when she—and she was certain, Maam—needed to hear him say it. Especially after little Freni had been taken.

A sharp pain cut through Barbara's breast at the memory of the tiny girl Maam had welcomed with such joy after giving birth to so many boys, and she directed a surreptitious glance in her mother's direction. Born too early, the baby had looked like a delicate flower, with silken skin as pale as milk and downy black hair already beginning to curl. But she had been too weak to live long.

Tears pricked Barbara's eyes. Frowning, she blinked them hastily away and concentrated on piling hot coals on the lid of the Dutch oven she had set on embers raked to the fire's edge. She could not imagine how she would bear the death of one of her babies, yet such tragedies happened all too often. Most of the families she knew had lost at least one infant or young child, if not several.

Barbara sensed clearly the pain her mother suffered every day since losing Freni. Could Daat not feel it? Most of the time, he seemed not to. Of course, maybe her parents talked about such things at night alone in their *Kammer*. Surely then he held her in his arms and comforted her.

She felt her cheeks flame at thought of the private things a husband and wife did together. A soft smile played over her lips, and all other reflections fled.

Only a few more weeks, and she would be free to explore the feelings that burned inside whenever she thought of Crist. She prayed the time would fly.

✦━━━━✦

"YOU *KINDER* HAVE HEARD the story so often that you can tell it better than I can," Jakob protested.

When they continued to plead, he finally gave in. While they filled their buckets with the rich, foaming milk, he recounted the story his children never seemed to tire of hearing.

As Anabaptists, he explained, they had been persecuted in Europe for baptizing only those old enough to profess a saving faith in Jesus Christ. They were also denied the right to own land for their refusal to join the state church and serve in the military. So in 1738 he and their mother, along with four-year-old Johannes and three-year-old Barbara, had left their home in Sainte-Marie-aux-Mines in Europe's Alsace region and traveled to Pennsylvania with other members of their Amish church.

The journey down the Rhine to Holland, then across the Channel to England, had taken all summer. That had been difficult enough. But the six weeks they had spent aboard the ship *Charming Nancy,* crossing three thousand miles of ocean with winter storms coming on, had strained their endurance to the limit. Many of their fellow passengers, both children and adults, had sickened and died before the ship reached the rapidly growing port of Philadelphia on the edge of the American wilderness. But by God's mercy, the four of them had made it through.

As soon as they could buy provisions, horses, and a wagon, their company traveled northwest to the frontier. At last they reached the Northkill community, named for the creek, or "kill," that wound down from the Blue Mountain and through the rich farmland on the valley's floor. There they had joined other church members who had come to Pennsylvania before them, including their Maami's brothers Jakob and Christian Buerki and their families.

Joseph squirted the last of his cow's milk into the bucket. "Were you ever afraid, coming so far to a strange land?"

Jakob set aside his brimming bucket, careful not to spill a drop. "We're yet human. But our *Gott* is a mighty fortress. Never forget that. We can always trust Him to bring us safely to our journey's end."

"Someday I'm going to take a long journey too," Joseph mused, his voice dreamy.

Jake carried his bucket over to his father. "It's better to make our home *guud* and safe and live the way we want to right here."

Jakob frowned. "You boys always stay close to home. If you run off into the forest or the mountains by yourselves, you'll come into danger and you may get hurt."

Joseph squared his shoulders. "I'm not afraid, Daati. Like you said, God will bring us safely home."

❦⸻❦

IT WAS FULL DARK by the time they finished the milking. Jakob sent the boys to turn the cows back out into the pasture. They returned to carry the heavy wooden milk buckets to the spring-house at the edge of the orchard, and he watched until they disappeared up the path around the end of the barn.

He shoveled out the last of the muck and readied everything for the early morning milking. In the barn's quiet dimness he brooded over the incident with the Indians. A shiver went through him at thought of what might have happened if he hadn't gotten home when he did.

Unsettling reports of confrontations with native warriors were circulating throughout the area with increasing frequency. Johannes had always been cautious, and Barbara would soon be married and under her husband's protection. But it seemed impossible to Jakob to keep his younger sons from wandering off, no matter how sternly he warned them of the dangers.

He understood the temptations that beckoned outside the borders of their peaceful, secluded community. But his responsibility to ensure that his wife and children remained faithful to the tenets of the church weighed heavily on him. If he failed in his calling as the priest of his household, they would be lost, and at the Judgment he would have to answer to Christ.

He wished mightily that he could talk once more with his own father, whose name he bore. He craved the counsel of that stern *Täuferlehrer* and close colleague of the "Patriarch" Jakob Ammann, the controversial reformer of the Mennonite Church from whom the Amish sect took its name. Jakob had been barely eleven when his Daati died, but he remembered him as always so sure of right and wrong, so unshakable in his faith in spite of the persecutions he had endured.

Jakob longed to learn from him how to protect his family both physically and spiritually. He wanted to ask how he would have handled the situation with the Indians, how he would answer Anna. But that was impossible.

Jakob sighed and shook his head. Anna was by nature emotional, but since little Freni's death she often seemed irrational to Jakob. She had always been protective of her family, but lately she became terrified at the slightest disturbance. And although she had been as anxious as he to flee persecution and start a new life in Penn's colony, over the past months she had begun complaining endlessly about their daily hardships and dwelling on memories of the life and relationships they had left behind in Europe.

Although they never talked about it, he knew that much of her distress had to do with Freni's death. A dull ache still took possession of his own heart whenever the haunting image of his small daughter's shroud-wrapped body came to his thoughts.

She was with God, he reminded himself. Grief couldn't bring the dead back to life. Better to work, and by working to keep such unhappy thoughts at bay.

He drew in a deep breath and released it, then slung the rifle and powder horn he had taken from Joseph over his shoulders by their leather straps. Lifting the lantern down from its hook on the overhead beam, he went outside.

Blitz was waiting for him, a pale shadow in the darkness under the barn's overhanging upper level. Her long, fringed tail beat the earth at his approach, and she gave a soft yip. He stroked her head before pushing the barn doors shut and dropping the iron bar into its brackets.

Whistling for her to follow, he held up the lantern to light his way and strode up the slope around the side of the barn, pointing his stride toward the candlelight that glowed from the windows of his home.

Chapter Three

CHRISTIAN SCOWLED at his brothers as they burst into the *Küche,* their cheeks reddened by their race up the slope from the springhouse in the evening chill. It seemed that he would never be big enough to join in the older boys' fun.

Why did they always leave him out? He tried so hard to win their acceptance and approval, but most of the time Joseph either ignored or made fun of him. Jake was much nicer, and Christian was certain that if he and Jake were the closest in age, Jake would include him.

When the door banged shut, Maami glanced up from the black iron kettle over one of two fires in the great fireplace. She took a second pewter bowl from the table in front of the hearth and ladled it full of steaming pork stew before handing it to Christian.

"You boys wash up for supper."

She said the same thing every evening when his brothers came in. Reassured that she was her normal self again, Christian inhaled the savory aromas of smoked pork and stewed vegetables that filled the house. It made his stomach growl.

Concentrating on holding the bowl level to keep the broth from spilling, he carried it to the long trestle table in front of the window at the far right end of the room. He set it carefully at Daati's place before hurrying back for the next one.

His brothers crossed to the dry sink next to the fireplace at the same time, and he didn't see Joseph stretch out his foot as he passed. Christian tripped, and would have sprawled headlong across the floorboards if Jake hadn't caught him in time.

"Ach, you're all right, Christli. Joseph was just teasing." Jake set him back on his feet and gently steered him toward Maami.

Christian twisted around to glare at Joseph, but Jake had already grabbed him and playfully dunked his head into the basin of warm water on the sink. When Joseph came up gasping for air, he slopped water onto the braided rug under their feet.

"Boys!" Maami warned, her voice sharp.

On his next trip to the table, Christian gave his brothers a wide berth. He watched as they wrestled for the piece of lye soap, laughing and splashing each other while they washed. As much as he wanted to ignore them, he felt a familiar envy clutch his chest.

His brothers' high spirits evaporated when Daati came inside carrying the lantern, the rifle and powder horn hanging from his shoulders. They toweled dry, studiously pretending they weren't watching him out of the corners of their eyes. But Christian could tell they were.

Without a word Daati set the lantern on the tall cherry hutch on the right side of the door, then detoured around the large loom that took up most of the space to his left. Opening the low cellar door at the rear of the *Küche's* side wall beneath the stairway to the second floor, he stepped down on the narrow landing inside. He added the rifle to the two others in the gun rack at the head of the stairs, then hung the powder horn on a peg above the fishing poles in the corner before coming back into the *Küche*.

Christian had seen Joseph sneak away from home with the rifle early that afternoon while Maami and Barbara were occupied baking bread. Now he had to bite his lip hard to stifle his gleeful anticipation of the reprimand Joseph was going to receive. He knew all too well that to appear to enjoy Joseph's punishment would earn him a share in it.

Holding his breath, he watched Daati take his tobacco pouch from the shelf above the settle, while Barbara bent over the second fire on the hearth, removing the hot coals from its lid. She transferred the last of the golden biscuits from the reflector oven onto a plate, covered them with a linen napkin, and set them on the worktable.

As Daati packed tobacco into his clay pipe, Barbara picked up a glowing coal with the tongs and held it out to him. He took it, nodded his thanks, and lit the pipe, puffing out a wreath of smoke. After throwing the coal back into the fire, he crossed the room to sit in the ladderback chair at the table's head.

Disappointed, Christian went to deliver the last bowl of stew to the table before slipping into his chair. Barbara set the biscuits beside Maami's plate and took a ground-cherry pie from the pie safe, while Maami sent Jake and Joseph to fetch cider from the large barrels stored in the cellar.

At last everyone took their places around the table. While they bent their heads over their folded hands, offering a silent grace, Christian surreptitiously watched his father, hoping for a short prayer so he could sooner quiet the rumblings of his empty stomach. But Daati apparently had much to thank God for that night and Christian had to wait.

Eventually, however, prayer ended, and they ate. Conversation around the table ranged from the difficulty of rounding up the cows to preparations for Barbara and Crist's upcoming wedding and the men's progress toward finishing the couple's new house.

On the surface everything appeared reassuringly peaceful and orderly, as it had all his life. But Christian longed to bring up the incident with the Indians. Since none of the others mentioned it, however, he was afraid to.

Although one question after another occurred to him, he swallowed each one along with bites of stew and biscuit, remembering Maami's angry glare when he waved at the warrior. In spite of his hunger, the food felt as if it was swelling in his throat. He took a generous swallow of cider in the effort to wash it down, but everything he ate seemed to lodge like a stone in the center of his chest.

As he studied the sober faces around the table, tears began to sting his eyes. He searched the room, unsure of what he was looking for.

The twin fires on the hearth were dying into cherry embers. Along with the muted light of the candles on the table, the wavering firelight sent long, misshapen shadows dancing eerily across the plank floor. A brooding darkness gathered in the room's corners and along the smoke-blackened beams overhead. The bunches of drying herbs, strings of dried fruit and vegetables, skeins of dyed yarn, and hand-woven baskets of various sizes that hung above them in the shadows, all comfortingly familiar until now, seemed suddenly as if they harbored threatening secrets.

Christian studied the neatly constructed boxes for salt and candles that hung on the wall above the dry sink along with the rack of wooden spoons, knives, and two-tined cooking forks, all Daati's expert handiwork. Everything looked much as it had before. But for Christian something essential had changed.

The day's events had stolen the sense of security he had always known in his home along the Northkill. And although he was only six, a new and strange sense of vulnerability left him feeling shaken.

✦━━━✦

BY THE TIME SUPPER was cleared away, it had grown too late family's usual evening occupations of weaving at the loom or spinning flax or wool yarn on the small and large spinning wheels. Instead, they gathered in the larger of the two rooms at the back of the house, the *Stube,* where they entertained company and began and ended each day with devotions. A sturdy door on the home's gable end gave access to the side yard and barnyard. On the room's interior wall another door opened into Maami and Daati's *Kammer.*

The *Stube's* furnishings were spare, but finely crafted. A five-plate cast-iron stove, which connected to the fireplace flue through the wall, provided warmth in cold weather. Daati's small writing desk and chair stood against the *Kammer* wall, and above it a shelf held a tidy collection of books and an ornate clock. This night its monotonous ticking chipped away at Joseph's nerves.

A sofa and two wing chairs upholstered in mustard brown woolen fabric clustered below the rear window, shuttered now against the night. On the small table beside one of the chairs rested the family Bible and a betty lamp. Daati took this chair as usual, while Maami settled in the other with a weary sigh. The children dutifully took their places on a plain bench between the chairs, facing the sofa.

Joseph's stomach churned. Still his father had made no mention of his disobedience. The longer punishment was delayed, the worse it would be, he knew. And in spite of the defiance Joseph could never seem to curb, Daati's disappointment and disapproval was harder to bear than a strapping.

"All the crops are harvested now except the corn, and we'll finish that by the middle of October," Daati said. "Then it'll be time for school to start. Young Ezra Mast has agreed to be schoolmaster again this year."

Christian clapped his hands. "Ach, *guud!*"

Joseph groaned. "I can read and do sums well enough, Daati! What's the good of being cooped up in school all day long when I could be helping you with the chores, and—"

Maami cut him off. "It's not the chores you're so interested in, but hunting and running around with the older boys who have nothing more to do than to make mischief—*ya?*"

Joseph squared his jaw. "*Nay,* Maami! I'm old enough to help now with the butchering and sausage-making and such."

Daati took the Bible from the table. "You won't be left out, Joseph. I suspect we can provide enough work to satisfy even you." He opened the Bible and found the passage he sought, then held it out to Joseph. "Since you're such a good reader then, you may read our Scripture tonight. *Hebräer*, chapter twelve."

Joseph rose and took the book, forcing himself to concentrate on the printed German script in the book of Hebrews. *"Darum auch wir, dieweil wir eine solche Wolke von Zeugen um uns haben . . ."* Wherefore seeing we also are compassed about with so great a cloud of witnesses . . .

He scowled at the words on the page as though they were his enemies and glanced repeatedly at Jake for help. When he reached verse five, he began to squirm.

"My son, despise not the chastening of the Lord, nor faint when thou art rebuked of Him: For whom the Lord loveth, he chasteneth, and scourgeth every son whom He receiveth. If ye endure chastening, God dealeth with you as with sons; for what son is he whom the father chasteneth not?"

"I guess you could yet endure some instruction in reading," Daati said without smiling. "A man must be able to read and understand the Bible, not only for his own sake, but in order to properly guide a wife and children in godly behavior."

Daati was not a good reader either, Joseph's thoughts protested. He often relied on passages of Scripture he had memorized or had his children read the more difficult portions. He was even unable to write the cumbersome German script Joseph had finally mastered through considerable toil.

He bit his tongue to keep his rebellious thoughts from spilling out. When he looked up he met Maami's reproachful gaze.

"Joseph doesn't figure up accounts so *guud* either."

Daati reached for the Bible. "If a man is to buy and sell goods to provide for himself and his family, he needs to know how to reckon numbers. So I expect it's best if you continue with your education a little while longer."

Heat crawled from Joseph's neck to his hairline. He surrendered the Bible to his father and resumed his seat between Jake and Barbara. He stared at the floor, grateful when Barbara squeezed his arm.

Daati set the Bible on the table beside him and sent Jake to fetch a tall, thick volume from the shelf above the desk. *The Martyr's Mirror* recounted the persecution of thousands of European Anabaptists during the previous two centuries and contained the joyful testimonies of believers awaiting torture and execution for their faith. Along with the two other books on the shelf, the *Ausbund* hymnbook and the *Wandelnde Seele* or *Wandering Soul, The Martyrs Mirror* was a fixture in Amish homes.

Joseph dreaded the reading. He wished he understood none of it, like little Christian, who was already yawning and rubbing his eyes with his fists. What was the good of any of it? Why couldn't they just have gone along with what the authorities wanted so everyone would leave them alone?

Daati leafed through the book and settled on a passage. He began reading slowly, with great effort., finally concluding: "This work must certainly not only be begun, but also finished, according to the example of the steadfast martyrs of God; with which finishing, whether it be brought about in a natural or a violent manner, according as liberty or persecution brings about, we must comfort ourselves."

"Daati," Christian whispered, "are we going to die?"

Joseph did not know whether the day's events or the evening's reading—or both—had prompted Christian's question. But he was suddenly angry.

"You're scaring him." His voice quivered.

Daati exchanged a sober glance with Maami. "We Amish try to follow all of God's commandments, and we prove our beliefs by the way we live. Those who are disobedient hate us for standing as witnesses against their sins. We do't wish to die or seek martyrdom, but we must be ready if God should require it of us. A faith that is abandoned when it is tested is no faith at all."

Jake's brow furrowed. "Did they really burn our people at the stake just because they wouldn't baptize babies or join the army?"

"Ach, they did worse." Maami folded her arms tightly across her bosom. "One of our friends in Sainte-Marie-aux-Mines said that his grandparents were driven into a house with other church members, including little children, and the building was burned down over their heads."

Barbara twisted her kerchief into a tight spiral, her eyes brimming with tears. "How do we know the English here will not do such things?"

Daati shook his head. "William Penn, who started this colony, promised that all who come here would be free to worship God according to their beliefs. That's why your Maami and I came all this way to this new land. Here we are safe. Nothing like that is going to happen to us."

When the clock began to strike eight o'clock, he studied the faces of his children until the chimes fell silent. "It's time for bed. Come, *Kinder,* let us say our prayers."

They gathered around his chair to kneel on the floor, heads bowed and hands folded as he prayed.

"O merciful heavenly Father, we thank Thee for letting us live through another day. We pray for all mankind throughout your world, for the governments and rulers of the nations. Do not permit them to shed innocent blood, but inspire them to rule according to Thy will, so that we who fear Thy name may lead quiet and peaceable lives here on earth. But if it be Thy will for us to endure hardship and persecution, then help us to remain steadfast in serving Thee.

"Now we ask that Thou wilt bless and protect us as we sleep. May we enter into this night's rest with grateful hearts and be ever watchful and ready for the return of Thy beloved Son, Jesus Christ, in whose name we offer this prayer: Our Father who art in heaven . . . "

Joseph dutifully repeated the Lord's Prayer with the others, echoing his father's amen before scrambling to his feet and heading for the door ahead of Jake and Christian. When Daati spoke, they halted and turned around.

"Did you shoot that fox then, Joseph?"

Joseph's cheeks burned. He dropped his gaze to the worn floor planks under his feet and shook his head.

"*Nay,* you wasted time that should have been spent doing your chores and helping your Maami."

Joseph forced himself to stand perfectly still while Daati leaned back in his chair and considered the ceiling.

"Tomorrow, after you clean up the damage the cows did in the cornfield . . ."

Joseph held his breath.

". . . you will stay home the rest of the day to take care of the chores, while Jake and I work with Johannes to finish cutting the last of his hay and your mother and sister help Katie with the baby."

Joseph's shoulders sagged, and a frown creased his brow. The way Johannes and Katie treated him made him feel almost grown up, and his newborn nephew had added another strong lure down the path to their homestead. Losing the chance to work with Johannes and to play with chubby little Jacob while Katie tended to her chores was stiff punishment indeed.

He opened his mouth to protest, but the slight shake of Jake's head caused him to close it again. Turning, he followed his brother up to bed with as much meekness as he could manage.

THE THREE BOYS RETREATED to the cramped front *Kammer* under the eaves at the top of the steep stairway. The room was chilly now that the fire had been banked for the night, with only faint warmth radiating from the chimney flue behind the head of the big rope bed the two older boys shared.

Joseph pulled the quilt up around his neck and wiggled into a more comfortable position deep in the thick featherbed layered over a cornhusk mattress. On the other side of the board partition, he could hear the muted sounds of his sister preparing for bed. The realization that she would soon be leaving for her new home brought back the sense of loss he had felt when Johannes had married and moved to his own home.

"It isn't fair that you get to go over to Johannes and Katie's tomorrow and I don't."

Jake rolled over and propped himself up on his elbow. "*Ya,* it is. Daati isn't being mean. Farming is hard work, and we all need to do our share."

"All we do is work! Don't you want to have fun sometimes?"

"We have fun all the time. What about the *apfelschnitzen* last week at Zug's?"

"*Ya,* and we had to go home to do chores and go to bed, while the older ones stayed to sing and play games."

Jake laughed. "In a few more years we'll be their age and get to stay up late and play games with the girls, too, you goose! What about Barbara's *Hochzeit?*"

"Her wedding is still weeks away! I don't want to stay here all by myself tomorrow, doing all the work while you're having fun."

"If you'd obeyed and gotten your chores done, you'd be going tomorrow. Didn't I warn you not to chase after that old fox?"

"It was just bad luck I didn't find him." Joseph rolled onto his stomach, buried his face in his pillow, and mumbled, "If I'd killed him, Daati wouldn't be mad."

Jake punched him on the arm. "He would, too, Joseph. Because you ran off, the cows got in the cornfield. Besides, even if you'd found the fox, you wouldn't have hit him."

"I would have! I'm as good a shot as you are."

Christian popped up in his trundle bed. "No you aren't! Jake shoots almost as good as Daati."

Ignoring him, Jake stretched out on his back, his hands behind his head. "*Nay*, not yet. But it takes more than shooting. You have to learn to track better too. As soon as we get the corn harvested, let's go hunting. I'll teach you to track as good as an Indian."

"Promise?" Joseph demanded, his eyes widening.

Jake grinned. "Promise."

Across the *Kammer*, Christian curled up under the covers. "I want to go too."

Jake shook his head. "You aren't big enough to handle a rifle yet. It's twice as tall as you are."

"I can learn how to track." A yawn muffled Christian's voice.

"Go to sleep," Joseph ordered. "We aren't talking to you."

"I wasn't talking to you either! I was talking to Jake."

"It's too dangerous for you yet, Christli. What if we ran into more Indians like the ones who came by here today? You can't run as fast as we can."

"Why can't we be friends with them? I'd like to wear leggings and moccasins and carry a tomahawk like they do. And paint my face, too. I bet they don't have to do any chores."

The room fell silent for several minutes. Finally Jake said,

"The Indians were our friends until the French soldiers started stirring them up against the English."

"But we're not English."

"We're not French either," Joseph answered. "Most of the Indians are on their side."

Joseph stared, frowning, at the sloped ceiling, wondering how the Indians could think it was all right to roam across his family's fields and take what they wanted. The previous spring, a couple of their calves had disappeared from the pasture, and Daati had found moccasin prints crossing the field.

"If they come back, I'll shoot them." He was surprised when he realized he had spoken aloud.

Jake yawned. "*Nay,* you won't. We Amish don't hurt anybody, and the Indians know that. Now go to sleep."

Joseph curled into a tight ball and closed his eyes. If the Indians knew they had nothing to fear from the Amish, wouldn't they leave his community alone?

Within minutes, he heard Christian's even breathing, but he could tell that Jake still lay awake. The muted voices of their parents drifted through the floorboards from the *Kammer* below. And although Joseph could not make out their words, he could tell they were arguing.

✦ ┄┄ ✦

HER HAIR FALLING LOOSE over her white linen shift, Anna jerked back the covers and flounced down onto the featherbed. "It wasn't enough that you gave them the bread Barbara and I worked so hard to bake—but my quilt yet!"

Jakob laid his breeches on the chair and turned to face her. "We have still enough to sustain us, Anna."

"They take food out of our children's mouths. You just hand over whatever they want when you should be taking care of us!"

"With Barbara marrying, we have one less to feed this winter. None of us will starve."

"Ach, I know you. If they come back again, you'll give them everything they didn't take this time."

Struggling to contain his annoyance, he went around to his side of the bed. "God has always provided for us, and He always will. As Christians, we're commanded to love our neighbor and give freely to all who ask of us. The Indians are our neighbors and God's children too."

"It's our children I'm worried about!" She drew her legs up onto the bed and attacked the covers the way she beat rugs on the clothesline. "We need all our quilts for the winter."

"Barbara has new quilts for her wedding. She won't need the one from her bed. We'll have enough to get by."

Anna wrung her hands. "But my quilt!"

He threw up his hands, still standing beside the bed. "What does it matter? It was old and worn out."

"It was our wedding quilt! I sewed it with Maam and my sisters and aunts. My closest girlfriends helped too. Their stitches were all in it, and I could tell who sewed each block." She blinked hard, tears glistening in her eyes. "It's been fourteen years, Jakob. That quilt was all I had left of them—and you gave it away to savages."

Chapter Four

Thursday, October 19, 1752

BARBARA SAT AT THE FRONT of Uncle Jakob and Aunt Mary
Buerki's *Stube* between her best friends, Bessie Beiler and
Mary Seiber, nervously rolling and unrolling the edge of her fine
white gauze apron. A matching *Halsduch,* or neck cloth, covered
her bosom. Beneath these she wore the indigo linen bodice and
petticoat she and Maami had painstakingly sewn for this day, and
a snowy linen *Haube* covered her hair.

Crist Stutzman sat facing her, flanked by his brothers Hans
and Jake. Certain that if she met his eyes, she was going to giggle in front of everyone, she clasped her hands together on her
lap and concentrated on God's laws about marriage and the
duties of husband and wife. The ministers had instructed her
and Crist on these subjects a short time ago in a separate room,
while the sober chant of hymns drifted through the walls.

Early that morning, dressed in their Sunday best—which
meant plainest—clothing, she and her family had ridden in the
wagon to her uncle and aunt's plantation, arriving just as the
congregation was beginning to gather. More than an hour had
passed and the first preacher had yet to speak. Bishop Hertzler

would preach second and, as usual, be in no hurry to finish, with several more preachers to follow. It would be noon for sure before she and Crist went forward to take their vows.

For months she had been certain that she was going to burst if their wedding day did not arrive quickly. But now, thinking of the ministers' sober charge about the duties and responsibilities of the holy relationship they were about to enter into, she felt nervous.

Although Crist was a few years older, they were both still so young. Before them lay a lifetime of labor in this untamed land, bearing and rearing their children to know and love God, and facing all the challenges of providing for their family on a frontier that might well soon erupt in war.

A chill went through her at the thought. How were they to prosper? Or even to survive?

A collective sigh and the muted rustle of movement filled the room, drawing her back to the present. She looked around at the grave, bearded faces of the men and the softer countenances of the women and children, and a deep comfort and assurance warmed her. Whatever the struggles they would endure in the years to come, she and Crist would not face them alone.

❖ • — • ❖

Joseph squirmed. The hard edge of the bench dug into the back of his thighs, just above the constricting leg bands of his breeches, and his shoes pinched his feet. He began to swing his legs back and forth to ease the discomfort and joined without enthusiasm in the congregation's drawn-out chant of the "Love Song" from the *Ausbund,* a staple at weddings.

The song finally ended, and the first preacher took his place at the head of the room. While he droned on and on about the marriage of Tobias and Sarah from the Book of Tobit, Joseph nudged his eleven-year-old cousin John Buerki, who sat on his right at one end of the crowded rows of benches at the back of the *Stube*. A grin and an answering shove rewarded his efforts.

Joseph let his gaze rove across the congregation, soberly dressed in tones of deep grey, walnut brown, dark blue, or purple. He calculated that he and John might be able to escape out to the barn unnoticed. They could pretend they needed to go to the privy. But if they headed for the *Stube's* outside door, they would have to pass too close to Daati, on the front row with Johannes and Christli—never a good option. And to leave through the *Küche* they would have to weave their way between the tightly packed benches that filled the larger room behind them, causing a commotion that would draw everyone's attention.

Joseph's shoulders sagged. Even if they made it outside, they would have to return quickly or risk interrogation after the service. And his cousin inevitably tattled. Besides, there was no use at all in broaching the subject with Jake, who sat on his left.

He swung his legs faster, fixing his gaze intently on Barbara's face, willing her to meet his eyes. The minute he captured her attention, he meant to contort his face into the silly expression that always made her laugh out loud.

But today, although a rosy blush colored her cheeks, Barbara's eyes were unusually sober, her characteristic smile suppressed beneath a mask of concentration. Blond-haired Crist, normally as easy-going and ready for fun as Barbara, appeared to have sunk into a state of equal gravity. He held himself ramrod straight, and his sturdy hands clenched his kneecaps as though they would fall off if he relaxed his grip.

Joseph decided that was what getting married did to you. Suppressing a snort, he looked around for another distraction.

His gaze fell on his eldest brother, who sat next to their father, his handsome, bearded face bemused. Johannes turned to smile at his young wife, who sat between her mother and Maami on the women's side of the room, rocking their tightly bundled baby.

Katie, Bishop Hertzler's eldest daughter, returned Johannes's look with a knowing one. The becoming pink hue of her cheeks deepened, and she tucked a stray strand of her light brown hair back under her *Haube*. Joseph suspected they were thinking about their own wedding day little more than a year earlier. He elbowed John and whispered for him to look at Johannes and Katie, then clutched his stomach and doubled over as though he was going to be sick, drawing a snicker from his cousin.

Feeling Jake lean into him, he straightened abruptly as his brother whispered into his left ear, "You'd better watch out. Anna Blanck is looking at you."

Joseph turned an anxious glance on the petite, blonde, nine-year-old daughter of Hans and Mattie Blanck seated one row up on the women's side between her mother and younger sisters. She had indeed twisted around to stare at him, eyes wide, one eyebrow raised mockingly.

The warm brown of her dress intensified the color of her emerald green eyes. He had never seen anyone so pretty. Friends of his parents from the Alsace, the Blancks had arrived in Berks County the previous year, moving in with Mrs. Blanck's parents while they built a homestead in nearby Heidelberg Township. It had quickly become Joseph's ambition to impress their oldest daughter.

Shouldering against him, Jake made kissing sounds, provoking Joseph to aim a hard jab into his brother's ribs, a blow the older boy would normally have returned with interest. This time, however, Jake winced and groaned, pressing his hand to his side as though mortally wounded. The commotion momentarily distracted Bishop Hertzler, who had risen to preach, and caught the attention of everyone on that side of the room. Including Daati.

Joseph instantly straightened, his expression as bright and innocent as a baby's. Nonetheless, Daati's intense gaze settled on him.

That was always what happened. No matter what his brothers did, he was the one Daati caught—even when he was a mere bystander.

He held his nonchalant posture until his father faced forward again. Then he let out his breath and relaxed . . . and met again Anna Blanck's eyes.

He felt the heat climb into his face. When she shot him a smirk, then deliberately flounced around and turned her back on him, he slid lower on the bench, wishing that he could disappear.

❦━━━❦

THE SERMON CAME TO AN END just when Joseph thought he might drop dead of boredom. The bridal party stood, the men facing the women, and the room filled with the shuffling of feet and creaking of benches as the congregation knelt for prayer. Joseph propped his elbows on the bench seat, hands folded and head bowed.

His thoughts never approached heaven, however. There was yet another sermon to come and the vows to get through before they could go back home for the wedding dinner. His stomach growled, and he despaired of surviving that long.

Suddenly Jake nudged him with his foot. Realizing that the congregation had risen, Joseph hastily got up and resumed his seat, arms folded across his chest.

He heard little of the final sermon and only wrestled his attention back to the proceedings when the bishop soberly asked Barbara and Crist to come forward if they still wished to marry. A prayer followed their vows, then the bishop joined their right hands and pronounced them husband and wife. The concluding hymn ended, and he and John escaped outside close behind Anna Blanck and her sisters.

She glanced over her shoulder as though she felt his gaze on her back. Settling his black felt hat on his head, he flashed a smile and was rewarded with one in return. Gathering courage, he winked. This time she turned away so fast that Joseph froze in his tracks.

John stopped too. "I think she likes you."

Joseph flushed but could not stifle a grin. He gave his cousin a punch on the shoulder.

"I don't care if she does or not."

He stuck his hands in his pockets. Whistling, he led the way across the yard to where the wagons waited, his stomach's complaints competing with Anna Blanck's attractions for attention.

✦ ····· ✦

THE BRIDAL PARTY'S OPEN CARRIAGE, drawn by a sleek black mare, led the procession of wagons and carriages back to the Hochstetler plantation for the wedding dinner. Barbara tried hard not to look at her new husband. Shy glances told her that he struggled to keep his eyes from her too. His arm curved possessively across the back of the seat behind her shoulders, however, and every time their glances met, his broad grin summoned her giggles.

When they arrived at the house, the two of them hurried into the *Küche* to welcome their guests. Several days earlier Daat and the boys had dismantled the loom and carried it and the spinning wheels out to the barn to clear space. Taking in the room crowded with sturdy boards set on trestles and covered with snowy linen cloths, she nodded with satisfaction.

She couldn't suppress a smile when Crist inhaled deeply the aromas wafting from the food her mother and the women of the congregation had prepared. The serving tables appeared to sag under platters filled with roasted and stewed meats; dishes of vegetables and noodles; plates of cheeses and breads; and pots of pickles, apple butter, and jam. Several cakes and fresh fruit rounded out the menu.

Long tables had been set up along the walls of the *Stube* to form a hollow square. As the wedding guests flooded into the house, Barbara's closest friends ushered her and her new husband to their seats in the *Braut Ecke,* or bridal corner, at the back of the *Stube.*

Maam had set the bridal party's table with her best tableware, accented by vases of bright golden and deep russet autumn flowers. Barbara threw her arms around her mother's ample shoulders and for a moment clung to her, eyes brimming with tears.

She and Crist took their seats on each side of the corner, with their attendants ranged beside them. Then the rest of the congregation filled the benches around the tables, overflowing into the *Küche.* The morning's solemnity quickly evaporated in the happy clamor of the meal, well wishes, and song.

✦ ┄┄ ✦

SEATED ACROSS FROM ANNA just inside the door into the *Küche,* Jakob found his eyes repeatedly drawn to his daughter and her new husband. They leaned together with shoulders and arms touching and fingers intertwined, talking little, but smiling much.

The memory of his and Anna's wedding day flooded his mind, arousing a piercing sense of guilt. What had he given his own bride but unending toil on the land? Both of them had started out with such hope for the future, such determination to provide a better life for their children. But the daily hardships they had to endure in this new country were taking a toll on both of them. Anna was unhappy, and he feared there was nothing he could do to change that.

His attention was drawn to the hum of voices and bustle of activity that filled the house as the young women who were serving kept dishes filled and goblets brimming with cider or beer.

At last the meal was cleared away, and for another hour the company sang traditional marriage hymns.

The newlyweds had already received generous gifts from him and Anna, the Buerkis and Stutzmans, and other church members, and as the afternoon waned, Barbara and Crist joined the children and young people for one last time, escaping outside while the adults visited. Soon the shouts of children playing games in the warm sunshine filtered into the room through the thick log walls and half-opened windows.

Jakob surveyed those who gathered in the *Stube* and *Küche,* enjoying this rare opportunity to relax and visit in the middle of the week. After a moment his gaze returned to Anna, who cradled their new grandson in her arms. Baby Jacob let out a wail, and immediately Katie appeared from the *Küche,* scooped him out of Anna's arms, and hurried off into the *Kammer* to nurse him.

Jakob was uncomfortably aware that Anna blinked back tears but was at a loss as to what he might say or do to relieve her grief. So he did nothing.

He was relieved when the Blancks came over to sit with him and Anna, the Buerkis, and Maudlin Stutzman. It was their first opportunity to visit at length since their arrival in Pennsylvania, and for some time all of them eagerly questioned the Blancks about friends and loved ones back in the Alsace.

The women soon excused themselves to join the clean-up efforts in the kitchen. Johannes, the bishop, and several of the other men drifted over to join Jakob, Dr. Blanck, and Jakob and Crist Buerki.

"I must compliment you on your fine plantation, Jakob. You've worked hard and prospered."

"*Gott* has blessed me indeed, Hans. My children and herds are straining the joists of my house and barn."

A gust of sympathetic laughter rippled around the circle of men.

Hannes Mueller settled on the bench beside Jakob. "Ach, that's a problem none of us would complain about."

Jakob clapped his hand on his neighbor's shoulder. "None of us can complain that I can see. I'm not the only one who needs more pasture for my animals—and more cropland too. And many of us have sons coming up who'll need land when they marry."

Blanck nodded. "I'm hoping the land I've warranted will prove to be as fertile as yours."

The *Stube's* outer door banged open and Joseph appeared with Christian on his heels. Hats in hand, hair disheveled and faces flushed, the boys planted themselves before Jakob. Johannes frowned and shook his head, but they stood their ground.

Jakob took no notice of his sons' fidgeting. "My acreage has produced well, but I have my eye on that piece of land to the north of my fields that may do even better. There's a spring and a good spot for an orchard too. I'm thinking about warranting it next year."

The bishop regarded Jakob with a skeptical smile, his head cocked to one side. "Then no doubt you'll build a bigger house and more barns to store your crops yet. But *Sprüche* 16:18 says,

'*Wer zu Grunde gehen soll, der wird zuvor stolz; und Hochmut kommt vor dem Fall.*'" Pride goeth before destruction, and a haughty spirit before a fall.

"Daati!"

Jakob stiffened but ignored Joseph's interruption. He studied the bishop's face, his jaw tensing.

Jakob Buerki cleared his throat. "I think we all agree that our plans have to line up with God's will."

"I don't intend to move outside the Lord's leading," Jakob said with a nod at his brother-in-law, "but if He opens a door for us, are we wrong to walk through it?"

"God promised to bless those who diligently obey his commandments."

Stephen Kurtz raised his stub of an index finger. "That's true, Johannes, but Job also had much land and many children and herds. And he lost everything when the Lord tested him."

"God tested Job," Jakob countered with a smile, "not because he was proud, but to prove that he was righteous."

Several in the circle raised eyebrows and exchanged glances, among them Bishop Hertzler. "Do you claim to be as righteous as Job, then? If you are, then you had better be on the lookout, for God will test you sorely."

The expressions of amusement in the group turned to low chuckles now. Although Jakob joined in the laughter, the bishop's rebuke stung.

"If it pleases God to test a man, he must bear it as best he can. Whether I know Job's sorrows or not, I can only pray that I learn his obedience too."

"Daati, there's a band of Indians—"

"Lots of them," Christian added, "and they're going real fast."

"They were crossing the far end of our pasture heading west toward Detweilers'—"

Jakob raised his hand. "You know better than to interrupt the grown-ups. Where are your manners?"

Blanck rested his hand on Joseph's shoulder. "I've heard reports lately of attacks on the other side of the mountains."

"The Delaware around here have always been peaceful. We keep good relations with all our neighbors, including the tribes. They know we're no threat—"

"But the French are stirring them up again, Jakob," Crist Buerki broke in. "A neighbor told me the other day that they pay fifteen pounds for every white scalp the Indians take."

Eagerly Joseph said, "See, Daati! Jake and I better track them a little way to make sure they don't try to hurt anybody."

"And what could you do if they did?"

"Warn everybody!"

"Ach, *ya,* always chasing prey, and never catching it. That's my Joseph."

Jakob bit his tongue as the heat climbed into Joseph's cheeks. The boy glanced quickly at the faces of the men surrounding them, then dropped his head and stared at the floor.

Before Jakob could speak, Christian's pleading voice broke into his accusing thoughts. "But, Daati—"

"You're just boys, and you have chores to do." Jakob nodded toward the window where the afternoon sun's pale rays poured in, slanting across the braided rug. "Better to do the work at hand than to go chasing off after shadows."

❧ ······ ❧

CHRISTIAN FOLLOWED JOSEPH across the yard, giving the scattered knots of children and grown-ups a wide berth. He nearly had to run to match Joseph's angry strides as they skirted the barn, but they reached the edge of the cornfield together. On the other side of the fence, long rows stretched toward the woods, pocked by the ragged stumps left after the corn harvest and laced with the trampled, drying remnants of squash vines.

When Joseph climbed the fence and perched on the top rail, Christian hung his arms over the rail below. He jerked erect when something whizzed over his head and plunked neatly into Joseph's lap.

Joseph glared at Jake, who approached down the path, and hurled the half-eaten apple back at his brother. Jake dodged and the missile sailed off into the grass.

"You're mad at Daati again. What's happened now?"

Joseph clenched his hands over the rail, his kuckles whitening. "Christli and I saw a party of Indians, all painted up like the ones who took our bread, crossing Johannes's pasture. But Daati wouldn't even listen to me. We can't say anything to him or we're being disobedient. But he was disagreeing with Bishop Hertzler, so what does that make him?"

"You shouldn't talk like that about Daati." Jake slanted a glance in their younger brother's direction. "Particularly not in front of Christli."

Christian looked from one to the other, eyes wide. Joseph pushed him away from the fence with his foot.

"What did I do?"

Joseph jumped off the fence rail and gripped him by the shoulder. "You'd just love to get me in trouble, wouldn't you? If you go telling tales—"

Jake grabbed Joseph's arm. "Stop it right now, or I'll tell Daati. We're not supposed to fight, and you know it."

Joseph tore his arm out of Jake's grasp. "Why does Daati have to act that way?"

Jake's frown gave way to a grin. "Ach, you're just mad because you wanted to impress Anna by chasing after Indians."

"I did not! I don't care a thing about her!"

"I saw you mooning over her. But I think she was more interested in Michael Speicher."

Joseph cocked his fist. "That's a lie! Take it back!"

Jake spun Joseph around and pinned his arms behind his back, knocking his hat off in the process. Fighting to break free, Joseph sent his brother's hat flying into the dirt as well.

They tussled, smashing into the fence post and dislodgiing the top rail, sending it to the ground with a crash. Christian danced from one foot to the other, unsure whether to run for help, join the fight on Jake's behalf, or stay out of the way and watch so he could tell his parents everything that happened.

Joseph pivoted sharply and broke Jake's grip. Hands free, he flailed at Jake's head.

Jake covered his head with his arms, laughing. "Okay, okay, I'm sorry! She only had eyes for you."

Grinning, Joseph brushed the hair out of his eyes. He retrieved his hat and beat it against his breeches to dislodge the dirt.

"We have to follow those Indians. We can't let them surprise us again or this time they might hurt us. Besides, you promised to help me learn to track like an Indian."

Jake climbed over the fence into the field and replaced the fallen rail, then clambered back out. He picked up his hat, brushed away the dirt and straightened the brim. After raking his fingers through his hair, he settled the hat back on his head.

"*Nay,* we need to get our chores done."

Joseph glanced at the sun, which still stood high above the western treetops. "It's at least a couple of hours before sunset, and we won't be gone long. We'll go just far enough to make sure they cleared out. Maami and Daati are busy with company. They'll never know. Daati didn't say we couldn't track the Indians, just that we have to do our chores, and we'll be back in plenty of time to get everything done before dark."

Jake frowned and shook his head. "If I let you run off into the woods alone, Daati will give us both a strapping."

"That's why you need to come. You can't let me go alone. If I get in trouble, it'll be your fault."

Jake leaned his back against the fence. Folding his arms over his chest, he gave Joseph a calculating look that slowly turned into a sly smile.

All three had discarded shoes, hose, and coats as soon as the church service was over, and now he reached for Joseph's hat.

"Give that here. Our hats will only get caught in the brush, so let's hide them under that bush behind the fence, where nobody will notice them. We can grab them on our way back."

Christian instantly offered his hat to Jake as well, but he shook his head. "You have to stay here, Cristli."

Christian's bright blue eyes blazed. "I want to go too!"

Joseph glowered at him, hands on hips. "You saw them already. We don't need you tagging along with us every time we want to go somewhere."

Jake bent over the younger boy and ruffled his hair. "You're too little. You can't go as far as we can, and if something happened to you, we'd be in big trouble with Daati and Maami."

"And if you breathe a word about this to anybody, you're going to be sorry!"

Christian stamped his foot. "But I saw the Indians first!"

"We'll tell you all about it when we get back," Jake assured him. "Just go play with your friends, and don't tell anybody where we've gone."

+———+

CHRISTIAN WATCHED HIS BROTHERS walk away, his lip quivering. As soon as they passed out of his sight behind the trees, where the path sloped gently westward toward Detweilers' plantation, he shoved his hat under a bush next to the fence and started after them.

He was careful to avoid dry sticks and drifts of fallen leaves that might crackle under his bare feet and alert his brothers to his presence, proud that he knew enough to take such precautions. They thought he was a nuisance, but he would show them.

He would follow until they turned back, and then he would jump out from behind the trees with a loud shout.

Wouldn't they be surprised—maybe even scared? He clamped both hands over his mouth to keep from laughing out loud as he hurried after them, imagining their astonished, fearful expressions.

Well ahead, his older brothers crossed from the fallow flax field into the pasture beyond. Christian crept along the hedgerows so they wouldn't spy him if they turned suddenly around. Often he peeked out from behind the heavy growth of thick briars and sturdy saplings to keep them in sight.

He shadowed them across Melchior Detweiler's adjoining fields to a shallow ford across narrow, rushing Northkill Creek, which wound northward across the cleared land to disappear into deep forest. By the time he crossed to the creek's far side, his brothers were already moving into the trees, and although Christian pumped his short legs as fast as he could, he fell steadily behind.

His chest began to ache from the effort. When the trail's steady ascent steepened, rising toward the looming mountain ridge still a mile distant, he lost sight of them altogether. Still he kept on going.

They were always leaving him behind, but this time he was going to show them that he wasn't a baby anymore. He was going to prove that he could track as well as Jake. Better, even.

They would see how grown up he was. And then they wouldn't leave him behind ever again.

Chapter Five

THE BOYS FOLLOWED the faint moccasin tracks leading them onward in single file into the deep forest. They had not gone far before the land began its gradual upward slope toward the long, sprawling bulk of the Blue Mountain straight ahead.

A halo of autumn sunlight glowed through the thinning golden foliage on the towering heights that drew steadily closer as they walked. It cast the Northkill's rocky banks and swirling water into blue shadow.

The awareness of time's rapid passing nagged at Joseph. But he had no intention of turning back until Jake insisted.

Jake stopped abruptly, then bent over and pointed. "See how these tracks are shaped? They're Delaware. Most of the tracks are like these, so the party you saw was mostly Delaware." He moved to the side of the trail. "But see these over here? They're bigger, but narrower. I took a good look at the tracks of those Shawnee who came by our place a few weeks ago, and these are shaped the same."

Joseph squatted and studied the two sets of tracks intently, fixing their outlines in his mind. "There are Shawnee with them, then."

"That's right. But look here." Jake moved farther ahead. "These look like they have different stitching along the sole. I've never seen any quite like them before."

"What do you think they are?"

"Maybe one of the Iroquois tribes. Could be Seneca. Some of their villages aren't far north of here, but they don't usually come this way. Not that I've seen anyway."

Joseph stood up, frowning. A blizzard of yellow and orange leaves swirled around them, and he shivered in the cool October wind, wishing he had worn his coat.

"Why do you think they're traveling together?"

"They're all allied with the French. If their officers are stirring them up, maybe they're heading off on a raid. Maybe the Shawnee came to get some of the Delaware to fight with them. There's been talk about it even at church."

As they continued following the warriors' trail, Jake added, "The English are worried about the French taking over all the land on the other side of the mountains and maybe even on this side too."

"The English want all the land for themselves. That's why they're worried. But it belongs to the Indians, doesn't it?"

Jake shrugged. "You could say the same about our land."

The ground steepened even more, rising toward a pass through the mountain range called *Kau-ta-tn-chunk* by the Indians. Seamed walls of rock and the forest's tangled growth increasingly hemmed them in.

Soon the creek's bank became so rocky that even Jake had trouble finding the warriors' trail. From time to time, however, he pointed out a thin branch that had been snapped off or the faint indentation where the moss had been trodden upon and had not yet sprung back.

In the lead, Jake crested a rise and stepped to the rocky precipice. Joining him, Joseph assessed the distance to the narrow gap in the ridge where the Northkill had its source, still well above them. After a moment he swung around to look out over the valley.

Far below, the great valley divided by the Schuylkill and Susquehanna rivers stretched into the hazy, limitless distance. Heavily wooded for most of its length, it revealed here and there a patchwork of pastures and cleared fields between stands of golden and russet forest, bounded by the shadowy lines of rail fences and hedgerows and dotted with cattle.

Closer at hand he identified the scattered plantations belonging to the Kurtzes, Zugs, and Detweilers as well as their own. Smoke drifted lazily upward from the chimneys of the expansive log houses, while to all sides the shadows of late afternoon stretched long fingers across the land.

The sun had disappeared behind the ridge, and Jake threw a calculating glance at the darkening sky. "We've gone a lot farther than I meant to. The Indians are on the other side by now. We'd better get back before anyone comes looking for us. If Daati finds out where we've gone, he'll take us out to the barn for a strapping."

Joseph slapped his brother's arm. "I'll race you!" He plunged back down the trail.

BARBARA GLANCED from Aunt Katrina to Maam, who hurried toward them.

"Excuse me, Katrina. Barbara, I've been looking for Christli to take the slop out to the hogs and gather the eggs, but he's nowhere around. Do you know if Jake and Joseph went to bring the cows up from the pasture? Maybe he's with them."

"You know, I don't think I've seen any of them since dinner. As late as it is, they should be doing their chores by now."

"Ach, with all the commotion they may have lost track of the time, and your Daat is going to be aggravated. Will you make sure they're down at the barn? I'd go, but we're not done clearing dinner away yet, and it's almost time to start supper for you young people."

"I'll go right now."

Barbara hurried outside. She saw Johannes striding purposefully up the path from the barn and went to meet him.

"Have you seen the boys?"

"I was just coming to ask you the same thing. The last time I saw them was at least a couple hours ago. I was going to ask Christli whether he wanted to come help me with my milking after he finished his chores, but I can't find any of them."

"You don't think they ran off together?"

Johannes shook his head. "It wouldn't be the first time Joseph forgot his chores, but Jake never does. Even if they took off somewhere, he'd make sure to be back in time."

The sound of voices brought both around sharply to see their father emerge from the outer *Stube* door. The Blancks accompanied him, trailed by Crist and his brothers. Johannes led the way to intercept them.

◆┄┄┄◆

CHRISTIAN'S EXCITEMENT was gone now. The trail climbed sharply and steadily upward. His body ached and he knew that every additional step he took increased the distance he would have to return.

Some time ago he had abandoned the cover of the underbrush and had begun to climb upward as fast as his short legs could carry him. Every ragged breath burned now, and weariness weighted his aching limbs so that every movement required greater effort than the last.

He crawled around a rocky outcrop and strained to see through the brooding forest. There was no one in sight. Still.

He began to run, tears blurring his sight. Branches smacked his face and brambles snagged his clothing as he tore through the brush, the rocky ground bruising his bare feet. The faster he ran, the more confused he became, until he had lost all sense of direction, not knowing whether his brothers' path lay ahead or behind . . . or neither.

Finally he stumbled to a halt. The only sound that reached him over his own gasps was the wind's faint whisper in the sparse canopy of leaves overhead, the muted creak of branches, an occasional birdsong. Unable to hear the hiss of the Northkill's tumbling waters, he realized with dismay that he had wandered away from it.

Untrodden forest loomed on all sides. His whimpers of panic quickly gave way to convulsive sobs.

Without warning a dark shape emerged from the brush directly in front of him. Several others followed it. There were five of them. Warriors. Their bodies and faces painted black and red. To Christian they looked just like the war party that had stopped at his home.

They showed no surprise, as if they had been tracking him. Their leader reached out to Christian, smiling.

Close up, the warrior's face was handsome beneath the war paint, with pleasing regular features and expressive brown eyes. Christian stood frozen to the ground, transfixed. Then the man clutched at Christian's hair.

He instinctively ducked and dodged away to plunge down the slope, stumbliing and sliding, too terrified to look back. Behind him leaves crackled and branches snapped, accompanied by pounding footfalls and a frightening, warbling war cry.

JAKOB USHERED THE BLANCKS and the Stuzman brothers outside. The last of the wedding guests had gone except for the immediate family and the youth of the church, who would stay for supper and the singing that would follow.

Blanck helped his wife and children into their carriage. "So you don't think these reports about Indian raids are serious enough to worry about, Crist?"

Jakob saw that his new son-in-law brightened at sight of Barbara approaching on Johannes's heels.

"Not as long as the Indians keep to the other side of the mountains." Crist brushed his curly blond hair off his forehead and settled his hat at a rakish angle. "The English who move over there ought to know they're taking a risk."

A blush rose to Barbara's cheeks when her eyes met his. Jakob stroked his beard, hiding a smile behind his hand.

"The treaty between the French and the British makes the Blue Mountain the border between their territories. If these settlers keep on laying stake to land on the other side, it'll come to a war."

Johannes came to a halt beside Hans Stutzman. "There've already been plenty of wars over this land, Hans, with a good many settlers getting killed or captured by Indians allied with the French. I'm afraid trouble is bound to reach us here, too, before the issue finally gets settled."

Jakob looked from his son to the others. "There's plenty of land on this side of the mountains. The English should leave the West to the French and the Indians so we can all live in peace."

"We'll pray they see it your way. Thank you again for your hospitality." Dr. Blanck shook hands with each of the men, ending with Crist. "May God bless you and your new bride."

He climbed into the carriage and shook the reins over the horse's rump. His daughter Anna leaned around her little sisters to catch Jakob's attention, mischief sparkling in her eyes.

"Say goodbye to your boys for me. I haven't seen them since dinner."

Jakob watched the Blancks' carriage roll down the rutted path, its occupants calling and waving goodbye. When horse and carriage disappeared around the far bend, he turned to Johannes and Barbara.

"Have you seen the boys?"

Johannes shook his head. "They're not in the barn, and they weren't in the house either."

The muscles in Jakob's jaw tightened. "Have the hogs been slopped?"

Barbara exchanged a glance with Johannes. "Maam couldn't find Christli to take the bucket down to the pen. She asked me to look for him."

Crist's smiling gaze rested on Barbara, whose blush deepened. "They're probably in the pasture rounding up the cows." .

"They ought to be half finished with the milking by now. Crist, will you, Hans, and Jake look in the barn again while Johannes and I go down to the cornfield? Barbara, stay by your Maam, but don't worry her about this."

Barbara hurried back to the house and the men separated. Jakob headed down the path past the barn with Johannes. Neither spoke.

When they reached the fence, Johannes grabbed his arm. "Daat—"

Jakob took two swift steps and pulled an object from under a bush at the side of the path. He held it up for Johannes to see.

It was Christian's small black hat, creased and smudged with dust.

＋—•----◆

"JAKE, JOSEPH! *Helfe!*" Help!

As one, both boys turned toward the sound of Christian's

screams. The undulating whoop that echoed through the woods raised the hair on the back of Joseph's neck.

They raced toward the sound, fighting their way through the dense undergrowth. "We're here!" Jake shouted. "Over here!"

Christian burst out of the trees, his face beet red, cheeks and forehead scratched and streaked with tears and trickling blood, shirt pulled loose from breeches smeared with dirt. He fell into their arms.

The warriors broke through the brush behind him. Jake thrust Christian into Joseph's arms and shoved them both forward.

"*Run!*"

They ran.

＊ーーー＊

FEAR TWISTED JAKOB'S GUT into a knot. "They're not in the cornfield either. Never have they run off like this. They know better."

The other men exchanged helpless looks.

Johannes pushed his hat onto the back of his head and threw another searching glance across the barnyard to the fields beyond. "They can't have gone far."

"When did you last see them?"

"In the *Stube* after dinner. When they told us about the Indians."

Jakob gritted his teeth. "I sent them to do their chores."

"We'll find them," Crist said.

He and his brothers went to search the orchard, the rest of the fields, and the pasture, while Johannes headed for his own plantation. Jakob watched them trot off, then returned to the house.

He peered through the open *Küche* door, careful not to attract the women's attention. Catching Crist Buerki's eye, Jakob beckoned his brother-in-law to join him outside, then curtly explained the boys' disappearance.

There was no need for Crist to say anything. His expression made it clear that he shared Jakob's apprehension. Whistling for Blitz, Jakob led the way toward the plantation's western boundary.

✦ ┈┈ ✦

IT WAS QUICKLY APPARENT that Christian could go no farther, and Joseph swung him up onto his back, hardly slowing his pace. Bent almost double, with his younger brother clinging to his neck in a stranglehold, Joseph crashed down the slope.

Behind him he could hear Jake urging him to greater speed. Full-fledged panic drove him forward until he feared he could not run another step and that they would never reach the valley.

How he kept his footing across the spongy carpets of pine needles, wet leaf mold, and patches of mossy rock was beyond comprehension. Yet he did.

Abruptly the path broadened and began to flatten out. He darted out of the forest and into Detweiler's harvested cornfield, dodging shocks as he stumbled toward the log house and barns just visible on the edge of a patch of woods. Every ragged breath seared his lungs like a hot brand.

"Joseph! *Halt!*" Stop!

By degrees Jake's voice pierced his panic.

"It's all right! They're gone."

Chest heaving, mouth dry, Joseph glanced back. Jake stood twenty paces behind, bent over with hands propped on bent knees, panting. Sweat dripped from his scarlet face and tangled hair onto the ground.

"We're safe," he gasped. "As soon as . . . we reached . . . the field . . . they gave off . . . the chase."

Joseph dropped to his knees and pried Christian's arms from around his neck. Convulsed by wrenching sobs, the child slid to the ground.

Joseph sucked great gulps of air into his lungs. Unable to still his trembling, he forced himself to turn completely around, his fearful gaze probing every direction.

They were all alone in the center of the field amid tidy rows of dry shocks. By every appearance, the warriors had never existed.

"I'm sorry!" Christian cried. "I didn't mean to—"

Jake staggered to Christian and dropped to the ground, catching him in his arms and rolling onto his back. "It's all right, Christli. We shouldn't have left you—shouldn't have gone at all. It's my fault, not yours."

Joseph fell to his knees beside them, sobbing and laughing. "We're a sight. We can't go home like this. And for sure we should have started the milking by now." He grimaced. "Daati's going to tan our hides."

Jake pushed Christian off his chest and scrambled to his feet, while Joseph helped Christian up. "Let's go to the creek and wash up, get most of the dirt off our clothes. Then we'll think up something to tell Daati and Maami."

BLITZ SNUFFLED THE GROUND, then headed straight to where the rushing Northkill crossed the neighboring plantation. In the soft soil of the stream's bank, they found a large number of footprints made by Indian moccasins and two sets of other, smaller impressions left by barefoot children. The first of these, moving together, merged into the Indian tracks. The smaller tracks of a single younger child zigzagged through the underbrush well off to the side.

Icy fingers of fear clutched Jakob's chest. "They went after those Indians they were talking about. But they didn't take Christli with them. He just followed."

"Jake won't go far."

Jakob pulled off his hat and wiped the sweat from his forehead with the back of his hand, trying to convince himself that his brother-in-law was right. Images spun in his mind, jumbled, but vivid: the painted, savage faces of the Indians a few weeks ago as they threatened his family; Joseph's excited expression earlier that afternoon when the boy tried to tell him about the Indians he had seen; his wounded look after Jakob belittled him in front of the men.

He stared into the shadowy forest, fighting to quiet his trembling. "It'll be my fault if something happens to them."

Crist shifted awkwardly from one foot to the other. "Ach, Jakob, 'he that spareth his rod hateth his son, but he that loveth him chasteneth him.' You've done nothing wrong."

"A man can do the right thing in the wrong way."

He was too much like his own father. He should not find it hard to be gentle with his boys. If they were so often *iverzwarich*—crosswise—with him, might it not be his own fault?

He struck his hat against the trunk of the giant hickory that spread its limbs over him and strode to the edge of the shallow stream. Before he could splash across to the other side, Crist grabbed him by the arm.

"*Nay.* We better get help."

Jakob clenched his teeth and jerked his chin in the direction of the plantation. "You go. I will find my boys. We're wasting time."

"*Ya,* we are," Crist shot back. "The more men we have searching, the sooner we'll find them. Let's go—now!"

Jakob's froze for a tense moment, finally yanked his arm from his brother-in-law's grasp and whistled to Blitz. Without a word, he stalked back in the direction of the house, Crist shadowing him and the dog bounding on ahead.

THE BOYS CROSSED THE CORNFIELD to the bank of the Northkill at the edge of the deep woods. In the trees' shade, the creek widened into a broad pool, where they often fished for trout and swam with Detweiler's sons.

Joseph pulled at the hooks that secured his shirt, intending to strip and jump into the water. A cry brought his head up.

"You're bleeding!" Wide-eyed, Christian pointed at Jake's leg.

Jake bent over to look at his bare legs below his breeches. A shallow cut ran along the outside of his right calf just below the knee, and from it a thick, crimson rivulet wound to his foot.

Joseph saw that his brother's footprints along the bank were edged with blood.

Jake laughed and shook his head. "I guess I was running too fast to feel it."

Joseph offered his kerchief, but Jake waved it away. He splashed out into the creek and began to lave water over the cut.

Joseph waded over to him and stopped, transfixed by the blood swirling away in the dark water. As he stared at the reddening stream, a deep unease gripped his chest..

"See—it's almost stopped already."

The bleeding had slowed to a trickle. Reassured by Jake's cheerful tone, Joseph climbed back onto the stream's bank with Jake close behind.

While Jake tied his kerchief around the cut, Joseph moved several paces away. He stared upstream in the direction of the mountain ridge, where black thunderclouds tipped with a threatening red light shouldered above the heights.

Through the branches overhead, he glimpsed the narrow notch at the summit of the heavily wooded ridge where the creek began. If they had gone a little farther, they would have reached it.

Someday he would follow the Northkill's course all the way to the gap and find out what lay on the mountain's other side, he decided. He wanted to see beyond their life in the valley, where nothing ever changed.

He turned his face to the freshening wind. His people had lived in this way for more than a hundred years, first in Europe, and even now in this new country that beckoned him to test himself against its challenges and dangers. But he wasn't afraid of the English, the French, or the Indians either, and he was determined to one day answer the call that coursed through his veins.

He became suddenly aware that the light behind the mountains was rapidly fading, blotted out by the gathering clouds. It had to be almost time for supper, and their chores remained undone with a storm coming on. By now their parents must be looking for them. He turned to meet Jake's concerned gaze.

"We better get going. I'll do the talking, *ya?* Whatever I say, back me up."

Jake's words echoed Joseph's thoughts and he quickly agreed, as did Christian. If they had any hope at all of avoiding a strapping, Jake was the one to do the talking.

They brushed off their clothing and stuffed their shirts back into their breeches, washed their faces and hands in the stream, and raked their fingers through their hair. When they deemed themselves presentable, they trudged back across the cornfield and by a roundabout route made their way home.

◆━━━◆

JAKOB AND CRIST MET JOHANNES hurrying toward them. "They're not at my place."

The cool wind was strengthening, rain scented, and Jakob peered up at the mountain. He sucked in a breath at the sight of the black storm clouds roiling above the ridge.

"It's blowing up a storm. We must get a search party together and head up the mountain—"

Blitz's sharp yip cut him off. She streaked up the path toward the orchard.

He could hear Jake calling the dog from a distance. Crist squeezed Jakob's shoulder hard, and he drew an uneven breath, feeling the tightness of his chest ease.

◆ · ——◆

JOSEPH HEARD BLITZ BARKING, then Hans and Crist Stutzman calling their names from different directions. Jake shot him and Christian a warning glance before answering. Moments later they saw Blitz loping toward them from the direction of the barn. By the time she reached them, their father, Johannes, and Uncle Crist appeared, quickly joined by the Stutzman brothers.

Jake raced ahead, and before Daati had a chance to say anything, he began to apologize for being late. They had been playing and ended up following the Northkill into the mountains. They had lost track of time, going farther than they intended, but they had learned a valuable lesson and were very sorry for the worry and trouble they had caused their elders, who were right to be angry with them.

Listening to his brother's breathless recital, Joseph shifted from one foot to the other, his gaze fixed on the ground. When Jake finished, Joseph dug his bare toes into the dust and held his breath, awaiting Daati's response, while the unspoken matter of the Indians hung between them like the storm clouds.

For a taut moment Jakob leaned into the wind and stared hard at the thunderclouds, clenching and unclenching his hands. When he finally lowered his gaze, he looked not at his boys, but at Crist Stutzman. There was an appeal in the young man's eyes that seemed to him a plea for mercy.

"Your chores have not been done."

His new son-in-law said quickly, "Hans and I will take care of the milking."

"*Nay*, it's your wedding day," Crist Buerki protested. "Go to your bride. My boys have run home to take care of our cows, and Hans and I will help the boys with the milking here. We'll be done by the time the womenfolk have supper ready."

"I'll slop the hogs!"

"Come on, Christli. We'll do it together, then you can help me milk my cows." Smiling, Johannes took his little brother's hand and led him off.

Jakob fixed the two older boys with a stern gaze that took in the kerchief tied around Jake's leg.

"It's nothing—a scratch only."

Jakob pointed his finger. "No more chasing after the Indians. And you must never—never—go through the gap to the other side of the mountains."

"We won't, Daati!"

"We promise!"

Jakob watched the boys run off toward the pasture. He was certain that they had not been truthful. Something had happened in the forest that they didn't want him to know.

For a long moment he studied the dark clouds shrouding the mountain. A flash of lightning illuminated the base of a towering thunderhead, followed within seconds by a distant rumble.

Shuddering, he turned and walked back to the house.

＋ ⋯ ＋

JOSEPH JERKED AWAKE, his heartbeat pulsing loud in his ears. Except for the faint reflection of starlight slanting through the window above the stairs, the narrow, cramped room under the eaves lay in complete darkness.

What had awakened him?

Then he remembered. He had dreamed that Daati had uncovered their deception and led them out to the barn, where the worn leather strap waited. But before he could punish them, an Indian war party materialized out of the night to capture them all and carry them far away up the Northkill.

He stared at the shadowy rafters above his head. *Lying seldom works and never makes you feel better. And now we have to worry about keeping our stories straight.*

He rolled over. The other side of the bed was empty.

Outside, Blitz began to bark. He could hear chickens squawking, then the outer door opened and closed softly.

Careful not to wake Christian, he slipped out of bed and crept down the steps far enough to see below the angle of the upper floor. In the darkness he could just make out Jake standing beside Maami, who sat on the settle with a coverlet wrapped around her shoulders. The next step creaked beneath Joseph's foot as he transferred his weight onto it, and they looked up.

"Ach, what are you doing out of bed too? It's only that fox bothering the chickens again. Your Daati went out to shoot it."

Joseph went the rest of way down the stairs and crossed to the fireplace. The embers on the hearth winked cherry red beneath the ashes but gave off no heat. He hugged his arms around him against the room's chill.

So Daati's going to shoot the fox just like that. I bet it runs off before he even gets close.

All three of them jumped when a rifle shot reverberated through the night. Joseph threw a questioning glance at Jake. The older boy grinned

For some moments they waited in silence until Joseph thought he was going to explode from the suspense. Finally footfalls sounded outside. He sprang for the door and threw it open.

Daati raised his eyebrows. "What are you boys doing up?"

He stopped in the doorway, hefting his trophy for Maami to see. It was the largest fox Joseph had ever seen, its thick fur a luxuriant red and white. Blood matted the base of its head.

"I'll skin it tomorrow and stretch the pelt to cure. It'll make you a good rug beside the bed."

Maami laughed, clearly pleased. "*Ya,* and this winter it'll feel so *guud* on my toes!"

Joseph stared at the limp form of the fox, feeling his father's triumph. Then, hands clenched, he crossed the room without speaking and went back up the stairs to bed.

Chapter Six

J AKOB HUNCHED HIS SHOULDERS against the biting wind and settled his hat more firmly to keep it from blowing off his head. The spongy ground, soggy from a heavy overnight rainfall, squelched beneath his shoes. His heavy woolen clothing offered little protection against the keen air that knifed through the thick layers, chilling him through despite the exertion of the long walk.

With every stride up the half-overgrown track twisting northward through the hills four miles from his plantation, a clearer glimpse of Fort Northkill's rude palisade walls emerged between the wet, lichen-encrusted trunks of the leafless trees. His closest neighbors of the church's militia-age men moved silently up the rise around him, their expressions variously stern, thoughtful, or anxious.

Johannes kept pace on Jakob's right, his broad, bearded face registering only a mild bemusement, while on his left sixteen-year-old Jake wore his excitement openly. Today his younger son's enthusiasm irritated Jakob, as did everything about this summons by the commander of the British army.

Where the path took a final turn through the trees, a group of church members who had ridden on horseback from a longer distance waited for them. They gathered in a loose cluster by their tethered horses to survey the fortification's palisade walls, hastily built the previous February as one link in a chain of forts extending along the Blue Mountain. The structure crowned a small rise a half mile from Northkill Creek, in the center of a clearing that stretched roughly two hundred yards to the edge of the forest.

Stephen Kurtz indicated the weathered stumps, small saplings, and low bushes that studded the clearing. "If they let it grow long enough, the Indians will have plenty of cover to reach the walls."

Isaac Kauffman grunted. "It's grown up even more since I came by here hunting last summer. Doesn't look like anyone's touched it."

Several of the men murmured their agreement.

"Some fortress," Crist Stutzman scoffed. "This place will provide little shelter against an attack."

Eyes narrowed, Jakob estimated that the palisade rose barely nine feet above the ground. He could make out gaps between many of the logs even from as far away as he stood. Although rudely constructed half-bastions perched precariously at each corner, they appeared ill situated for soldiers to effectively cover every angle of the walls during an attack.

He jutted his chin in the fort's direction. "You can yet see through the walls at places."

Johannes stamped his feet against the cold, his grin broad. "It wasn't built by us Amish. We'd let the logs dry before we set them . . . and use straight ones to begin with."

Jakob suppressed a laugh. "The Indians don't bother to attack these forts anyway. Why fight armed soldiers when they can fall on us farmers while we're out working the fields—or in our homes at night too?"

"The militia patrols the area," Crist pointed out. "Barbara and I see scouts pass by our place pretty often. It's only a small force, and they can't be everywhere at once."

His older brother, Hans, snorted. "If we see them, so do the Indians. And they go where the scouts are not."

"Just Tuesday Andrew Wolbeck's daughter was taken from their home." Moritz Zug's voice was low and thick with emotion.

"*Ya*," Benedict Lehman said, "and we heard from the neighbors that a war party attacked Nicholas Long's family Wednesday last. Not far off from here."

"They say two men were killed and Bernard Motz was carried off. There were at least twenty Indians, and they set fire to the house with the women and children down in the cellar. Praise *Gott* the militia came in time to get them out." Rudy Detweiler pulled off his hat and ran his fingers through his hair, then nodded in the direction of the fort. "They brought them here."

A tense silence fell over the men.

Jakob studied the armed guards visible through the fort's open gate and at the top of the bastions. A militia company commanded by Lieutenant Samuel Humphreys garrisoned the fort, but today that small force was bolstered by soldiers in red coats.

Driven by the raw wind, low-hanging dark clouds scudded across the bleak grey sky. Jakob shivered. British soldiers would be even less sympathetic to the refusal of the Amish to take up arms than the local militia and their English neighbors were.

"Didn't I say we shouldn't come?" Hans Lantz growled. "This *Herr* Loudoun who took over after the Indians killed General Braddock sends his recruiting parties out to all the forts in the area to drag us into King George's war, when he's shown no interest in either making peace with the French or defending these western settlements where all the attacks are going on."

Crist Buerki folded his arms across his chest. "*Ya,* Loudoun wants to make us part of his army, and then march us away to wherever he sees fit, like Louisbourg up in Nova Scotia. By all accounts, there's no fighting there to worry about."

"I read that Benjamin Franklin said Loudoun is like Saint George on a tavern sign." Jake paused, grinning. "Always on horseback, but never riding on."

A gust of laughter rippled through the group.

Hans Gnaegi did not laugh with the others. "In the latest *Pensylvanische Berichte* Christoph Sauer says that the provincial council intends to make us slaves by forcing us and our sons to become soldiers. Then they'll increase our taxes to help the British fight this war."

"Before we could even settle in this colony, we had to pledge allegiance to the British king. Surely it comes as no surprise that he now expects us to fight for his cause, just as the kings did in Europe."

Gnaegi rounded on Crist Beiler, shaking his head fiercely. "We gave up everything we had in the old country to come here so we could live in peace. If we answer this summons, we only give them a chance to arrest us."

Crist Buerki cut him off with a raised hand. "If we don't make an answer to them now, they may tear us away from our homes in the sight of our wives and childrenas they did back in *der Schweiz.* You want that?"

At his reference to the suffering the Anabaptists endured in Switzerland because of their faith, the group again fell silent.

Jakob's mouth went dry and his neck cloth felt suddenly too tight. He had been only eight years old when his father was imprisoned on returning to his old homestead in Switzerland to help other members of the church escape severe persecution. Jakob vividly remembered the physical and emotional hardships his family had suffered for years until his father's release.

"Whether they arrest us or not," Crist continued in a stern voice, "we are commanded to submit to the government *Gott* has instituted, as far as we are able, in obedience to His will. What we propose is reasonable. May the Almighty show us favor before these *Englishe.*"

Jakob could not help thinking of the fear on Anna's face early that morninng. The war had gone on for two years now, with no signs of ending, she had wailed. If the raids continued, all of them would have to give up their homes and move away like so many other settlers already had.

Jakob's shoulders drooped. A few families from the church had gone back east, fearing for their lives. But if they moved, they would lose everything. And if they stayed, they were in danger of being attacked, perhaps murdered. Or what could be worse: made captives and carried far away to an unimaginable fate.

His thoughts returned to the same weary track they had followed for months, but the more he thought about it, the more impossible it seemed to decide either way.

Before leaving with his older sons to walk to the fort, Jakob had cuddled his little Annali, barely six weeks old. He had made sure the younger boys got their chores done. He had led them all in prayer for God's protection.

He was forty-four now. The prospect of walking away from all he and Anna had worked so hard to build and starting over—as they had when they came to this country across thousands of miles of ocean—left him feeling defeated. Yet almost every day they heard of another raid, more deaths, more children carried off. How could he expose his family to such danger?

"The letter was sent by Colonel Weiser. He's German like us, and he has proven to be trustworthy. Maybe we can convince him to speak on our behalf." Jakob paused only slightly before continuing, his voice hoarse with emotion, "*Gott* has given us an opportunity to witness to these unbelievers. He is faithful. We must be faithful too."

He stared hard at the fort. Just then a detachment of grenadiers emerged from the forest opposite them. There were perhaps two dozen of them, all clad in brick-red uniforms with buff facings. Each man wore a tall, stiff, elaborately embroidered cloth cap shaped like the bishops' miters Jakob remembered from the Alsace.

The soldiers' uniforms appeared worn, but the muzzles of their shouldered muskets gleamed in the pale light, summoning bitter memories of the political and religious wars back in the Old Country. Sensing the heightened tension of his companions, Jakob's heart sank further.

Lantz waved his arm at the grenadiers. "But if we support these soldiers, we're helping them to kill."

Jakob watched the soldiers march in tight formation toward the fort's gates, his jaw set. "We all agreed to this compromise. We will not fight, but we can pay a tax and supply the army. They need food and clothing as much as they need soldiers. Our offer is fair."

"But it's not our way! We're called to peace."

"You heard what Bishop Hertzler said, Hans. It's our Christian duty to be a neighbor even to the soldiers. Are we not commanded to do good to our enemies?"

Jakob's son-in-law made an impatient gesture. "They don't want us for neighbors, Jakob. They want us for soldiers."

Johannes's expression registered uneasiness. "*Ya,* but these men from the militia are endangering their lives to protect us. They're our neighbors whether we agree with them or not."

"Protect us?" Kurtz countered. "Tell Andrew Wolbeck and Nicholas Long how well they protect us."

"Enough!" Jakob snapped. His voice sounded much harsher than he intended, and he raised his hand in apology. "How shall we live in peace with the English if we fight amongst ourselves? Each of us must do what he thinks right in this matter."

He glanced meaningfully at Johannes, Jake, and the Stutzmans, before nodding in the direction of the fort. "I'll go talk to this English captain. When we came to this land Penn guaranteed us the freedom to live according to our convictions. I'll tell the captain about Penn's promise if he does not know it."

Fists clenched, he wheeled and set off toward the fort. He did not have to turn to know that the footfalls following him were those of his sons and the younger men. After all, those who had been born in this land and the majority who came with their parents as young children had never experienced firsthand the persecution their people had suffered in Europe. They had never seen a parent arrested and imprisoned in harsh conditions. They had never been driven out of their homes or had family members and neighbors martyred for the faith.

But Jakob and most members of his generation had. He knew that it was not just conviction causing their consternation, but also fear based on experience.

When he threw a quick glance back, he was relieved to see that the older men had fallen into step behind the younger ones, though several still appeared to brood. He drew a deep breath and consciously relaxed his own frown. But as he stepped across the ice-crusted stream that wound from the spring outside the fort's walls and advanced to the open gate, he wished that he didn't feel as though they were all walking into a lion's den.

JOSEPH LOOKED UP when ten-year-old Christian climbed up beside him on the settle, his German primer in his hand.

"It isn't fair Daati wouldn't let you go to the fort with the men. I'm big enough to help Dr. Blanck load that ewe into his wagon."

Joseph glanced at Maam, who sat across the *Küche* at the smaller of the two spinning wheels, spinning a bundle of flax into fine thread. "Only those old enough to join the militia were ordered to come to the fort. I won't be sixteen for a couple of years yet."

"It wouldn't have hurt for you to go along too."

Joseph shrugged. "It's all right, Christli. I don't mind."

His father's refusal to let him go with the men to Fort Northkill had stung at first. But the explanation that Dr. Blanck was coming today to fetch the ewe he had been promised had put a different slant on things.

Joseph stared dreamily into the warm glow the crackling fire spilled across the floor's planks. *Maybe he'll bring Anna along.*

Anna occupied an increasing share of his thoughts lately. If only he could see her more often. But since moving to a plantation near Womelsdorf all the way south in Heidelberg Township, the Blancks were no longer members of the Northkill church. They were good friends of his parents and visited regularly, however, though not nearly often enough to suit Joseph.

Did Daat suspect his feelings toward Anna? His stern expression that morning when he cut off Joseph's protests at having to stay home had given no hint. But Joseph knew there was not much his father missed. He smiled, pleased to think that might be the reason Daat had insisted he stay home.

He grabbed Christian's arm. "Let's make sure the ewe is ready to go when An—Dr. Blanck gets here."

Christian bounced to his feet, apparently not noting Joseph's mistake. "Ach, *ya!* That's a good idea."

With his younger brother on his heels, Joseph strode to the pegboard by the outer door. "Maam, we're going out to the barn to check on that ewe. Daat wants us to take extra good care of her so the wagon ride to the Blancks' plantation doesn't hurt the lamb she's carrying."

Maam turned a sharp gaze on Christian. "Have you finished your studies?"

"*Ya,* Maami!"

The baby's hungry wail sounded from the *Kammer* as she nodded her approval. "*Guud* then," she called over her shoulder as she bustled from the room. "Only stay close by in case the Blancks come while I'm nursing Annali. There've been yet more attacks not far off from here the last few days, too, so you boys be sure never to go running off."

"We won't." Joseph handed Christian his coat before pulling on his own.

They stepped outside, and Joseph motioned Christian to a halt. Blitz came bounding up from the direction of the barn to join them. While the dog waited patiently, ears pricked and tongue lolling, the boys stood shivering in the wind, watching and listening for any unusual movement or sound.

Finally reassured, Joseph led the way to the barn. Christian fell into step with him.

"Why do the Blancks want one of our ewes?"

"They want to start their own flock. Daat says the wool from these Leicester Longwools makes the finest cloth, and we're the only ones around here who breed them—along with Johannes and Katie, of course."

"Maybe she'll have twins next spring."

Joseph returned Christian's grin, his steps buoyant at the thought of the coming visit. "*Ya,* maybe so!"

If Anna was sitting on the wagon seat beside her father when Dr. Blanck drove into the yard, it would more than make up for the disappointment of not getting to go to the fort with the men. If she wasn't . . .

Joseph didn't want to consider that possibility.

JAKOB AND HIS COMPANIONS gathered inside the gate, keeping their distance from the soldiers and the other men from the area who crowded the fort. The small expanse of beaten earth that functioned as a parade ground was obstructed only by a narrow log cabin of the same quality as the palisade. Jakob tugged at his beard, thinking what poor shelter the structure would afford in bad weather, especially considering its lack of a chimney.

He watched the British grenadiers form two orderly queues along the palisade to his right and draw stiffly to attention, with their captain at their head. On the fort's opposite side the militia company, garbed in dun-colored coats over homespun hunting shirts and buckskin breeches, drew up in creditable formation.

Tall, young Lieutenant Humphreys took his place at their head, his rugged features and stern and his bearing as ramrod straight as that of the grenadiers.

Jostling each other between the two detachments milled the men of the neighborhood who, like Jakob and his companions, had been summoned to Fort Northkill on this day. Many were German like themselves, members of the local Lutheran or Reformed churches. The sprinkling of English settlers obviously found the plain dress, unbound hair, untrimmed beards, and reserved manners of the Amish to be an even greater source of amusement than they did the few Quakers who were present. Jakob ignored them and turned his attention to two men who stood nearby, speaking in German.

"Did you hear the governor sent most of the militia all the way to Shamokin? It's wilderness over there, with few settlers. Here in Berks County, where we're under attack, they leave us exposed!"

"And now they want us to enroll in the militia," scoffed the younger man. "Who knows where we'd end up, leaving the Indians to raid our plantations and murder our families."

"Weiser says Loudoun thinks us Germans will support his regiment because they have Dutch and Swiss officers."

"They can go to blazes!"

Lantz pressed close behind Jakob. "We've been kept waiting more than an hour already. When is this captain going to show his face?"

Jakob's eye caught movement at the cabin. Its sagging door was thrown open to reveal a slight young British officer, who paused on the threshold. Behind him stood Colonel Conrad Weiser, the stocky, sixty-year-old commander of the militia, who was well known and respected among the Germans in the area.

The red-coated officer looked down his pinched nose at the waiting men. He took his time pulling on fine riding gloves, then swaggered to the center of the muddy ground in front of the house, carefully skirting a shallow puddle. Weiser strode straight through the puddle after him, heedless of the mud splashing on his boots, his expression reflecting something less than pleasure.

As soon as the colonel vacated the doorway, several grenadiers emerged, carrying trestles and a board out of the cabin. Within moments they had set up a table, placed several sheets of paper along with pens and an inkpot on its surface, and arranged two folding camp chairs behind it. Jakob shifted to get a better look at the camp chairs so he could evaluate the usefulness of the design.

The grenadier lieutenant drew Jakob's attention as he marched briskly across the parade ground, one of the grenadier lieutenants took a seat behind the table. Lieutenant Humphreys stalked over to take the chair beside him, his manner giving the impression that he wasn't looking forward to the next few hours. The two men neither looked at nor spoke to each other.

The captain surveyed his audience for a moment, lip curled, then began to speak in a thin, high voice. Although Jakob understood much of the language from interaction with his English neighbors, the officer's rapid speech and accent made it difficult for him to catch more than an occasional word.

He leaned toward Jake and Johannes. "What does he say?"

Their companions gathered around them, straining to hear over the low murmur that had begun to rise from the crowd.

"As far as I can make out," Jake said, "he says this Loudoun needs soldiers to fight England's enemies and they're here to enroll us all in the militia."

"This is something we don't know?" Crist Buerki questioned under his breath.

Johannes scratched the back of his head. "It sounds to me like he's trying to get everyone fired up to go fight. He says everyone who enrolls will get a generous bounty now and land grants when the war is over."

Jake scowled. "He says it's our duty to England and to our families to protect our wives and children from the French."

They were interrupted by a small group of men who pushed past and walked through the gate, their expressions dark. Jakob watched as they strode rapidly away, not looking back.

Jut then the commanding officer of the grenadiers shouted an order. Four of the tall, muscular soldiers broke away from the rest of the detachment and moved quickly to the gates. Pulling them closed, the soldiers dropped the heavy iron bar into place.

❖━━❖

CHRISTIAN SIPPED HIS CIDER, studying the blushing couple over the rim of his cup. They sat at the opposite end of the table, sharing the cake and cider Maami had placed before them. After an awkward silence, during which Anna and Joseph repeatedly stole glances at each other, only to look hastily away, both began to speak at once, then stopped, staring at each other in surprise.

Anna giggled and pressed her fingers to her lips, a pink hue covering her cheeks, her green eyes sparkling. "I'm sorry. You go first."

"No, you. It was my fault." Joseph sounded like he was choking on a bite of cake.

Christian regretted devouring his portion so quickly since Joseph seemed completely oblivious to his presence. But he was determined to make his cider last as long as possible so he would have an excuse to remain at the table. Although he had seen the older boys at church act in the same strange manner when the girls came around, he was nonetheless amazed at the transformation in his brother.

Maami was engrossed in her conversation with Dr. Blanck. The murmur of their voices and the moaning of the icy wind around the eaves made it hard for Christian to make out what Anna and Joseph were saying. Fascinated, Christian watched Anna concentrate on mashing the cake on her plate into crumbs with her fork.

He shifted, drawing his legs up under him on the chair, hoping to hear better. As he did so, he accidentally shoved his plate into his cup, nearly spilling it—and prompting Joseph to look up with a scowl.

A muted cry sounded from the *Kammer*. Both boys froze. When the baby let out a loud wail, Joseph flashed a look of appeal in Christian's direction. He pushed out of his chair before his mother could move.

"I'll get her, Maami."

When he returned, cuddling his little sister, Dr. Blanck rose to stand beside his chair. From the *Stube* they could hear the clock strike the last quarter before four.

"It's getting late already, and we have yet a long road home," he said. Christian noticed that although he spoke to Maami, his kindly face was turned toward Joseph and Anna. "We're keeping you from your baby and these boys from their chores."

Smiling, Maami stood up. "Don't stay away so long next time, Hans, and be sure to bring your dear wife along so we can visit."

Joseph sprang to his feet, almost overturning his chair, and hurried to bring the Blancks' cloaks from the pegboard.

"We'll come soon. And you come visit us too. The door is always open to you and your family." Dr. Blanck included Joseph and Christian in his warm glance.

Joseph flushed, appearing to suppress a smile. While they bundled up against the rising wind and misty rain outside, Maami released a sigh and glanced toward the window before taking the fussing baby from Christian's arms.

"Ach, Jakob should be back by now. I hope there's no trouble with the soldiers."

Dr. Blanck gave Maami a reassuring smile. "The English have no reason to make trouble for us. I'm sure the men will all be home soon."

After they had gone, Christian shadowed Joseph outside to drive the cows up from the pasture. "You're in love with Anna, aren't you?"

Joseph swung around and lunged at him, making him stagger backward. "Shut your mouth! You don't know anything. Go back in the house with Maam, where babies like you belong."

Hot tears filled Christian's eyes. "Take care of the cows yourself then!" Turning away, he stomped back up the path.

COLONEL WEISER FACED JAKOB, his legs spread apart, one hand propped at his waist while he rubbed the back of his neck with the other. "The captain expects you men to join the militia."

"You told him we do not bear arms or kill?"

"I explained your beliefs, *ya*. He says he does not accept any excuses, and that as British subjects you have a duty not only to protect your families, but also to defend the interests of your king." Weiser spread his hands in appeal. "You would be serving under German or Dutch officers."

"Would those be the same Germans and Dutch who drove our people out of Switzerland, the Palatinate, the Alsace, and other places—that is, when they did not imprison or kill them?"

"Why should we provide protection for able-bodied men who refuse to defend themselves?"

Although the colonel's steady gaze remained sympathetic, his mouth had settled into a firm line. Jakob could feel the tension rising among his companions as they exchanged glances or shifted from one foot to the other.

"We came here because William Penn guaranteed that his colony would afford freedom to live according to one's beliefs. Are you and this *Englisher* now telling us his promises were false?"

Weiser studied Jakob for a long moment before returning to the table, where the line of willing recruits was short in spite of the handful of coins being handed over for each signature. While Weiser consulted in English with the British captain, who stood behind the two lieutenants, Jake and Johannes eased closer. After several minutes both quietly rejoined Jakob and the others.

"Weiser is explaining that our religion will not allow us to fight. The captain talks too fast, but I think he says we are only stupid German peasants."

Jakob did not need Johannes to tell him that. The British officer's manner showed nothing but disdain for the Amish men ranged before him. And the murmur rising from his friends told Jakob that he was not alone in his assessment.

Glancing around, he raised his hand in a plea for patience. "It doesn't matter what he thinks, only what he does."

After several minutes, Weiser returned. "The captain says if you do not enroll, you will receive no protection. The army and the militia will not endanger their lives to save those who will not fight."

Jake turned his back to the colonel, his hand cupped around his mouth. "The captain called us stupid, lazy cowards who are loyal to the French."

Jakob gritted his teeth and took a slow breath. The men pressed in close, looking from him to Weiser with scowls while they muttered to one another.

"We will supply the soldiers with food, clothing, and other necessities," Jakob said loudly enough for all of them to hear. "We will pay a tax, if the British king requires it. And we will care for our neighbors who have suffered loss, so the English will not be burdened. But God commands us not to kill. We will not take another's life under any circumstances. No matter who commands it."

Weiser's eyebrows rose. He hesitated, then swung around and returned to the captain to explain Jakob's offer. Hostility radiated from the British officer, and they could hear his voice across the parade ground.

Johannes grasped Jakob's arm. "Weiser is only telling him about our offer, not what you said about our refusing to kill."

"The captain says he will arrest all of us and force us to fight."

Jakob stared at Jake, keenly aware of the barred gate at their backs. He felt like a rabbit in a snare awaiting the trapper's return.

Johannes leaned in closer. "Weiser is telling him what good farmers we Amish are, and that we produce good wool cloth too. He says that the army needs supplies as much as it needs men, and that the captain would do well to accept our offer."

Jakob felt a hand clamp his shoulder and looked around. Crist Buerki gave him encouraging nod.

"We're under the protection of a Ruler far more powerful than the British king."

Jakob let out a rueful laugh. "I doubt either the king or his officers hold that opinion."

He glanced back at the table as the captain wheeled and marched over to the officer who commanded the grenadiers. Smiling, Weiser strode back to Jakob and his party.

"I persuaded the captain that better troops can be found back east, and he's agreed to your offer."

Jakob relaxed, his tension evaporating.

"I'll send out a party next week to gather the supplies for the army. You'll also provide wagons to transport the goods to Loudoun's regiment."

"*Guud.* We'll supply all that's needed."

He spoke with more confidence than he felt. Weiser was a fair man and a valuable ally. Still, Jakob had heard reports of the British demanding so much in taxes and goods that forced to pay suffered greatly. He couldn't help fearing that the Northkill Amish would face greater hardship than before, while still remaining vulnerable to attack.

While he and Weiser spoke, Jakob noticed that Johannes drifted closer to the captain and the commander of the grenadiers, who were deep in conversation. When the gates were opened and they left the fort, he came to walk at Jakob's side, his expression sober.

"This captain says that those who suffer from the raids deserve it because they chose to settle on Indian lands. But he thinks all the trouble this has made for the British will be worth it because the officers will make a fine profit from the taxes and goods we supply for the army."

Jakob snorted. He was not surprised. What else could one expect of the English?

❖┄┄❖

JAKOB STRODE BESIDE JAKE along the rutted track, a few steps ahead of Johannes. Jake had already equaled—and soon would surpass—Jakob's height, he noted. His son's lithe, muscular form testified to the powerful man he would grow into.

They had parted from the rest of the men a short time earlier at the Kurtz plantation, and while they walked, Jake kept his head bent, the broad brim of his hat partially shading his face. Jakob sensed that he was troubled.

"Daat," Jake said after some moments, "Were you afraid, facing those men?"

"*Ya.* But a man must do what's right even when he's afraid."

"But if we're attacked and we don't defend ourselves—"

"We must ask *Gott* to defend us. A man cannot kill another without having his heart scarred by it."

Johannes strode up beside them. "The way of Christ is not to meet violence with violence, but to overcome evil with good."

Jakob directed an approving glance at his eldest son. "We came to this land to live in peace, according to *Gott's* command. His laws are higher than man's laws, and we belong to His kingdom, not to the kingdom of this world. We'll not turn our backs on peace because others do."

Jake said nothing more but his pace increased. Jakob let him take the lead, and a strained silence fell.

Dark shadows were gathering beneath the spectral treeson either side of the path. Jakob pulled out his pocket watch and checked the time. The heavy cloud cover made it feel later than it was, but by now Joseph and Christian should have brought the cows up to the barn for milking. If any Indians lay in wait for them, they would not see them in time.

In time for what? To raise a weapon against them? To run away?

The forest gave way to gently rolling fields. Noting no sign of danger, Jakob shook off his unease. Where the path branched, Johannes took leave of them, turning toward his plantation.

Many a night Jakob had lain awake, questioning whether he should move his family away from danger. But by daylight, he could not help seeing how good this land was. It was *his* land, the first land he had owned since Anabaptists were prohibited from buying property in the old country. And this new section, warranted the previous year, was even more productive than his first homestead, which Johannes and Katie now occupied.

He and Jake turned past the fallow cornfield. Ahead of them loomed the bank barn, half again larger than the old one to accommodate more crops, implements, two wagons, and a new carriage. A larger milking parlor occupied the lower level, along with additional stables for the two carriage horses he had acquired this past spring.

How could he leave now? Would there not be dangers anywhere they moved? Where would he find land as fertile? And when would it stop? Could he never hope to put down roots into soil that belonged to him?

Jake motioned toward the lantern light glowing in the milking parlor's windows. "I'll go help Joseph and Christli finish up."

Jakob up down the slope beside the barn and along the path toward the expansive log house his sons and church members had helped to build two years earlier. When it came in sight, he stopped to admire it, as he had many times before.

A substantial stone bake oven and a large garden lay steps from his home's front door. Behind the house, rows of young fruit trees curved around the base of a broad hill, and a springhouse, stocked with crocks of milk, butter, cheese, and eggs, spanned the small stream that bubbled from the spring. On the opposite side of the barnyard from where he stood loomed a tall smokehouse, its log walls already blackening from the smoldering fires over which hams and sausages cured. At the barn's far end a granary bulged with corn, while generous stores of wheat, buckwheat, and rye filled huge bins on the barn's upper level, and hay spilled over the edge of the loft. He had even constructed a still and a cider press, all built with the same exacting precision as the buildings.

Finally his gaze drifted back to the house and settled on the light streaming through the downstairs windows. He smiled. Every window in the house could be closed from the inside with sturdy shutters of solid wood that slid into recesses built into the casement. He had learned about these "Indian shutters" from a Dutch neighbor and added them when they built the house. It had seemed a small thing at the time, but after the brutal raids of the previous winter, it had gone far toward calming Anna's fears. And that was not a small thing.

Not only were his granaries overflowing and his flocks and herds expanding, but so too was the number of his grandchildren increasing. And just weeks ago Anna had presented him with a new daughter, a red-haired, blue-eyed baby named after her mother.

In spite of the dangers, their lives overflowed with blessings. To abandon all that had been given them now would be an act of unbelief.

A yawn made Jakob suddenly aware of the toll the long day had taken on his emotions and energy, and he headed for the house. Anna would expect a full report on the events at the fort, and he prayed he that would not fall asleep before he could tell her about the day's success.

Chapter Seven

Monday, September 19, 1757

CAREFUL NOT TO BRUISE the ripe fruit, Joseph transferred apples from his basket into the large basin directly in front of Anna Blanck until the pile was in danger of toppling. He prayed she would not suspect that from the moment he had entered the crowded *Küche* every movement had been calculated to attract her attention.

She stopped slicing an apple and looked up as though surprised to see him, her smile radiant. When he returned a stiff nod, soft color rose to her cheeks.

Quickly she returned her attention to her conversation with Bessie Mueller and the other girls at the table, one of several that crowded the room. Joseph worked hard to keep from beaming at the warmth of her glance.

He felt as clumsy as Daat's young oxen when they had been yoked for the first time last spring. During the past year he had gained another three inches in height, though not in breadth. He now stood just a shade shorter than his father, so lean his joints jutted from his frame at awkward angles.

At times it felt as though he wore an oversized suit of clothes. His lanky body seemed an alien thing with a mind of its own, especially when attractive members of the opposite sex were around.

Particularly if one of them was blonde, green-eyed Anna Blanck.

He squeezed onto the bench next to John Detweiler and opposite the girls. His friend jabbed him with his elbow and gave him a knowing smirk. Joseph arched his eyebrow in return and let his gaze drift across the table to Barbara Speicher, on Anna's other side, then back again. John suddenly discovered an intense interest in chopping the apple he had taken from the bowl. Joseph grabbed a knife and followed suit to keep his eyes from wandering back to Anna.

Arriving on foot or driving buggies or carts, the youth of the Northkill community, along with a number of parents, had gathered at the Hochstetler plantation a few hours earlier to spend the afternoon cutting up apples from the year's bountiful harvest. While the adults took charge of barn raisings and the frolics following threshing and corn husking, *apfelschnitzen* was the highlight of the autumn for Amish youth.

Joseph had hardly been able to contain his excitement when Maam and Daat had announced plans to host one of the events. During the endless interval until the first of their guests finally arrived that day shortly after noon dinner, he had suffered such an agony of anticipation he all but made himself sick.

Fearful his parents might neglect to invite the Blancks, he had repeated more than once that they might enjoy the frolic. To make doubly sure the message reached them, at the earliest opportunity he had also mentioned to Anna's close friend Bessie that the Blancks would be welcome to join them. When the Muellers' horse cart had turned into the yard that afternoon with Bessie and Anna sitting beside him and the entire Blanck family following in their wagon, he felt as if he might burst with happiness.

As quickly as the apples were sliced, Maam, Barbara, Katie, or one of the other women whisked the filled basins away and replaced them with empty ones. A portion was set aside for drying, while the rest simmered in huge iron kettles hung over fires out in the yard. The mouth-watering tang of apples, cider, and quince sweetened with molasses cooking into apple butter that drifted through the open door and windows made Joseph's stomach growl in anticipation.

Daat, along with Johannes, Jake, and a number of their neighbors manned the cider press, where the Spitzenburgh, Swaar, and Guelderleng apples were being crushed. Several full barrels had already been carried down to the cellar or loaded onto Johannes's wagon, while still more barrels waited to be filled.

Most of the other boys had drifted outside to help sort apples or carry the heavy baskets to the house, but Joseph found more attraction in the work going on inside. At the moment the festive hum of conversation and laughter and the heady aroma of apples underlaid with wood smoke filled his senses. Keeping his head bent and his brow furrowed in pretended concentration, he darted quick glances around the room.

The spacious *Küche* bustled with clusters of women and girls occupied in preparing the ripe apples for cooking. Maam and Magdalena Blanck kept a keen eye on the applesauce gently bubbling in big kettles over three low fires on the great hearth. Meanwhile, toddling from one to the other with happy squeals, his eleven-month-old sister, Annali, and the other small children held the attention of the older unmarried girls.

Joseph sneaked a glance across the table at Anna. When their eyes met, he hastily transferred his attention back to his work, heat creeping up his neck. He chopped vigorously, falling into an unconscious rhythm with John at his side.

"You're going to turn those apples into mush," John noted, his mouth suspiciously puckered.

"Then they won't need to be cooked, will they?"

Hearing Anna's giggle, he looked up. She blushed but this time held his gaze.

He couldn't wait until their work was finished. After a simple supper the young people would be allowed to linger for singing and games long after their parents went home and Maam and Daat retreated to their *Kammer* for the night.

Joseph's pulse quickened in anticipation, and fantasies of romance raced through his mind. He had just turned fifteen last month, and Anna would be fifteen in a few months too. It would not be much longer before they were old enough to marry.

He knew, however, that he was not the only boy in the Northkill community who had noticed Anna Blanck. Not to mention the boys in her home community at Womelsdorf. How could he expect to attract her interest when every time he tried to talk to her his hands sweated, his face flamed, and his voice cracked?

He felt a light kick under the table and looked up, ready to retaliate against John's assault. Instead, he caught Anna's smiling gaze.

"Oh, I'm so sorry. Did I kick you? I didn't mean to—"

"That's all right. It didn't hurt."

"Ach, *guud.* I've been sitting here so long cutting apples that my foot went to sleep and I was trying to wake it up."

He nodded, hoping his expression conveyed suitable sympathy. "It isn't good to sit still so long. If you want to go outside for some fresh air, I'll go with you. The sun's gone down behind the ridge, but it's warm still."

He could hardly believe the words had come out of his mouth. He was even more amazed when she turned around on the bench and stood up as though she had been waiting for him to ask.

Smoothing her apron over her petticoat, she came around the end of the table. "That's a wonderful idea. I haven't seen your orchard yet. Do you have apple trees only?"

Realizing his jaw hung open, he snapped it shut and jumped to his feet. He felt the stares of the others at the table, who made no attempt to hide their amusement.

"No, we have peaches and cherries too. Jake, Christli, and I helped Daat transplant the saplings before we even moved onto this plantation, and they grew fast. This is our first crop, but most of our apples came yet from the old orchard."

He forced himself to stop babbling. He rarely spoke so much in one stretch, and certainly never to a girl. She smiled up at him, however, then led the way to the outer door.

He grabbed his black broad-brimmed hat from its peg and set it squarely on his head. When Anna had donned hers, too, he draped her black shawl over her shoulders, feeling even more stupid when his work-roughened fingers momentarily caught in the fine weave. To his immense relief, she seemed not to notice.

Before he could push the door open, however, Annali wobbled away from the cluster of girls who had been playing with her and wrapped her chubby arms around his leg to steady herself. He stooped to pry her hands from his breeches.

"Annali, you stay here. I can't play with you right now."

Anna picked up the squealing infant. Lightly touching the copper-red curls that peeked from beneath the child's tiny gauze cap, she settled her on her hip.

"What a pretty girl you are! Where did you get your beautiful red hair?"

"Maam says her Maam back in the Alsace has red hair."

He shot a glance at his mother, who carried a heavy basin filled to the top with sliced apples. As though she read his mind, she came over to them, set her burden on the nearest table, and reached for the baby.

"Ach, let me take her, Anna. You two go on."

Annali clung to Anna, however, and she laughed with delight. "Oh, she's no trouble at all. We're only going for a short walk, and we'd love to take her along, wouldn't we, Joseph?"

Joseph forced a smile. "*Ya.* Sure."

"*Guud,* then. If she fusses, bring her back."

Assuring Maam that they would, Anna waited for Joseph to open the door. He complied without looking at her or his baby sister, who happily cooed and waved her arms as though she knew that she had just ruined everything.

✦ ┄┄ ✦

CHRISTIAN SPRAWLED BACKWARD onto the ground, the breath knocked out of him. Eyes wide, mouth hanging open in dismay, he scrambled to his feet.

Joseph stood on the step behind Anna, one hand on her shoulder, the other on the baby, steadying them, while Blitz danced around them in excitement. "What's the matter with you? You could have hurt someone!"

Little Annali squirmed and her face puckered. Anna bounced her on her hip, patting her back until the child stuck her thumb in her mouth and laid her head on Anna's shoulder.

The younger children who had been trailing Christian gathered around, but Joseph ignored them. Stepping from behind Anna, he grabbed Christian and shook him.

"You should look where you're going."

Christian jerked his arm out of Joseph's grip, his chin jutting out. "I didn't see them—"

Joseph glared at him. "You didn't look."

Anna touched Joseph's arm with her free hand. "It's all right, Joseph. He didn't mean to run into us. The children were just playing. Thanks to you, no one got hurt."

Joseph's expression softened. "Just see that you're more careful from now on and don't go running through here."

Christian ignored his brother and concentrated on brushing the dust from the seat of his breeches.

Anna ruffled his hair. "I hope you didn't' get hurt when you fell, Christian."

He looked up and returned her smile with a shy one.

Joseph took Anna's arm. "Let's go."

As he escorted Anna away, she glanced over her shoulder to wink at Christian. His smile widened, and he led the children off to play under the trees in the side yard.

Anna was nice, he reflected, looking around at his small flock of followers. She treated him almost like a grownup. He wouldn't mind at all if she and Joseph got married someday.

As usual, Christian had been assigned to watch over Jacob and John, Johannes and Katie's sturdy five- and three-year-olds, and delicate, pretty Mattie, Barbara and Crist's four-year-old daughter. They had soon been joined by several others of the younger children from the church who always seemed drawn to Christian like a lodestone.

Unlike many of the boys his age and older, he always took time to play with the little ones. They had just finished a game of fox and hens, with him as the fox, of course. More often than not, he ended up being the one to chase the others, but he didn't mind. He always made sure not to run so fast that he caught the smallest children too easily as they scurried away, squealing in delight.

He scanned the eager faces surrounding him and felt his chest swell. He enjoyed the children's company and basked in their admiration.

Although he was no longer the baby of the family, he was still the youngest boy and small for his age. Daati and Joseph— even Jake sometimes—pushed him aside. At the thought, hurt and resentment welled up.

He always got stuck with the chores no one else wanted to do, while Jake and Joseph were entrusted with more grownup and challenging responsibilities. But these children looked up to him. They vied for his attention. They never criticized or made fun of him. When he was with them he felt capable, even important.

So when they pulled him down to the grass to pile on top of him, Christian joined in their gales of laughter as he struggled to break free—but not too hard.

❖┄┄┄❖

JAKOB WAITED FOR RUDY Detweiler to finish scooping the last of the apple pulp out of the huge, circular stone trough. When the young man finished, Jakob helped him spread the fragrant paste across the top of the pile already in the press. After they leveled the sticky mass, Rudy deftly freed the ends of the burlap from the wooden frame and folded them in over the pulp, snugly overlapping them before removing the frame.

Jakob stepped back to assess the height of the stack of pulp-filled burlap squares, called the "cheese." Stroking his beard, he nodded in approval. While he and the others watched, Johannes and seventeen-year-old Jake applied themselves to the chain that pulled the windlass lever, their faces heating with the effort.

Creaking loudly, the giant screw revolved, compressing the stack and sending rivers of juice sluicing down the drainage racks and into the tank below. When the flow had slowed to a lazy drip, Jakob motioned to his sons to halt.

"Looks like we're done. We'll end up with more than eight full barrels out of this first crop. Not so bad for a day's work." He went to unhitch the Belgian from the gearshaft that turned heavy stone rollers to grind the apples spread in the trough.

Rudy's father, Melchior, came over to help with the harness. "*Ya*, we've all had a good harvest this year—even when you figure all we had to supply for the British troops."

The other men were already pulling the cheese apart to shake out the lengths of burlap and shovel away the almost dry pulp. Johannes and the two Stutzman brothers carefully tipped the fragrant, foaming apple juice into the remaining barrels.

Jakob Mast leaned on his shovel. "You were right about this piece of land giving a good yield, Jakob. And it looks like your livestock have increased twofold at least."

Straightening, Jakob stretched his aching back. "I can't complain. I got good strong colts from both my mares this spring, and all my cows but one dropped calves. My sheep and hogs more than doubled too."

A bull's low bellow drifted up from the lower barnyard a short distance away, accompanied by the scrape of horns against fence rails.

Dr. Blanck smiled broadly. "That's not the only bull that's been among the cows."

He tilted his head to include Johannes and Crist Stutzman. Both men flushed, though their chuckles matched those of the others.

Jakob led the Belgian to the watering trough and waited while she drank her fill. "*Ya, Gott* has filled my quiver with grandchildren. And my Anna finally got that girl she's been wanting for so long."

Hannes Mueller elbowed Jake. "Another year, and Jake here will be warranting land, I expect. My guess is Barbara Hooley will likely take a husband around that time."

Jakob threw his son a sharp look, but Jake raised his hands in protest, his handsome face wreathed in a smile. "I'm sure she'll make some man a fine wife."

The men laughed.

"The rumor is that you're sweet on her," Crist Buerki put in.

"That's news to me—and to Barbara, too, no doubt."

Jake's expression remained supremely innocent. With unhurried calm, he reached for the Belgian's reins, to all appearances oblivious to the others' teasing remarks.

Suppressing a smile, Jakob watched him lead the horse around the side of the barn to her stable in the lower level. In the past year Jake had grown taller than Jakob, taller even than Johannes.

Turning back to his friends, he shook his head. "If things hold as they are, with the increase in all our families, we'll soon have to split off a new congregation."

Crist Stutzman pulled off his hat to scratch his head. "This war may change that yet. Already a number of families from this area have moved away because of the Indian attacks, leaving household goods behind along with the crops in the fields and even livestock. I hear plenty of talk that others are seriously thinking of leaving too."

"Did you know the troops were pulled out of Fort Northkill last week?" Hans Zug asked.

"Pulled out?" Stephen Kauffman's features registered alarm.

"All of them. One of *die Englishe* just east of us came by this morning to tell us the British shut the fort down. He says Colonel Weiser is concerned about it, but there's nothing he can do."

Johannes leaned his back against the wagon. "That should worry all of us. Why, Frederick Myer and his wife were killed and scalped back in June not three miles from here, and the children were all carried off."

"*Ya,* and a couple months before that George Gisinger and Adam Miller were both killed."

Detweiler rounded on Mueller, his expression grim. "And don't forget that Baltzer Smith's daughter was taken captive."

"Things have been quiet since July, though," Blanck said hopefully. "Maybe the French are pulling the Indians back."

Crist Buerki lowered himself onto the end of Johannes's wagon, his legs dangling over the edge. "*Ya,* back to Fort William Henry on Lake George up in New York. Did you hear how the French burned it down last month and massacred all the prisoners? There will likely be even more trouble in this area now that they have the British on the run."

Jakob shrugged. "Having soldiers stationed out here hasn't protected anybody so far."

Jake rejoined the men. "If the Indians aren't afraid when soldiers are out scouting for them all the time, what are they going to do if they have a free hand?"

For a long moment, no one spoke. All around the circle, the men's faces settled into tense lines.

At last Blanck broke the silence. "I suppose they need the troops at the other forts since there've been more killed in those areas lately."

Kurtz snorted. "Last year that British captain said they'd leave us to the Indians' mercy since we Amish won't help them fight. Looks like he meant it."

Jake shoved his hands into his pockets and shifted from one foot to the other. "How can we expect the English to fight for us when we won't fight for ourselves?"

"*Gott* yet knows our need and will protect us. We Amish are no threat to the Indians, and they have no reason to attack us."

"Yet still some of our people have been attacked, Jakob," Zug pointed out. "Are we testing the Lord too far by staying here? Maybe it makes sense for us to move back closer to Philadelphia until the war is over."

Jakob's mouth tightened. "*Ya,* and leave all we've worked so hard for, and then have to start all over again. I think we're better off to trust *Gott* to care for us in this place where he brought us to."

Several of the men voiced agreement, and one by one, they returned to their work. But a cloud of unease hung over them, dampening the formerly festive atmosphere.

Jakob tried to concentrate on cleaning the press, but he could not shake off the nagging question of what he would do if his home was attacked. It was all too easy to tell a neighbor how to respond when his life and the lives of his loved ones hung in the balance. It was an entirely different matter to personally face the tomahawk.

In the end, he could only pray that he would never come to that hour of decision. And that he would have the courage to stand firm if his obedience was ever tested.

Chapter Eight

JOSEPH WAVED HIS ARM toward the south end of the orchard. "The peaches are from there on over. We'll begin picking them later in the week."

Anna balanced baby Annali on her hip and tilted her head to survey the straight rows of young fruit trees that stretched out all around them. "I expect Jake will be warranting his own land before long. Bessie claims he's sweet on Barbara Hooley."

Joseph felt a pang of envy. "I'll soon be old enough to buy a plantation too. There's still plenty of good land here along the Northkill, but I'm thinking about moving on the other side of the mountains once the war is over."

He stole a sidelong glance at Anna, worried that his words sounded boastful. Reading admiration in her gaze, however, he gathered his courage.

"Anna, I've been wondering—"

Just then the baby crowed and bounced in excitement, waving her arms and legs and leaning backward to look up at the leaves rustling in the wind overhead. Anna nuzzled her neck, making Annali wriggle and laugh.

"Such a big girl, you are! By next year you'll be helping your brothers with chores and even picking fruit, *ya?*"

Annali reached for Joseph, and Anna held her out. Suppressing a sigh, he took her, his irritation melting away the instant her arms went around his neck and her soft cheek pressed lovingly against his.

"Up you go, Annali!"

He tossed her toward the branches just over his head, then caught her safely in his arms. She squealed in delight, and, laughing, he threw her up again.

"You'll make a good father someday, Joseph." Anna's smile warmed him all over.

He wanted to answer that she would make a good mother, too, that she was the prettiest and kindest girl he had ever met, that he thought of her to the point of distraction, that the dream of his own home included her as the keeper of it. But the words refused to reach his tongue.

Just looking at her addled him. In the months since he had seen her last, back in the spring, she had blossomed from a girl into a young woman. She had grown taller and more slender, and her body had begun to develop a womanly fullness. Even her face had perceptibly thinned, her cheeks losing their childishly round contour so that the delicate lines of her cheekbones now emphasized her large eyes. He could gaze into those emerald depths for the rest of his life.

Into his mind flooded the common talk between the young men during covert meetings behind one or another's barn during church services and other gatherings. Frank and often ribald, their conversation invariably turned to speculations about the things a man did with a woman in the privacy of their *Kammer.*

The physical part of sexual relations was no mystery to Joseph. Growing up on a plantation, he had often seen a male animal covering a female. He had watched, even helped, with the births that followed. At the same time, those joking, embarrassed, boastful discussions between his friends had given him the sense that there was considerably more to the intimacy between a woman and a man than there was in the coupling of beasts.

He tried to wrest his thoughts under control, but with Anna standing so close to him in the concealment of the orchard, he couldn't help wondering how it would feel to hold her blossoming form against his own. Feeling his body respond to his thoughts, he feared that Anna would notice his discomfort.

Yet his longing for her went far beyond physical desire, powerful as that was. Could she ever feel for him what he felt for her? When she reclaimed the baby, he was engulfed by the vision of her as his young bride with their firstborn in her arms, and his throat tightened until it ached.

"Ach, what a dear little sister you have," Anna sighed, tickling the gurgling baby under her chin. "I do so love babies, don't you?"

"Anna—"

She looked up at him, her rosy face wreathed in an expectant smile that held every promise he could ever dream of. "*Ya,* Joseph?"

The rising wind rattled down the lanes of the orchard, hissing through the leaves and softly creaking the branches overhead. The shadows had deepened. He felt the gooseflesh rise on his arms, and what little courage he had felt vanished. He cleared his throat.

"It's getting dark. We better go back inside."

Her smile faded. She bent her head, snuggling the baby closer.

"*Ya,* your Maami and the others are most likely getting supper ready. Everyone must be wondering where we are."

She hunched her shoulders against the wind. He ached to put his arm around her and pull her to his side. To keep her warm. To protect her. Merely to touch her.

While he hesitated, she turned and started toward the house, little Annali's head bobbing sleepily over her shoulder. He fell into step beside her, cursing his awkwardness and brooding over his lost opportunity to confide in her all the tender emotions of his heart.

*　⊷┄┄┄⊶*

"JOSEPH! COME HELP carry these kegs down to the cellar."

Joseph swung around. Jake stood beside Johannes's loaded wagon, beckoning, while Daat and the other men busied themselves cleaning the cider press.

Joseph gave Anna an apologetic smile. "I've got to go help them."

"Do you want me to save you a place at the table?"

He nodded, beaming. "It won't take long. I'll hurry."

Determined not to stare after her, he went to join the men. Dr. Blanck gave a sly smile as Joseph passed by.

"Seems to me Jake won't be the only one warranting land in the next couple of years."

Joseph hurried to help his brothers and brother-in-law carry the heavy kegs of cider into the house, pretending he hadn't heard the remark and trying to ignore the knowing looks the men exchanged.

After they wrestled the last keg down the steep cellar stairway, the others hurried back up to the *Küche,* drawn by the savory aromas of supper cooking. Joseph lingered, however. He sat down on the steps and wiped the sweat from his brow with his kerchief, studying the familiar scene in the dim light of the betty lamp Johannes had left on the stairs.

The cellar extended the full length and width of the house, dug so deep that even a tall man could easily stand erect in it. Great hewn beams supported the thick floorboards overhead, and a huge, rectangular stone pillar extended from ceiling to floor at the center, forming the foundation of the *Küche's* massive hearth. Dry and cool even in hot, humid weather, the space was walled and floored with neatly fitted field stones kept scrupulously clean.

The walls extended aboveground far enough to allow for a narrow window at each end to provide ventilation. The sturdy Indian shutters were closed over these openings now in preparation for the coming cold weather as well as to keep out intruders, whether man or beast.

To each side along the cellar walls, rows of shelves held stoneware crocks of honey and maple sugar, fruit preserves, sauerkraut, and pickles. One section held wooden boxes of beeswax candles that Christian had helped Maam dip earlier in the month, while crocks filled with fresh apple butter already crowded another shelf, with room for more below. Large bins lined the cellar's back wall, ready to receive the abundant harvest of late apples, cabbages, and root vegetables soon to come; buried in sawdust this store would supply the family through the winter.

On a low platform along the far end wall, barrels of wheat and rye flour and parched and ground corn flanked hogsheads of corned beef and salt pork. Alongside these stood the kegs of fresh apple juice, which would ferment into tangy, refreshing cider during the coming weeks.

When he built his own homestead, Joseph decided, he would have a cellar just like this one, if not larger. He and Anna would fill it with the bounty of the land beyond the mountains.

He roused when he heard someone enter the stairwell above him. "Are you going to sit there all day?" Johannes called. "Supper's ready."

Joseph pushed to his feet and ran upstairs. Eagerly he scanned the crowded *Küche* for Anna.

The last of the adults and their younger children were preparing to leave after a hasty meal of leftovers. The girls from the church, Anna among them, were already hurrying to set the trestle tables for the youth.

Joseph's mouth watered as he scanned the plates of cold beef and sliced bread, small crocks of pickles and preserves, and an assortment of pies. His stomach growled, and he winced, hoping no one overheard.

After they ate supper the young people would sing and play games well into the night, while the rest of the family went to bed. When Joseph's gaze met Jake's, he couldn't stop a grin of anticipation.

✦ ⋯⋯ ✦

"GET BACK TO BED right now!"

From the shadows of the upper stairway, Christian smirked at Joseph. "You better leave me alone or I'll tell everyone you've been doing more than just kissing Anna."

Joseph climbed another step, fists clenched. "That's a lie, and you know it."

Christian puckered his mouth and made kissing sounds. "I watched you kiss. Everybody knows you're in love."

Joseph felt Jake's hand on his arm. "Christli, you're just jealous because you're not old enough to stay up. Now get to bed before I tell Daat you're bothering us."

"If you wake Daati up, he'll make everyone go home."

Joseph gritted his teeth. He knew Christian was right.

Jake started up the stairs, a determined glint in his eyes. Before his foot came down on the second step, however, Christian vanished upstairs.

Standing on the step below Joseph, Jake gave him a wink. "It's no secret you're sweet on Anna. Every time she gets close to you, you blush or trip over your feet or knock something down."

"You're a fine one to talk. You ought to see how you look when Barbara Hooley walks by."

Jake laughed and shrugged, and Joseph's annoyance disappeared as quickly as their youjnger brother had. Together they went to rejoin their friends.

An hour of hymn singing had followed supper, with the boys and girls seated across from each other at the tables, taking turns choosing hymns. Although Joseph sang with the others, his mind was not on the words. He could tell he was not the only one who was distracted. At the end of each hymn before another was chosen, a hum of conversation filled the *Küche* as everyone talked and joked, boys and girls self-consciously eyeing each other. And no one was in a hurry to resume singing.

Because of the continuing threat of Indian raids, instead of gathering outside on the barn's expansive threshing floor as they normally would have, the young people had been directed to remain inside the house with the door barred and the heavy interior shutters closed over the windows. Joseph had all but burst with impatience until Christian was finally sent to bed and Maam and Daat took Annali and retreated to their *Kammer* for the night. Left to themselves, the young people's restraint eased, and the hymn singing soon ended.

They had removed the trestle tables and arranged the benches along the walls, boys engaging in horseplay with each other to impress the girls, who gathered in giggling clusters to share confidences about whom they would choose as partners for the evening's games. At last they lined up across the *Küche* from each other, the boys facing the girls. One at a time, alternating between girls and boys, each called out the name of the one they favored.

Noting Jake's unhesitating choice of Barbara Hooley, Joseph had gathered his courage. The choice came to Anna first, however, and he waited in agony while she coyly scanned the row of boys as though trying to make up her mind. At last she called out his name, and he hurried to stand beside her, banging his shin on a bench in his haste. He sheepishly joined his friends' hoots and laughter.

When Anna's teasing gaze met his, he had to struggle to control his breathing, certain that everyone in the room could hear his heart's pounding. By some miracle, her fingers closed over his, and trembling, he gently squeezed her hand. She was so small and delicate that he was afraid he would inadvertently hurt her in his clumsiness.

Giggles and whispers had filled *Küche* when everyone took their place for the first game. When they returned to their seats at its end, it took several heartbeats for Joseph to realize that Anna had lifted her face to his. He hesitated for a moment, paralyzed by fear and desire. Then, holding his breath, he closed his eyes and bent over her.

Exhilaration flooded through him when their lips met. To his astonishment, she did not draw away, and he lingered, savoring the sweet innocence of her kiss before they both pulled back.

He had hardly been able to look at her, terrified that he would see disappointment or contempt in her eyes. Instead, when he gathered his courage, there had been unmistakable warmth in her gaze and her lips curved upward in a sweet smile that left him weak kneed.

For the next hour, nothing could sour Joseph's mood or dampen his ardor, not even Christian's teasing. While the games continued, that kiss lingered, ruling his heart and mind. He could finally dare to believe that Anna felt for him what he felt for her. And as heady images of their future together spun through his head, he wished passionately that the evening would never end.

✦ ⋯⋯ ✦

"It's time now for your friends to go home."

"Not yet, Daat!" Joseph pled.

"It's almost midnight. The sun will be up in just a few hours yet. Besides, with the danger from the Indians, your friends should not be out so late."

Clad only in his long shirt, with his uncombed hair and beard sticking out in untidy tufts around his head, Daat was clearly the object of the muffled titters coming from the young people nearest them. Embarrassed, Joseph transferred his imploring gaze to Jake.

"Can't they stay just another hour, Daat? There haven't been any raids right around here for months, and we young people don't need so much sleep."

Jakob shook his head firmly and turned to their guests, raising his voice so all could hear. "We all have chores to do in the morning. It's time to go home now. Stay together on your way and be on the lookout for any danger."

Joseph stalked outside with Jake to see their friends off. The sliver of the first quarter moon had set more than an hour earlier, and, faintly visible in the starlight, he saw that streamers of rising mist cloaked the surrounding forest and orchards. The girls shivered and clutched their shawls tightly around their shoulders.

Blitz got up from her usual post on the front step to accept their affectionate pats as she let them pass. In the dim lantern light, the white dog appeared ghostly, with her pale, fringed tail waving and her white fangs gleaming in her grinning mouth. Many of the young people paired off, the boys driving the girls home in their light carriages. Joseph helped Anna into the Muellers' carriage for the drive to their home, where she was staying overnight.

He watched until the bobbing light of the carriage's lantern disappeared around the bend down the lane. Then, pushing past Jake and Daat, he grabbed a candlestick and stormed upstairs to his *Kammer.*

He wished he didn't have to share the space with anyone. Tonight of all nights he wanted badly to be alone.

To his relief, Christian lay curled in a tight ball on his own side of the bed, sound asleep. Joseph set the candlestick on the small bedside table and as quietly as possible removed neckcloth, breeches, shoes, and hose. Leaving on his long shirt and his drawers, he sank gingerly onto the mattress to avoid disturbing his younger brother. He drew up the quilt, then leaned over to blow out the candle.

He had left the door between the two upstairs rooms open, and he could hear Jake in the front *Kammer* also getting ready for bed. After several minutes the soft glow of his candle extinguished, and quiet settled over the house.

Fingers interlaced behind his head, Joseph lay on his back staring up at the attic floorboards overhead until his eyes adjusted to the faint starlight streaming through the window. Of all nights for Daat to end this party, this was the worst. Frolics often lasted most of the night, and Joseph had wanted this one to go on forever. But as usual, Daat had to spoil everything. He never listened, at least not to Joseph.

What would it have hurt for me to spend just a little more time with Anna? Why must you always be like an oak? Why can't you—just once— bend a little?

Weariness tugged at Joseph's eyelids, but his thoughts drifted back to the unforgettable moment when his lips and Anna's had met for the first time. Against his will, a little at a time, the border between consciousness and slumber blurred, until at last the familiar details of the room faded into blackness.

Chapter Nine

Tuesday, September 20, 1757, 2:47 a.m.

A N INDEFINABLE FOREBODING jerked Joseph awake. His eyes snapped open, and he stared at the shadowy ceiling above his head, blinking to clear his sleep-blurred vision.

How long had he slept? Darkness shrouded the room, and instinct told him it was well past midnight.

Every sense fully alert, he strained to make out what had shocked him from slumber, but he could discern no unusual sound. Outside, the autumn wind whispered through the dry, thinning leaves of the surrounding forest. Moaning faintly under the eaves of the house, it creaked the planed boards that clad the upper story's exterior.

Becoming aware that clammy sweat beaded his forehead, he wiped his brow with the back of his shirt sleeve. Christian lay motionless beside him, his breathing slow and regular, and Joseph relaxed, reassured that everything was as it should be.

The events of the previous evening flooded back into his mind, prompting first pleasure, then seething anger at his father. He turned his back to Christian. The younger boy did not stir.

A sudden, unearthly howl brought both boys bolt upright at the same instant. Heart hammering, hair on end, Joseph rolled off the bed as Blitz set up a furious clamor.

"Joseph, what—?"

Christian's voice shook, and Joseph bent over him. "Hush! Stay here and don't make a sound."

He groped across the room and through the doorway that separated his and Christian's *Kammer* from Jake's.

He could just make out the faintly lighter rectangle of the window at the head of the stairs. Skimming the wall with his hand, he crept cautiously toward it at a crouch. In the darkness, he bumped hard into Jake and let out a grunt.

He felt Jake touch his finger to his lips to silence him. Then Jake pressed back against the wall at the gable's end, straining to catch a glimpse of the yard through the window without exposing himself to view from below.

Abruptly Blitz's barking escalated abruptly to a snarling, baying frenzy. Before Joseph could move, Jake bolted down the stairs. Joseph sucked in a lungful of air and raced after him, only dimly registering that Christian crowded on his heels.

❖ ────── ❖

FINGERS FUMBLING in his haste, Jakob dragged on his breeches. Anna huddled on the bed behind him, the quilt clutched to her bosom.

"Vass iss los?" What's going on?

Blitz's howls caused the breath to choke in Jakob's lungs. In her cradle beside the bed Annali began to whimper, then let out a wail. Anna reached to quiet her.

Jakob grabbed the door handle. "Stay here!"

He heard the creak of footfalls descending the stairs and tore open the *Kammer* door. Across the *Küche,* the front door swung wide, Jake's tall, lean form silhouetted against the pinpricks of starlight in the black sky outside.

Transfixed, Jakob stopped in his tracks. Before he could find breath to cry a warning, a tongue of red flame leaped from the darkness, and the deafening explosion of musket fire rent the night.

In suspended horror he heard Jake's sharp outcry, saw him stagger, then sway back against the outer door and slam it shut. The metallic ring of the iron bar dropping into its bracket punctuated the harsh, shuddering rasp of Jake's breaths.

Three strides brought Jakob across the *Küche* to catch his son as he sagged toward the floor. Holding him upright, Jakob propped him against the doorjamb.

Something struck the outside of the door with a thud that rattled the window panes on either side and drove the two of them several paces backward together. Outside, Blitz uttered a single agonized yelp, then began a repeated, high-pitched yelping that chilled Jakob's blood. Abruptly the dog's keening ceased.

Cold sweat trickled down Jakob's forehead. Feeling numb, he clutched Jake to his chest, both gasping in short, shallow pants. A dim ray of candlelight bloomed behind him, and he was suddenly aware of Annali's terrified screams and Christian's convulsive sobs.

He threw an imploring glance toward the *Kammer* door. Anna's voluminous white shift gleamed faintly as she rushed to him, a candlestick in one hand and their screaming daughter clasped in her other arm. Joseph and Christian pressed in close, helping to support Jake.

"Is he all right?" Christian quavered, his voice unnaturally high.

Jakob shook his head, his throat too tight for speech. With Anna hovering over them, they helped to Jake hobble into the *Stube.* Anna set the candle on the small table while they lowered him onto Jakob's chair. Jake groaned, his face pasty white and gleaming with sweat in the wavering light.

The dark stain that soaked Jake's shirttail, creeping steadily outward, sent a bolt of cold fear through Jakob. Setting his jaw, he gingerly pulled the fabric back.

A thick rivulet of blood streamed from the wound on the boy's upper thigh, marking where the musket ball had entered. He bit his lip and focused on pulling the ample length of Jake's shirttail tightly around the leg in the hope that the sturdy fabric would stanch the flow of blood, though he knew it could not do so for long.

All of them startled when the case clock on the wall shelf began to toll three o'clock. The normally reassuring sound of the chimes unnerved Jakob.

What are we to do, Gott? *Help us!*

Joseph hurried to the *Stube's* outer door and made sure it was securely bolted. He swung around when a second shot shattered the nearest *Küche* window, exploding shards of glass against the outside of the heavy shutters as the ball tore into the solid wood with a hollow thud.

Anna and the baby shrieked simultaneously. Joseph scurried back to his parents, and Jakob pulled them roughly down to crouch on the floor by the sofa. The swift movement to the floor caused Jake to gasp and moan and his wound to bleed more profusely.

A flurry of shots followed, cutting through the front *Küche* windows and lodging in the shutters, door, and thick log walls. They cowered behind the furniture, while Annali screamed and Anna wailed, covering her ears.

As abruptly as it had begun, the firing ceased, the sudden quiet as unsettling as the repeated crack of gunfire had been. Anna's cries gave way to muffled sobs, and the baby clung to her, whimpering.

Huddled with them on the floor, shaking, Jakob knew he must not allow Anna and the children to see his terror. For their sakes he had to stay calm, maintain control, and think clearly. If he did not keep his wits about him, they would have little hope of survival.

He gripped Anna by the shoulders and forced her to meet his stern gaze. "Keep Annali quiet and watch over Jake while the boys and I try to find out how many of them there are."

Quieting, she drew a shuddering breath and nodded, staring at him wide-eyed, her loose hair flying around her flushed face, the baby clutched tight against her bosom. Jakob squeezed her shoulders and stood.

He motioned to Joseph and Christian to follow him. Stooped, he led the way into the *Küche's* large, shadowy space, the boys crawling after him on hands and knees. When he reached the front wall, Jakob crouched between the hutch and the window to the left of the door.

"Stay low," he told them in a hoarse whisper. "Go upstairs and look out the window. *Schtill!* Don't let them see you."

Their faces tense, the two boys nodded and moved past him.

Jakob cracked the shutter open just enough to see outside. When his vision adjusted to the darkness, he saw directly across the yard a number of indistinct forms huddled together on the far side of the bake oven's black bulk. Several times the faint red glow from the embers inside was briefly obscured as one or more of the war party passed in front of it.

As Jakob watched, a man clad in the breechclout and leggings of a warrior strode out of the shadows. Starlight glinted on his musket barrel and rippled across the blade of the tomahawk hanging from his belt. His head was shaven except for a topknot on its crown, and his tall, lean body was streaked with paint that appeared black in the darkness.

Another form, clad in buckskin, came to stand beside him—a white man, soon joined by another. Frenchmen. They seemed to be in charge of the party, and Jakob concluded that they were conferring about what to do next.

The dense shadows cast by the surrounding trees made an exact count of the attackers impossible. Maybe a dozen. Maybe more. It made little difference.

He shifted cautiously, and a ghostly form sprawled on the ground not far from the *Küche* door caught his eye. Heart racing, he realized it was Blitz, and a wave of nausea washed over him.

He heard Joseph and Christian slip back down the steps behind him. Keeping his expression impassive, he inched the shutter closed and led the way back into the *Stube*.

Anna sat on the floor where they had left her, the baby lying against her shoulder, hiccupping. Jake stretched on the floor beside them, clutching the bloody hem of his shirt around his leg. When they came back into the room, he looked up, his face taut with pain.

"What's going on?"

Joseph shrugged. "We weren't able to see much through the trees. A couple of warriors went around the end of the house. That's all."

At Jakob's terse report, however, all of them paled.

Suddenly Jake caught his breath and bent over, his fingers digging into his thigh. Anna rose and thrust the baby into Christian's arms. She hurried through the *Kammer* door and quickly returned, carrying one of her petticoats and a pair of scissors.

She lumbered to her knees beside Jake and began to cut the linen into strips. Expertly she bandaged Jake's leg, gently shushing his muffled groans as she drew the strips tight. Blood soaked through the cloth at the site of the wound, but within moments the flow ceased.

"See, you're going to be all right."

Joseph's attempt at cheerfulness fell flat. Jake looked away, jaw clenched.

"They killed Blitz, didn't they?"

Joseph glanced over his shoulder at Christian, who cuddled Annali, his lips compressed in a firm line. He was trying hard to be brave, Joseph realized with a pang of sympathy.

Maam and Daat exchanged worried glances, but neither responded.

"What will they do now?" Christian persisted.

"I'm not waiting to find out." Rising, Joseph nudged Christian's shoulder. "Come on."

Christian immediately returned Annali to Maam. Avoiding Daat's frowning gaze, Joseph headed into the *Küche*. He cautiously felt his way to the cellar door with Christian at his heels.

All his senses strained to detect any noise or movement outside. The uncanny quiet worried him, and for once he was grateful to have his younger brother close. He quickly found the rifles stored at the top of the cellar stairs, and with Christian carrying the powder and shot, they returned to the *Stube*.

Joseph handed one of the rifles to Christian. "You prime and load while I load mine and Jake's. Here's yours, Daat." He extended a rifle to his father.

Jakob stared at the weapon. Its wooden stock had been worn smooth by his own hands, but he eyed it as though he had never seen a rifle before and had no idea of its use.

The clock's single chime emphasized the foreboding silence outside. Could only a quarter of an hour have passed since the attack began? An irrational hope overwhelmed him. Might the Indians have gone?

Into his consciousness filtered the barely perceptible crackle of dry leaves and the light scrape of something dragging against the wall under the window behind him. The hair on the back of his neck prickled.

Someone was creeping along the rear of the house, separated from them by only the width of a log.

"Take it, Daat. If we fire at them, they'll leave!" Joseph's whisper was urgent now.

Jakob looked from Joseph to Christian, both clutching rifles, then to Jake, who sat slumped on the floor, his bandaged leg extended stiffly in front of him. Finally his gaze found Anna, huddled beside their wounded son. She clutched Annali in one arm, her free hand pressed over her mouth, her eyes fixed on him in an unspoken plea.

Before him rose the vision of words written as though in letters of fire: *Thou shalt not kill. Vengeance is mine saith the Lord.*

All his adult life he had struggled to conceal from others his worst impulses. To sternly bring heart and mind into conformity to God's command. To earn God's favor and pardon by doing what was right.

But now, when they were under attack by an implacable enemy bent on their destruction? Was he to leave the ones he loved to God's mercy, not knowing what the outcome would be? Could he trust God to save them as he had the three Hebrew boys in the fiery furnace and Daniel in the lion's den?

And if God did not? He had not saved His own Son from the cross. Or the martyrs from the sword.

Could he face the likelihood that all of them would be killed, that his wife and his children would die because he did nothing?

Everything in him screamed to take the rifle Joseph offered and shoot those who threatened his family, to stand between the savages and the ones he was responsible to protect. But God's command forbade it, and the weight of that charge staggered him.

He pressed his lips together and drew in a breath that felt as though it seared his lungs. His hands shaking uncontrollably, he wrenched his gaze to his son's face.

"*Nay*," he rasped. "Put down your guns. God commands us not to kill."

Joseph shook his head, the color draining out of his face. He opened his mouth, but before he could speak, Jake cut him off.

"If we don't do something, Daat, they'll kill us all."

"*Gott* will protect us, even as he did the Hebrew children in the midst of the fire. We will trust Him to provide a way of escape."

"You don't need to kill anyone." Anna spoke rapidly, her tone reflecting desperation. "If you just shoot at them so they know we have guns, it'll scare them off, and they'll leave us in peace."

Euphoria flooded over Jakob at the simple solution she offered. But as quickly as the emotion rose, it evaporated.

"If we shoot, we risk killing by accident. Or we may drive them to attack again, and then will we have the strength to stop shooting? *Nay*, we cannot be halfhearted and expect the Lord's favor. The only way of obedience is . . . obedience."

He groaned the last word. Motionless, Anna and the children stared at him, clearly stunned, their eyes accusing him.

Shaken, he cried out in anguish too deep for words, *Ach, Gott, save us! Take my life, if need be, but protect these innocent ones!*

Joseph became aware that he still held out the rifle. Lowering it to his side, he studied his father's bearded face and stocky form in the same way he had peered through the upstairs window just minutes before. Searching for a way of escape he had not found. And that he did not find now.

He and Jake were skilled riflemen, and Christian could hit a target most of the time. Daat could easily drop a deer from a hundred yards. Or a fox.

His heart contracted. They had more than enough ammunition to drive the Indians off if only Daat would listen to reason.

"Ess iss nett unser vek," Daat said. It is not our way.

Joseph regarded him blankly. *Not our way? Then our way is foolish!*

He wanted to shout the words. Clenching his hand around the rifle until the metal fittings bit into his palm, he looked from Daat to the weapon, then back to Daat.

For as long as he could remember, Joseph had heard the story of how, when Daat had been only eight years old, his father had been arrested for returning to Switzerland to help other believers after the Anabaptists had been driven out of that country. Maam and Daat had come to this New World because they believed Christ taught them to either endure or escape from persecution rather than resisting it.

He knew these things, but still he froze in disbelief as his father pried the rifle from his fingers, then took the one he clutched in his other hand. But when Daat reached for Christian's weapon as well, Joseph stepped between them.

"Daat, *nay!*" He gestured at his mother and baby sister, at Jake and Christian. "Will you let us all die?"

"Should we do a wrong thing because others do?"

Rage rose in Joseph's chest, nearly choking him. Helplessly he watched his father wrench the other rifle from Christian's grasp, pick up the powder horn and bag of shot, then stride across the room to prop the weapons in the far corner.

Joseph clenched and unclenched his fists. Was there no room for common sense in his father's convictions? Was he stubborn enough to sacrifice even his family in obedience to . . . what? A God no one could see or hear?

Joseph saw Jake suddenly cock his head and half turn as though he heard something. At the same instant the faint sound of something striking the outside of the house filtered into Joseph's racing thoughts. It seemed to come from upstairs.

Daat had stopped in the center of the room and now placed his hand on Maam's shoulder. "Have faith," he urged. "*Gott* will yet provide a way of escape."

✦——✦

CHRISTIAN GLANCED through the *Stube* door into the *Küche*. "I smell smoke!"

"Ach, they're going to burn the house down yet! Do something, Jakob!"

Daat raised his hand to still her words. "*Bleib schtill!*" Stay quiet!

To hear his parents speak so sharply to each other alarmed Christian almost as much as the danger outside. He wanted to escape, find a place to hide, but the realization that there was no place of safety left struck him forcibly.

"I think it's coming from upstairs," he blurted out.

"We'll go find out what's going on."

Joseph jerked his head at Christian and ducked back into the dark *Küche*. Christian ran after him.

A muted, orange glow drew them to the opposite end of the room. The moment they reached the stairway, Christian saw light shimmering through the window at the top of the steps. Thin wisps of grey steam rose from the window frame.

Joseph sucked in a breath. "The warriors must have fired burning arrows into the house!"

Christian stared upward, the sickening realization dawning that the flames were cooking the moisture out of the wood and would soon burn through into the interior. How long before the glass would get hot enough to explode?

Already his throat was becoming raw from the acrid smoke that clogged it. When Joseph pulled his shirttail up over the lower portion of his face to cover his nose, he did likewise, then groped after him up the stairs to crouch on the landing just below the wavy glass panes scorching in the heat.

Joseph crawled to the other side of the window and stood up, pressing against the wall as he craned his neck to look out. His pulse beating loud in his ears, Christian cautiously pushed to his feet and strained to see through the window. on his side

Shadowy figures dashed through the side yard, carrying what appeared to be bundles of straw and smoldering torches. He clamped his hand over his mouth to stop an outcry when one of the figures threw his bundle against the side of the house below them and touched his torch to it. The straw erupted in flames.

Farther out in the yard, another black form fitted a flaming arrow to his bow and raised it toward the top of the house. The arrow sprang from the bowstring, sliced a blazing arc through the early-morning blackness, and buried its head solidly into the board wall at the window's lower left. Orange-red tongues sprang from the dry wood and licked hungrily toward the conflagration just below Christian.

He turned toward Joseph in alarm and saw that his brother was staring through the door into the other *Kammer*. It also was illuminated by fiery light streaming through the window at the opposite end of the house.

Christian plunged back down the stairs and raced into the *Stube*. "The upstairs is on fire, and they're setting more along the walls!"

Joseph crowded close behind him. "Daat, please! We have to get out of here! Let me and Christli take the rifles! You don't have to do anything."

With an effort, Jake pulled himself upright. "I can shoot too."

Joseph gave him an eager nod. "If we fight back, they'll run off—I know they will! Then we can make it to Johannes's house and warn them."

For an instant, his father's hard gaze eased, and Christian thought he would yield. But then Daati's beard jutted upward in a gesture Christian had seen hundreds of times, and he felt as though a stone lodged in his stomach.

"*Nay!* There are too many of them for us to fight in any case. And even if we could escape, they might follow us, and we'd bring danger to your brother and his family—"

The sound of glass breaking at the top of the stairs on the opposite side of the house cut Jakob off. It was immediately echoed by the splintering of the glass panes in the *Kammer* window directly overhead.

Anna's desperate, beseeching gaze met his. The smoke was rapidly thickening, leaving no time to think.

"Down to the cellar—*schnell!* Joseph, on your way push the water barrel over to douse the *Küche* floor. Christian, help him. Anna, take the baby downstairs. I'll bring Jake."

He tried to appear confident, but his commands felt pathetically feeble, and doubts shadowed his mind. Was Joseph right? Could they save their lives by resisting evil instead of submitting to it? Was it possible to fight back without claiming life? Was saving innocent lives a greater good than their revered doctrine of non-violence?

Smoke snaked into the room, but no one moved. They all stared at him, mouths agape.

"Go!" he shouted.

They obeyed hesitantly, preceding him into the *Küche*. He encircled Jake's waist with his arm and brought him to his feet as gently as he could manage. Together they hobbled after the others.

Shocked at how dense the smoke at that side of the house had become, he began to choke and cough, as did Anna and the children. He heard the thump of the water barrel hitting the floor, then felt water sluice around his feet. The barrel was large, but how long could the few gallons it held hold back an inferno?

The smoke, heavy with the stench of burning oak logs, obscured everything around them as they traversed the *Küche,* eyes stinging, bare feet slipping on the floor's wet planks. Jakob fought to keep his footing, every sense focused on holding Jake steady, on getting to the cellar stairs and finding shelter from the flames crackling overhead.

Just beyond the fireplace he and Jake came upon the others, clustered fearfully together. Annali, for some time drowsing against her mother's breast, had awakened and again begun to scream and thrash.

Through the black haze boiling directly ahead, he could see a leaping angry yellow glare. Narrow strips of light flared in the cracks between the planks cladding the upper story and the crumbling chinking of the log wall below it.

"Hurry!" Jakob cried.

Anna rounded on him, bloodshot eyes narrowed. "The stairway is on fire! If we go in the cellar, we'll never get out alive!"

Chapter Ten

"IT'S OUR ONLY CHANCE," Jakob shouted over the din of the fire and the children's cries. "The cellar walls are stone. If we can hold out until sunrise, they'll go away and leave us be!"

By then maybe the militia at the fort will see the smoke and come drive the war party off.

Even as the desperate hope leaped into his mind, he remembered that the soldiers had been withdrawn from Fort Northkill several weeks earlier and sent to Fort Lebanon miles farther away on the other side of the mountain. Biting his lip hard, he stifled a groan. It was on God they must depend, not man.

He got them moving again into the stairwell, slamming the cellar door shut behind them, then urging them down the steep, narrow steps. In the stifling air of the constricted space, they felt their way, breaths rasping, while above their heads the thin cracks between the upper stairway's risers and treads admitted a faint tracery of fiery light. Jakob all but dragged Jake, groaning, down the last few steps, and at last the cellar's moist coolness enveloped them.

Groping through the darkness, Jakob stubbed his toes on random wooden kegs and pottery crocks in his path. He blundered on until he reached the great central fieldstone pillar that formed the foundation of the massive *Küche* fireplace. Using it as a guide, he moved beyond it, supporting Jake on one arm as he felt his way with the other.

He did not stop until he shepherded Anna and the children to the far end of the cavernous space, as far from the heat and smoke as it was possible to go. When he came to a halt he felt the others press close around him.

He lowered Jake to the stone floor, taking care not to cause him more pain. Straightening, he reached out to touch each head or shoulder to assure himself that none was missing. When he laid his hand on Annali's head, her screams quieted to shuddering sobs.

Danke, Gott . . . *danke! For the moment we are safe.*

Gradually his eyes adjusted to the darkness. Faint bars of light blurred the edges of the shutter that closed the single small window above his head. A dull glow above the stairway at the cellar's opposite end provided the only other illumination.

For the first time it occurred to him to wonder about their young guests, who had left not many hours before the attack began. Several had an hour's ride before they reached home. Had they all made it safely?

What about Johannes and Barbara and their families? Were they under attack too? Others of their community?

Resolutely he shook off his frantic thoughts. He could not allow himself to worry about anyone else now. He had to focus on these lives, this crisis, if they were to make it through.

A resounding clatter high above sent a tremor through the house, momentarily deafening them. Screaming, they fell to their knees, arms shielding their heads against clouds of dirt jarred loose from walls and floorboards overhead that filled the air and sifted down on them.

Jakob pulled Anna to him. Both crying out for God's protection, they gathered the children into their embrace, sheltering them from falling debris with their bodies. Jake lay sprawled under them, his gasps of pain stabbing through Jakob's heart. The instant the shower subsided, he anxiously sought the boy's form.

The roof has come down, but the second floor must yet be standing.

"How long . . . will it take for the house . . ?" Anna's whisper choked and ended in a wheezing cough.

Jakob pressed his lips to her ear, forcing a calmness he was far from feeling. "The walls and beams are thick. It'll take some time before they burn through."

Mentally he calculated, *An hour, at the most.*

Joseph tilted his head to catch the muffled roar of the flames above their heads. "The floorboards will burn through between the beams first. Then everything will fall on us."

In the cellar's gloom he could make out Daat's face clearly enough to see that he glared at him. Joseph pressed his lips together hard and gritted his teeth.

The smoke and dust-laden air had already grown perceptibly warmer, the glow above the stairway brighter. With his arm he wiped away the sweat beaded on his brow and squinted at the others. Trickles of perspiration wove muddy tracks down their dirt-smudged cheeks.

He could feel his younger brother shaking. When coughs wracked Christian's body, Joseph drew him more tightly against him.

"Daat, we need some air." His throat was raw, making speech painful.

Daat levered himself upright. "If we pull one of the hogsheads over here, can you stand on it and unlatch the shutter, Christli? Then you can look outside and tell us where the Indians are."

Christian glanced apprehensively at Joseph, then at Daat before nodding, eyes red-rimmed. Quickly the three of them wrestled a large, half-empty hogshead over to the window. Christian scrambled atop the barrel, while Joseph helped Daat to steady him.

Unlatching the shutter, Christian eased it open a degree at a time, spilling a faint shaft of light through the swirling streamers of smoke that had begun to collect beneath the *Küche* floorboards. A trickle of fresh air cooled Joseph's sweaty forehead. Gratitude flooded over him, and a measure of hope—immediately extinguished by the undulating warble of war cries.

Christian slammed the shutter closed and glanced around, his face taut with fear. When Daat took hold of his leg, Joseph saw that his hand trembled.

"Did anyone see you?"

Christian shook his head, sweat dripping from his hair, his breath coming in pants.

"Look again. Carefully. Don't let anyone see you!"

Christian swallowed, pried the shutter open again, and pressed his eye to the crack. "There's lots of smoke. . . . Oh . . .

there are three Indians coming this way! They have rifles!" His voice shook with panic.

"We should have brought ours! We could hit them from here!"

Daat motioned Joseph sharply to silence before turning back to Christian. "What can you see?"

After a tense moment, Christian said in a choked voice, "The barn and smokehouse are on fire. Everything's burning. The chickens . . . they're all dead."

Jakob pressed his eyes shut. *Gone. All gone. Everything we worked so hard for.*

And what does it matter compared to our lives?

Behind them a smaller crash than the first brought them all around, gasping. At the cellar's far end the stairway to the upper floor had burned through and collapsed onto the cellar stairs, bringing the entire structure down and exploding blazing boards outward. Embers cascaded into the sawdust-filled vegetable bins on the back wall, and they burst into flame with a hollow whoosh.

Only distantly aware of his wife's and daughter's screams, Jakob stripped off his shirt. "Boys, roll that cider keg as close to the fire as you can get and break it open!"

Together they sprang to the nearest keg, rolled, pushed, and pulled it toward the bins until the heat grew too intense, then clawed open the lid with their bare hands. Jakob plunged his shirt into the foaming liquid, then stopped. Evaluating the blaze, he threw aside the sodden fabric and motioned to Joseph and

Christian. As one, they heaved the heavy keg onto their shoulders and dumped its contents into the first bin, quenching the conflagration.

Wasting no time, they grabbed another keg and doused the second bin. When they had broken open a third keg, Jakob retrieved his cider-drenched shirt and began to beat out the burning boards from the stairs, while the boys stripped off their shirts and sprang to follow his example.

By the time the fires were extinguished, a cloud of bitter, burnt-cider-tinged smoke filled the upper third of the stone-walled space. Jakob could see it rapidly expanding, descending progressively lower as it consumed the air like a living thing.

Coughing and gagging, he and the boys crawled back to the others, bare-chested, their sweat- and cider-soaked linen drawers plastered to their skin. Jakob's soot blackened hands were scraped raw, blistered, and bleeding. He sagged, spent, to the floor beside Anna and Jake, and Joseph and Christian huddled up against him.

Her small face bright red, streaked with tears and dirt, Annali drooped on her mother's shoulder, eyes closed, breath rasping, too exhausted even to whimper. Her diaper and tiny gown were soaked through, and the odor of stale urine soured the air. Anna rocked her back and forth, muttering desperate, incoherent prayers.

Jake clutched his wounded leg and drew himself into a ball. "How much . . . longer . . . can we stay . . . here?"

Jakob squared his jaw. "At daylight they'll leave. It won't be much longer now."

Did he speak nonsense? With anguish he had never felt before, he prayed for God to preserve them.

All concept of time's passing had been torn away. Had it been an hour since the attack began? Two? Three? Surely it must soon be dawn. If the Indians withdrew into the forest at the sun's rising, and if the fire did not consume the house too quickly, they might yet escape.

If only they could hold out that long.

Dense smoke hung just above their heads, forcing them ever lower in the search for air. Left slightly ajar, the shutter admitted a stream of cool, fresh air that cleared a narrow column along the wall to the floor, and they all pressed into it.

As he listened to the roar of the fire overhead, Jakob mentally reconstructed the image of his home's framework, every inch familiar from the work of building it with his own hands. He tried to imagine what parts of it still stood.

With increasing frequency, additional crashes signaled the collapse of a side wall or a supporting beam. Each time Anna, and the children startled and pressed fearfully together.

All at once, with a shuddering, thundering impact that caused even the stones of the cellar's walls and floor to quake, the second floor supports gave away and what was left of the upper story caved in onto the first floor. Jakob clutched his screaming family to him, while a shower of flaming splinters and incandescent coals erupted through the open stairwell on a blast of searing air. Dirt, ashes, and hot cinders rained down on their heads, and the remaining bins across the cellar burst into geysers of flame.

When the downfall settled, Jakob rubbed his burning eyes and squinted up at the massive beams that supported the first floor of the house. The breath left his lungs.

In the center, on either side of the huge pillar of the hearthstone's foundation, the beams had begun to smoke. And buckle.

◆━━━━◆

THE CELLAR HAD BECOME A HELLISH PIT of suffocating smoke and melting heat.

Joseph gave up all hope of escape. This place that only hours earlier had seemed to him a bounty-filled haven was certain now to be their graves.

Working in dogged silence, Daat tore strips from the remnants of their shirts. He tied one around his head, covering his nose and mouth, before helping each of them to do the same. With his mask in place, Joseph felt his breathing ease slightly.

He watched in blank despair as Maam gently placed one of the strips on Annali's beet-red face as she lay limp and unresponsive in her arms. He could barely make out the rise and fall of his baby sister's small chest.

The flaming bins had finally sunk into ashes, but in several places the first-story floorboards were burning through, dropping red-hot cinders into the gloom where they cowered. Again and again Daat soaked his fraying shirt in cider and quickly beat them out.

Down the cellar's length, Joseph could see the great beams sag. Terror constricted his throat at the thought of the heavy logs collapsing on their heads. It could only be a matter of minutes now.

Christian pulled himself back up onto the hogshead beneath the window and stood, his legs trembling from exhaustion. He inched open the shutter, and as he peered out into the first light of dawn, his mouth fell open.

"Maami, Daati, they're going to the woods! They're going away!"

Daati shoved a smaller keg over beside the hogshead and leaped onto it. Anxiously Christian watched him scan the cornfield and what could be seen of the woods below the house. After a moment he stepped down and faced the others.

"Christli's right! It's almost sunrise, and they're taking off."

Christian saw the last of the Indians disappear from sight among the trees. Sobs of relief welled from his chest.

"We can get out now! Let's get out!"

Above them the fire's pitch suddenly increased. He felt Daati's hand grip his bare leg.

"Quick! Crawl through, but be quiet and don't let anybody see you. Make certain they're all gone. If it's safe, I'll hand Annali out, and you carry her away to the bake oven as fast as you can, then come right back."

With Daati lifting and pushing him from behind, Christian squirmed through the window opening and fell onto the ground. His lungs felt as though they would burst. He tore off his mask and drew in great gulps of fresh air.

Crawling a short distance away from the foundation wall, he fearfully scanned his surroundings. No Indians were anywhere in sight.

Shimmering waves of heat radiated from the charred remnants of the log walls above him, while gouts of orange flame drove roiling, grey-black smoke into the cloudless, steadily brightening sky. At the far end of the yard, the barn and smokehouse were reduced to smoking ruins, and broken parts of the cider press and the still lay strewn across the ground along with the bloody forms of dead animals.

"Christli?"

"There's no one!"

"Then haste!"

His arm across his face as a shield against the fierce heat, Christian scrambled back to the window. He grabbed Annali's limp form from Daati's arms and ran to the broken walls of the bake oven. She lay where he placed her on the grass, as motionless as a rag doll.

He hurried back, dropped to his knees, and crawled to where Joseph had collapsed on the trampled grass several feet from the foundation. Without speaking, his brother clutched him, and they clung together, sobbing, their tears mingling on their soot-streaked cheeks.

"Now Jake!"

At Daati's urgent whisper, they crouched as close to the window as the heat would allow. They grabbed Jake by the arms, and with Daati pushing from behind, dragged him free. Ignoring his cries of pain, they pulled him as far as they could from the burning building. He sprawled across the grass, all but insensible, fresh blood blooming through the bandage around his leg.

"Take off your shift!"

Anna clutched the fouled, sweat-drenched linen around her, eyes widening. "*Nay,* Jakob, the children! I cannot—"

He ducked, dragging her out of the way as a fiery length of floorboard crashed down. Thin wisps of steam rose from her hair, and he could feel the intense heat searing his own head.

"There's no other way! You cannot get through that window wearing it!"

A sheen of sweat glistened through the ash and soot smeared across her scarlet face. She threw a hopeless glance at the narrow opening, began to sob.

"I'll never make it! You go before the floor gives way!"

Jakob jutted his chin. "I'll not leave you. Now hurry!"

When she stared at him as though paralyzed, he caught the top edge of her shift and ripped the thin, frayed garment from neck to hem. She screeched and grabbed at the cloth, but he tore it out of her hands.

Sagging in the scorching heat, she stood before him, naked and weeping. "No, Jakob! Please!"

He bit his lip, then swung around and thrust the wadded shift through the window. There was no time to comfort her. He stepped up onto the small keg and with his bare hands wrenched the window's shutter and frame loose from the stones, then cast them to the fire. Turning, he reached for her hand.

More flaming boards fell, crashing, all around them. Terror drove her to clamber up beside him.

He reached out the window and motioned to his sons. He could not imagine how they were going to get her through that narrow window, knew only that they had to. And there were surely only seconds left.

Joseph grabbed Maam's right elbow, while Christian took her left and Daat pushed from behind. Joseph kept his head turned away and saw that Christian also averted his eyes.

Maam squirmed and clawed at the dirt, while he and Christian pulled with all the strength remaining to them. Without warning Joseph lost his grip on her sweat-slick arm and fell backward hard, jerking his brother off balance.

"Joseph! Christian!" Maam braced her hands on the ground and fought to drag herself out of the window.

"What happened?" Daat's shout reached him faintly over the fire's roar.

Joseph pushed back onto his knees. He caught Maam's outstretched arm as Christian scrambled back into position.

"It's okay! Push!"

For a long, horrifying moment, Joseph was certain they would never get her out, that both his parents would perish in the flames. Then suddenly her upper body slid forward, only to catch again at her broad hips. Another concerted heave, and she slipped through the opening with so much force that she propelled them across the grass together.

Christian rolled onto his back, convulsed in a spasm of laughter, while Joseph fought to quench his own mirth.

Jakob clawed through the window with desperate haste. Kicking to break free, he dragged himself as far from the burning house as he had strength to go, gesturing to the others to follow.

He heard a roaring thunder and turned back in time to see the last walls and beams and burning rubble of the house break through into the cellar. A phosphorescent geyser of flames erupted skyward, followed by a dense coil of black smoke that ascended high into the brightening heavens, raining sparks, cinders, and ashes for yards to all sides. He rolled into a ball and covered his head with his arms while debris showered around him.

When the hot rain at last subsided, he rolled over onto his back, panting, oblivious of the searing prickles of cinders as he sucked in the freshening air. Then he began to laugh and weep, a wave of exhilaration flooding through him.

Danke, Gott! We are safe! We are alive! Your way is right after all!

Within moments the deafening roar of the flames diminished to a seething hiss and crackle. Although his throat and lungs were raw from the smothering smoke and acrid vapors rising from the inferno that had been their home, Jakob's senses seemed extraordinarily alive. Sounds were clearer, colors more brilliant. Every sensation achingly keen, he thrilled to the distant robin song that welcomed the morning and gazed, laughing, up to the pair of red-tailed hawks that skimmed down the windstream, high in the sky's transparent blue.

At last he rolled over and pushed erect. He staggered on unsteady feet toward Anna and the children. Their faces were scarlet from the hours in the cellar's heat. Besmeared with mingled sweat and soot, ash and dirt, their bloodshot eyes red-rimmed in their blackened faces, they looked like demons from the pit.

None of them had ever appeared lovelier to him than at that moment.

Anxiously he lifted his gaze to the southwest, in the direction of Johannes and Katie's plantation. No smoke rose above the trees there, nor over the low hills to the southeast, where Barbara and Crist lived. Again he breathed heartfelt thanks for his children's safety.

It was then that he heard it, and icy fingers squeezed the breath from his lungs. He swung back to Anna and the children, read in their faces what his numb mind refused to believe.

They had heard it too: the eerie, high-pitched keening of a jubilant war cry.

Chapter Eleven

THE WARRIORS BURST out of the orchard, the first red light of sunrise washing over their supple, fearsomely painted bodies and glinting across their weapons in a ripple of fire as they raced through the slanting bars of light and shadow that spilled between the eastern trees.

Joseph swung around with the first chilling cry. At sight of their attackers rapidly closing on them, instinct took over and he ran, racing through the trampled garden and around the far end of his home's ruins, arms, legs, lungs pumping harder than he thought possible. In full flight he darted around the springhouse and into the trees at the base of the steep, wooded hill behind the smoking foundation, crashing heedlessly through the underbrush, his only thought to gain safety.

Relentless footfalls gained on him. Frantic, he scrambled upward with strength borne of terror, wriggling beneath bushes, clutching at mossy rocks, saplings, any handhold he could find to heave himself higher. With the hill's summit in sight, too spent to go farther, he veered behind a massive, fallen tree trunk and collapsed to the moist leaf mold, his harsh gasps and thudding heartbeat blocking out all other sounds as he pressed into the ground, shaking, waiting for the death blow he knew must come.

By degrees, as breathing and pulse settled, he became aware that he was alone, that the sounds of pursuit had ceased, that there was no sign of movement between the trees. Other sounds pierced his consciousness then, screams of agony and anguish, and, sobbing, he gripped the leaves and moss beneath him and sought to burrow deeper into the earth in unreasoning terror of spinning off into the abyss if he lost hold. A flood of abject horror and crushing remorse rolled over him, a searing tide of shame that he had fled, leaving his helpless family to their attackers.

At length he forced his hands to relax, his leaden limbs to bend. It seemed to him that his panicked flight must have taken an hour. Reason told him that it had spanned not even a minute, that only moments more had passed since he took refuge behind the log.

Dread filled him. Painfully he levered himself up to crouch behind the rotting, moss-covered log to watch between the trees the scene that played out in the now sun-drenched yard below.

✦ · · · ✦

"Nchutièstuk!"

Jakob struggled to his feet. Turning in a circle in the effort to keep his face to the warriors who coursed around him, he desperately signed the word for friend.

"Nchutièstuk!" he repeated again and again.

Their attackers responded with even fiercer shouts and hostile glares, eyes narrowed in triumph and anticipation. The two warriors who had raced after Joseph emerged from the trees, and as they passed the bake oven, one of them stooped with a careless motion and buried his hatchet in Annali's limp form. The baby shuddered, blood spurting from her back, then lay still.

Anna scrambled upright and swung to Jakob, the tattered remnants of her shift clutched around her. "Stop them, Jakob! Do something to make them stop!"

They were completely surrounded now. As Jakob stepped toward her, two warriors blocked his path. One grasped him from behind and twisted his arms back, forcing him to his knees.

"Daati!"

Christian's scream reached him as from a great distance. Jakob tried to squeeze his eyes shut, but, paralyzed by terror, he could not.

Yards away, Jake had struggled half erect, his bandage saturated with blood, his ashen face furrowed with pain and horror. Bending over him, one of the warriors kicked him over onto his stomach, grasped his sweat-drenched hair, and knelt with one knee on the boy's neck, strangling his outcry. With the gleaming blade of his knife, he sliced a circle around Jake's skull and in the same fluid motion gave one quick jerk and lifted the scalp lock over his head, streaming blood.

"Nay!"

The breath left Jakob's lungs in a rush. Sweat stung his eyes as he stared at Jake's motionless form, bile rising in his mouth. Gagging, he sagged forward against his captor's restraining hands and vomited.

"Maami! Daati!" Christian squealed, straining against the warrior's hold with what little strength he had left.

He shrank away from the tomahawk raised over his head, looking up in mute appeal. For a terrifying moment the man stood suspended, staring down at him, a black shadow outlined against the bright rays of the sun at his back. Then slowly he lowered his weapon and dragged Christian to his feet.

"Jakob! *Helfe!*"

Christian wrenched around. Close to the house, Maami wove clumsily back and forth, dodging two warriors' clutching hands. Suddenly she lost her balance and stumbled to her knees. One of the warriors thrust his knife deep into her breast, whooping as a bright crimson fountain splattered across his face and chest.

Mouth agape, Christian watched his mother topple forward onto her hands, a scream gurgling in her throat. The second warrior shoved her prone to the ground. Grabbing her long hair, he deftly wound it around his wrist, pulling hard as he held her shoulders down with his foot and sliced through her scalp with the knife clenched in his other hand.

Darkness filmed Christian's eyes. The breath left him, and he went limp in his captor's arms.

Held upright in the warrior's grip, Jakob stared blankly at Christian, desolation washing over him. The war party danced around him, waving their bloody weapons and the scalps of his wife and children above their heads, while he awaited the blow that would end his own life, praying that death would come quickly.

Chapter Twelve

"JACOB'S GOING TO DRIVE the cows up to the barn for me this morning." Johannes yawned as he stuffed his shirttail into his breeches. "He's getting big enough now to help with the livestock."

The sturdy five-year-old returned his conspiratorial wink with a broad smile. "*Ya,* Maami, I can drive the cows all by myself."

Katie looked up from stirring a gruel of parched corn in a small iron pot set on a tripod over the flames. "He's so little yet, Johannes," she protested, her face rosy in the flickering firelight. "The Indians—"

"Until these troubles die down, I'll go with him and make sure there aren't any war parties around."

Katie let out a sigh. "Our babies grow up too quick."

"They do, but we don't want them to stay little forever, do we?"

Katie's cheeks dimpled as she shook her head. "I'll feed Frany and John then, and have your breakfast ready when you finish the milking. Please be careful."

"We will."

Giving her an affectionate smile, he bent to pry Frany's chubby fingers from his breeches leg. He swung the squealing infant up to give her a hearty kiss before handing her to her mother. Three-year-old John jumped off the bench where he perched and reached up his arms.

"Me too!"

Chuckling, Johannes complied, then headed outside with Jacob trailing happily on his heels. The early-morning breeze felt refreshingly cool on his face, and in the western sky the last of the stars were fading into the rapidly advancing dawn.

Halfway across the barnyard, he stopped so abruptly that Jacob collided with him from behind. Johannes laid his hand on the child's head to steady him and drew in a deep lungful of air. He frowned and tilted his head.

The odor of wood smoke carried on the light northeast wind was much stronger than a cooking fire at his parents' house a quarter mile away could produce. He swung sharply to his right and glanced toward the trees to the northeast. At sight of the dark plume of smoke rising over the treetops into the brightening sky, he sucked in his breath.

Surely Daat wouldn't be burning brush so early in the morning.

Jacob was looking up at him with a fearful expression, and Johannes squatted beside the child. "Go inside the house and tell your Maami I'll be back in a few minutes. I'm going over to *Grossmaami* and *Grossdaati's* house before we drive the cows up."

"I smell smoke," Jacob said in a small voice, looking apprehensively toward the column of smoke hanging above the trees. His lower lip trembled.

Johannes kept his voice steady. "*Ya,* and I'm just going to make sure everything's all right. Don't worry your Maami, now."

His eyes large, Jacob shook his head, then turned and ran back into the house.

Johannes stood and forced his steps to an unhurried pace until the path curved between the trees, blocking the view from the house. Then he ran, heart pounding so hard he felt light-headed.

Halfway to his parents' plantation he heard the savage warble of war cries. The hair on the back of his neck and arms prickled, and he raced the last hundred yards to where the lane turned into Daat's pasture. There he staggered to a halt.

On the rise directly ahead, wind-drifted clouds of smoke swirled incandescent cinders high into the hazy pink streamers of dawn, alternately obscuring, then revealing, the ruins of house, barn, and outbuildings etched in fiery light against the darkly wooded hill and orchards behind them. The mutilated corpses of animals lay scattered across the barnyard, while half-naked warriors danced around them, waving their weapons in the air.

He clutched the nearest tree to keep from falling to his knees. *"Ach, Gott, nay!"*

He shrank in among the trees and underbrush that bordered the lane. Although his legs shook so hard it was an effort to press forward even at a crouch, he clawed his way through the bushes to a thick tangle of vines and saplings beneath an ancient, towering hickory and sagged against its trunk.

Peering out fearfully, his hand pressed to his mouth to keep from retching, he searched desperately for his parents and siblings while the Indians gathered in the kitchen yard. At last he caught a glimpse of Daat and one of his brothers—Christli, he guessed from the boy's size—in the midst of a threatening circle.

Off to one side lay a pale body. *Maam,* he realized at once, a wave of sickness breaking over him. Nearby lay another huddled body, whether Jake or Joseph he couldn't tell. Nor could he see Annali anywhere.

The sharp crackle of sticks and dry leaves off to his left brought him around with a start. Heart pounding, he crouched lower, straining to see through the heavy growth.

Two figures, one tall, one short, moved stealthily toward him from tree to tree. As they drew nearer, he saw that it was a man and a woman, then identified his neighbors to the west, Jakob Kreutzer and his wife. With a quick glance toward the distant war party to assure himself that the Indians took no notice, Johannes straightened and raised his hand through the vines to attract the their attention.

They froze, staring toward him in alarm until he struggled to his knees and motioned to them. Visibly relieved, they hurried over to crouch beside him.

"We heard gunfire, then saw smoke." Kreutzer craned his neck, squinting through the underbrush. "They burned your folks out!"

Sick at heart, Johannes nodded, his stomach lurching. "Everything's gone . . . "

He glanced anxiously back at the ruins. Those who held his father pulled him to his feet, while a small party of warriors headed up the hill behind the house. Off to one side a couple of tall, muscular Indians held Christian slumped between them.

Frau Kreutzer grasped his arm in a painful grip. "I see your Daat and Christli, but—"

"Maam's . . . dead. The other . . . it's either Jake or Joseph." Johannes buried his face in his hands, weeping, unable to watch the Indians put the rest of his family to death.

He felt Kreutzer's hand squeeze his shoulder. "We need to call help—raise an alarm."

Johannes straightened and pressed his fingers to his throbbing temples. "There's no time. The soldiers are all gone from Fort Northkill, and Fort Lebanon is too far away."

"They're carrying them off!"

At *Frau* Kreutzer's urgent whisper, Johannes looked up to see the Indians driving his father and brother up the hill. When they disappeared from sight between the trees, Johannes swung around to throw a fearful glance toward his own home.

Frau Kruetzer followed his gaze. "You better get your family into hiding. There may be more of them roaming through here."

"Go!" Kreutzer urged. "We'll watch and come warn you if we see any of them head in this direction."

Johannes sprang to his feet and fought his way back through the underbrush to the turning of the path. When he was certain the war party could not see him, he ran for the house as fast as his legs could carry him.

Chapter Thirteen

T O JAKOB'S DISMAY, their path led up the hill where Joseph had disappeared. He stared straight ahead, following the leading warriors with no outward show of emotion, while inwardly his mind raced as he beseeched God for Joseph's safety. He could not bring himself to look back toward the bodies of Anna, Jake, and the baby sprawled across the trampled yard of what had been a blessed home.

The party came to a halt near the hill's crest, and Jakob's heart sank even further. After a brief scuffle in the underbrush ahead of them, several warriors dragged Joseph from behind a fallen tree trunk. Fighting their grasp, the boy glanced at Jakob, terror and defiance mingling with supplication in his eyes.

"Daat! Helfe!"

His cry, as much accusation as plea, ripped through Jakob's heart. "Do what they tell you!"

He wrenched around to seek Christian, but caught no glimpse of him among the warriors. When he returned his gaze to Joseph, the boy's eyes bored into Jakob's with what seemed to him judgment and disdain. Then Joseph his head turned away.

Jakob's guard jerked him roughly forward. Despair seized him. His eyes stung with hot tears, but he hastily blinked them back, knowing that if he and his boys were to survive, they must never allow their captors to see any sign of weakness.

"Don't fight them or they'll kill you!" he called.

The cold steel of a musket barrel thrust hard against his bare back. He managed to keep his balance and plodded forward as they angled along the ridge of the hill and down its western flank.

By the time they descended among the fruit trees, Jakob's bare feet, already blistered by the fiery heat of the cellar's stone floor, were painfully bruised and scratched by rocks and sticks. Remembering stories he had heard of Indians killing captives who hindered their swift pace, he gritted his teeth against the pain and lumbered on, praying he and his boys would find strength to keep from falling behind.

At the foot of the hill, they splashed through the small rivulet that trickled from the spring to wind through the orchard. As Joseph stumbled into the water, he gave in to exhaustion and dropped to his knees in the shallow stream, repeatedly sluicing cool water over his face with his cupped hands. He brought more to his mouth and drank, not caring what penalty he might suffer.

No one moved to stop him, however, and Daat and Christian followed his example. The Indians also took turns quenching their thirst, while keeping watch for pursuers.

The memory of standing in the orchard with Anna Blanck and little Annali just hours earlier came to his mind suddenly, and he a chill fell over him. He had sensed someone watching them then and questioned now whether the Indians had already lurked behind the trees, waiting for the moment when they would wreak death and destruction upon his family.

✦┄┄✦

WHAT ORDEAL DID THEY FACE NOW? Imploring God to keep his boys safe from whatever lay before them, regardless of what happened to him, Jakob followed his captors to the far edge of the orchard, where it bordered Detweiler's field. There the party's leaders detoured to retrieve several bulging rawhide pouches that lay beneath the trees' heavily laden branches, and realization dawned: But for the ripening peaches, their attackers might have retreated quickly after their bloody destruction of the plantation, sparing his family. It was all Jakob could do to keep from breaking down in tears.

In fierce resolve he focused his attention on their captors. Besides the pouches filled with fruit, they also gathered other packs that he guessed held provisions for their journey. They had come a long way, he concluded, dread filling him.

How far did they mean to take the three of them?

He clenched his jaw and again looked around for his boys. They were held under close guard, as was he, and all of them were kept apart from each other.

He started when the two buckskin-clad Frenchmen he had seen the night before emerged from among the trees, along with a third. Scouts, he guessed. Armed with tomahawks and muskets, they were shorter than the Indians, dark haired and dark eyed, with swarthy complexions. Green cloth leggings covered them thigh to ankle, and they wore blue knit caps on their heads.

Their return heightened his anxiety. *What will they do with us? Are we also to be slaughtered? Will they torture us? Will they carry us away? If so, will we be separated, never to see each other again?*

He had only questions. And he feared the answers.

JOHANNES TORE OPEN THE DOOR.

Katie sprang to her feet with a startled cry, clutching baby Frany to her breast. She stared at him, the color draining from her face, then hastily set the baby in the cradle. Pushing aside young Jacob and John, who clutched at her petticoats, she rushed to him.

"Johannes, what—"

He gripped her shoulders so hard she winced. "Maam and Daat's place is under attack. Grab some blankets and bring the children. We've got to get you all out of sight."

Her mouth dropped open, and she gasped. "Are they—"

He could tell by her expression that she read the answer in his face. Shaking his head, he urged her to hurry.

When the children began to wail, he gave them a stern look and put his finger to his lips. "Silence! Come now, quiet as you can. There's no time to waste."

Their sobs subsided, and he caught John into his arms, waiting only long enough for Katie to gather the baby and a couple of blankets. Then, urging Jacob ahead of him and keeping Katie at his side, he brought them down the sloping path past the barn. With each step he looked apprehensively to every side until they gained the shelter of the stand of heavy brush at the pasture's far end.

✦┄┄┄✦

JAKOB WATCHED, GUT KNOTTED, as the French scouts conferred in low tones with the war party's apparent leaders. At last the Indians began to draw clothing from their packs and distribute it to their captives.

Into Jakob's blistered hands were thrust a threadbare linen shirt, greasy and stiff with sweat; an equally dirty piece of cloth he took for a breechclout, with a longer strip that appeared to be a sash; leggings; and badly worn moccasins. With an abrupt gesture, his Indian guard signed for him to put them on.

Jakob looked to his sons and said hoarsely, "Do whatever they want—"

His guard's snarled warning cut off his words. The warrior grabbed Jakob's arm and dragged him roughly around so his back was to the boys.

Staggering, Jakob cringed and drew in a shaky breath as the horrifying scene in the kitchen yard rose vividly before his eyes. These men held all power over him and his boys. To resist them could only result in disaster. He would take his own advice and be careful to do whatever they wanted.

At the same time, he must show no weakness. He knew the Indians respected courage and strength. By gaining their favor he and his boys might yet survive what lay ahead.

And, if God willed, they might find a way of escape.

Gingerly he stripped off the scorched, tattered remnants of his linen drawers, thankful that the spring's cool water had eased the raw flesh of his hands. Enduring his captors' derisive laughter at his clumsiness, he fumbled with the breechclout until he managed to secure it around his soot-streaked loins with the longer strip of cloth. He drew on the leggings, and, by casting surreptitious glances at the warriors' garb, soon had them securely attached to the sash by their worn leather thongs.

This done, he pulled the shirt on over his head, shrinking from its greasy feel and fetid stench. It hung below his waist, but pulled tight across his shoulders. The moccasins he slipped onto his aching feet in silent gratitude. Without them, he knew, it would be impossible for him to journey far.

Several warriors stood around him, blocking his view of the boys. He prayed they also obeyed their guards.

He no sooner finished than his guard shoved hard to the ground and bent over him, scalping knife in hand. The breath left Jakob's lungs in a gasp. He steeled himself for the death blow even as his mind protested that surely they had not been clothed only to be killed.

In suspended horror he shrank away from the rough fingers that gathered his hair tightly in a bundle. But the knife's razor-sharp blade merely traced the contours of his scalp, dropping lengths of hair down his shoulders, back, and face. He shivered in the light breeze that evaporated the sweat from his exposed skull, a surge of relief flooding over him.

Finished, the warrior scraped the knife along Jakob's jaw, cutting away his beard. Jakob felt a thick substance trickle over his head and the back of his neck, stinging the nicks drawn by the knife. When the man moved around in front of him, Jakob saw he held a leather pouch from which he dipped a red liquid that he smeared over Jakob's face and neck.

He was being painted red. A sign that he was a captive? That he was condemned to die? An effort to disguise him as an Indian in case the war party encountered soldiers or other settlers? He could make no sense of it.

His task completed, Jakob's guard jerked him to his feet. Jakob ran his fingers along his jaw, taken aback by the smoothness of his face. It was the first time he had been clean shaven since he married, in conformity to the teachings of the church. He pulled his hand away and stared, dazed, at the blood-red paint that stained his fingers.

Anxiety welled up in full force, and he again looked around for his boys. His fear eased when he saw that neither made any effort to resist the warriors.

Clad in Indian clothing, they also had been shaven bald, their heads entirely painted red. Laughter bubbled in Jakob's throat at the thought that they all looked like hideous turkeys with red wattles. As quickly, a storm of bitter grief almost brought him to his knees.

He was given no time to mourn, however. His guard seized him, and another warrior began to tie his hands together with a rawhide thong. Without thinking, Jakob wrenched away and gave his head a vehement shake.

Instantly the two warriors brought their faces close to his, shouting and waving their arms in threatening gestures, while the rest of the party gathered around them, scowling and muttering among themselves. The Frenchman Jakob took to be the leader of the small detachment strode over to them, his face contorted with anger.

Sudden inspiration struck Jakob, and he waved his hand toward the laden peach trees. "We'll need food."

He made motions as though he was picking the ripe fruit and eating it, then repeated the words in broken French, praying that they understood his meaning. When the scout came to a halt and considered him through narrowed eyes, Jakob made a show of agreeing to the warriors' vehement demands that he go with them.

He pointed to Joseph and Christian, then to the warriors' packs bulging with fruit. "*Ya,* we will go with you. We will not make trouble. Only let me take some of the peaches for my boys to eat."

The warriors' tense postures and fierce expressions relaxed as they looked from Jakob to the peach trees to the boys, then at the Frenchman. When he nodded in agreement, the first warrior signed for Jakob to gather fruit, while the other brought him an empty rawhide pouch.

Jakob bowed and thanked them. He took the pouch and strode to the nearest tree with a confidence his trembling legs belied. With every step, the fear that the stroke of a tomahawk or the sharp stab of an arrow would be his last sensation raised gooseflesh on his arms.

Joseph and Christian quickly joined him, evidently ordered by the Indians to help. *You are still with us!* Jakob breathed. *Oh, Gott, keep us safe!*

Motioning to the boys to do the same, Jakob began to fill the pack with fruit that was not quite ripe, taking care not to bruise the flesh. The boys worked without speaking, their expressions blank and unreadable, their movements hampered by the shirts that hung loose from their shoulders to their knees.

Jakob's mind raced, trying to calculate the impossible: Where were they going? How many days might their journey last? Would their captors give them food, or would these peaches be all they had to eat?

The pouch was quickly full, and Jakob shouldered it, bending under its weight. Immediately their guards separated them and drove them forward, motioning them to silence with gestures and threatening looks. They crept out of the orchard and crossed into Detweiler's pasture, the lead warriors and French scouts moving stealthily ahead of them, every muscle tense as they scanned the area for signs of danger.

The golden sun hung above the eastern treetops now, steadily brightening the cloudless azure sky. The air had begun to warm, save for the dark shadows beneath the trees, where the light breeze chilled Jakob. All around him amid the lingering wildflowers pulsed the drone of bees, and as their feet brushed through the long weeds, grasshoppers sprang away with a dry, whirring sound.

Jakob glanced distractedly after the insects, his chest aching so painfully that he feared it would burst. How was it was possible that this morning could appear so pure? he wondered. How was it possible that he still lived when violence and death had stolen from him so much that had been precious to him?

For what purpose, Gott? he demanded. *How does this glorify You?*

There was no answer but the sigh of the wind through the dusky treetops and the muted rustle of dry leaves underfoot. And so he stumbled on, heart and body numbed with grief.

Within moments he heard ahead of them another sound: the gurgle and hiss of water. The winding, tree-shaded course of the Northkill lay across their path, its waters tumbling over rocks and bare tree roots, scouring its winding streambed as it rushed down from the mountain ridge, then angled southeast to Tulpehocken Creek, from where it flowed at last into the Schuylkill.

But they were headed in the opposite direction, following the Northkill's course upward to pass within half a mile of the abandoned fort, then to the gap in the Blue Mountain's long, sprawling ridge, and into the unknown wilderness beyond.

✦┈┈➤

JOHANNES EDGED around the far side of the barn, every sense alert for any sound or sight of the war party. Before he could reach the path to his parents' plantation, the Kreutzers crept out of the woods and hurried to meet him, relief etching their features.

Kreutzer caught him by the arm. "The Indians carried them off. They headed west into Detweiler's field."

Frau Kreutzer looked years older than the last time Johannes had seen her. "They were moving real fast. We followed as far around to the orchard as we could, keeping to the trees, and it looked to us like they had Joseph with them." She dropped her gaze to the ground. "We didn't see Jake."

Johannes swallowed hard. "Then he's the one who . . ." The words choked in his throat. "But Daat, Joseph, and Cristli are still alive?"

"*Ya,* in *Gott's* mercy." She stopped abruptly and clamped her mouth shut in a tense line.

"Let's pray they're given mercy, then, until we can find them and bring them home."

Kreutzer shook his head. "They'll be far off before we can get a party together to follow after them. Even if we track them down, it'll come to a fight to get your father and brothers loose—if the Indians don't kill them to keep them from us."

"We cannot fight them and risk more killing. We must find another way." Johannes searched the shadows of the surrounding woods. "Have you seen any others?"

Kreutzer stroked his beard. "*Nay,* but that doesn't mean there aren't any around."

Johannes's gaze was drawn to the heavens, where several buzzards circled, dark, foreboding shadows hovering low above the treetops. *Frau* Kreutzer's spare body tensed.

"We must take care of your Maam and the others before . . ." She broke off, then quickly continued, "I have a couple of quilts to cover them over with. I'll go get them right now."

Johannes bent his head. "*Danke.* I'll go get Katie and *die Kinder* and take them to her folks. They don't need to see all this." He swiped the back of his hand across his brow. "I'll stop by Barbara's and let her know too."

Shoulders bowed, he buried his face in his hands. *Frau* Kreutzer drew him into her embrace.

"Go to your family. We'll take care of this for now."

Kreutzer cleared his throat. "We'll warn Detweilers too. And the others close by."

Johannes reached blindly out to him, and Kreutzer took his hand and squeezed it hard. Without another word Johannes headed back to his family's hiding place.

Chapter Fourteen

THE WAR PARTY BROKE THROUGH the trees onto the bank of the creek. At this time of year the Northkill's waters ran low, easily waded where their path intersected it. The leading warriors were already across, moving rapidly northward along the far bank, Daat in their midst.

Joseph stared at the misty bulk of the ridge looming above the trees two miles ahead of them. It was the same path he and Jake had taken on the day of Barbara's wedding five years earlier, following it toward the narrow gap over the Blue Mountain.

With an impatient grunt the warrior behind Joseph shoved him forward. But when he stepped into the creek, the cool water trickling over his feet brought him to a halt again. For a long moment he gazed upstream, his chest aching, but his heart too numb for tears.

Just around the bend from this crossing, he and Jake and Christian had waded into the pooling water after eluding another Indian band. Now, glinting in the long rays of the rising sun, the Northkill appeared as red to Joseph as when Jake had bathed the blood from his wounded leg on that long-ago afternoon.

Had not Joseph felt a premonition and dismissed it? Now it had come true.

He tried to swallow, but the dryness of his throat made it impossible. Another shove from behind sent him sprawling full-length with a splash. He scrambled to his feet, shaking off the water, ready to fight. But when his guard shook his tomahawk in Joseph's face, he swung hastily away.

Splashing through the ankle-deep water in the creek's center, he slipped on the mossy rocks of the streambed and banged his knee so hard on a protruding boulder that it drew blood. He clawed awkwardly onto the bank on the far side, nursing his sore leg.

The vow he had made that afternoon at the creek that one day he would travel beyond the Blue Mountain haunted him. He was finally going to find out what awaited on the other side, but now he felt despair and fear at the prospect, not glad anticipation.

A deep sense of powerlessness and vulnerability oppressed him. Head down, he limped along the stream toward the flank of the looming ridge, hands clenched until his fingernails dug painfully into his palms, limbs weighted with weariness and despair. A paroxysm of wrenching grief and helpless rage squeezed the air from his lungs and left him gasping.

Angry thoughts wore a weary circuit in his brain: Daat was responsible for this destruction. They could easily have driven their attackers away. If Daat believed so strongly that killing was wrong, could he not at least have allowed his wife and children to defend themselves against an enemy so merciless and cruel?

Hot waves of shame rushed over Joseph as an accusing voice reminded him that he had run away to save himself, leaving his family to the Indians' slaughter. He should have kept his rifle and shot at their attackers, tried to create a diversion to distract them, raced to the neighbors to sound an alarm—*something!* Anything would have been better than cowering behind that fallen tree, paralyzed by fear and guilt.

His mind argued that any attempt at resistance would only have resulted in his own immediate death, while his heart cried out that he should have died too. Why had he and Daat and Christian been spared, while the others were killed?

He roused from his tormenting reflections to note with a shock that at some point after they crossed the Northkill the Frenchmen had disappeared. He and Daat and Christian were alone with the war party, entirely at the mercy of these savages with no one who might be persuaded to intercede on their behalf.

His fearful gaze focused on the warrior who shadowed him, scowling as he urged Joseph to a faster pace. A Delaware and surely the cruelest of his family's murderers, he was short but powerfully built, with a head that seemed too large for his body and stern features that Joseph found both ugly and frightening. In his seamed face, deep-set eyes glittered with a malevolent light, and the barbaric designs tattooed into the dusky skin of his face, chest, and arms enhanced his savage appearance.

With a start Joseph realized that he was the warrior who had driven his knife into Maam's breast. Hatred for his captors and equal rage at his unyielding father seared through him as he forced his aching legs to an unwilling run.

THE TRAIL WOUND ever more steeply upward onto the flank of the mountain. Jakob forced his steps to match the warriors' rapid strides, praying that his boys could keep up the swift pace. It was still early, and although it seemed to have consumed a lifetime, he reckoned that no more than an hour could have passed since they had escaped from the cellar and been overtaken by their attackers.

With each step the fruit-filled pouch he carried bounced against his hip. Favoring his stinging hands, he shifted it from one shoulder to the other, worrying that the peaches would be ruined before they had gone far. He had no way of knowing how long their journey might last, and this small store of fruit might well be the only food he and the boys had to eat.

He glanced at the warriors loping easily along on each side and noted that several also carried bulging pouches. They moved in a steady rhythm that swung their burden back and forth instead of side to side, he noted.

He adjusted his stride to match theirs and after a little practice was relieved to find that the pouch no longer struck his hip. Its easy swing not only provided better balance but also eased the strain on his back.

He did not find it as easy to allay other burdens. Did anyone yet know what had happened? Were Johannes and Barbara and others of the community raising an alarm? Would they try to find and rescue them? If so, would their efforts result in more tragedy?

A little more than halfway up the mountain, the leading warriors broke through a dense stand of pines into a clearing and came abruptly to a halt. As the rest of the party closed with them, Jakob caught sight of a white man.

It was Hannes Mueller. He held an ax and the ground around his feet was littered with branches and chips from the tree he had evidently chopped down.

At sight of the war party, the young man's eyes widened. He glanced wildly from the Indians to their captives, confusion and fear etching his features.

For a suspended moment Jakob's heart stood still. Then he shouted, his voice coming out in croak: "Hannes, run! *Schnell!*"

Mueller stiffened in alarm and lifted his ax as though he meant to threaten the Indians. At the same instant, the warrior on Jakob's left raised his rifle and fired.

The ax flew out of Mueller's hands, blood spurting in its wake. Uttering a strangled cry, he grasped his bleeding hand with the other, swung around, and fled into the woods.

The lead warriors conferred briefly before the entire party resumed the steady climb toward the mountain's summit as though nothing unusual had happened. Jakob soon realized that no one intended to pursue Mueller, and the tension went out of him, replaced by relief and a tentative ray of hope.

Hannes had escaped. He had to have recognized Jakob—at least his voice. He would surely tell Johannes and Barbara that they were alive, that they were being carried over the mountain. And they would put immediate efforts in motion to find them, to rescue them, to bring them home.

If he and the boys could only endure.

THEY FOLLOWED the dwindling rivulet of the Northkill, climbing so steeply upward through the heavily wooded, rock-strewn cleft that Joseph's legs burned and the breath rasped in his throat. As though immune to hunger, thirst, and fatigue, with blows and shouts the warriors drove their captives up the last few yards to the narrow gap in the ridge.

When they at last reached the crest of the rise, Joseph's steps arrested against his will, and he cast a longing glance back the way they had come, his mind warning that he dare not linger. The vivid image of the day he and Jake had looked down into the valley from a promontory some distance below pierced him to the soul.

Sick at heart, he found the thin ribbon of smoke that marked the ruins of all that had once been safe and secure and known. Unable to bear the sight, he turned quickly away, trembling in every limb.

Would blood and death be his last memory of home? Would he ever return, ever see Barbara, Johannes, and his little nieces and nephews again?

The vicious blow of a rifle butt staggered him, cutting off his anguished thoughts and driving him down the path. He fell into step, teeth clenched to keep from rubbing his aching shoulder. And as the party descended the ridge's western face, the darkly shadowed mantle of the surrounding forest gathered them into its chill, obscuring folds.

Chapter Fifteen

"BARBARA! CRIST! *Kumm schnell!*" Come quickly! Her breath catching, Barbara swung around as Johannes burst through the door. His eyes were bloodshot, his hair and clothing in disarray.

She dropped the measuring cup into the bowl with a clatter, scattering rye flour across the worktable. "*Vass ist's?*" What is it? The babe in her womb gave a sharp kick, and she pressed her hand to her swollen abdomen.

"Maami?" Mattie's lower lip trembled.

On the hearthstone, two-year-old Anna dropped the wooden spoon she had been happily banging against a small bowl. Eyes wide, she scrambled to her feet and ran to clutch Barbara's petticoat. The baby, Mary, lost her grip on the chair at the far end of the table and sat down hard on the floor. Her face puckered, and she began to wail.

Barbara hastily lifted Mattie down from the stool beside her and hushed the younger children. Carrying an armload of firewood, Crist pushed through the door as she turned back to Johannes. Crist looked from one to the other, then hurried to drop the wood into the woodbox before straightening to face his brother-in-law.

"What's going on?"

Johannes braced his arm against the frame of the nearby loom, fighting to catch his breath. "Maam . . . and Daat . . . the Indians . . . "

Barbara stared at him, openmouthed. She had never seen such raw emotion on her brother's face, and darkness gathered at the edges of her vision. She staggered, feeling the two older girls dragging at her petticoats.

Crist strode quickly to her side. "They've been attacked?"

Johannes pushed away from the loom and joined them at the table. "They burned the house . . . the barn. . . everything. They—"

"*Nay!*" Barbara cried. "I don't believe you!"

"*Everything's* gone?" Crist's tone was incredulous. "You don't mean—?"

Johannes could only nod, his breath coming in gasps.

"Your folks—the boys—they're—" Crist stopped abruptly, drawing in his breath. He glanced toward Barbara, then hastily away.

Barbara focused on his taut face, her gaze pleading. *Bitte, Gott. Bitte* . . . Please, God. Please . . .

"They took Daat . . . and Joseph and Christli." Johannes broke down in wrenching sobs.

"Maam?" Barbara whispered.

He shook his head, tears streaming down his cheeks into his beard. "Jake and Annali too."

Barbara heard someone keening as though from far away,

dimly realized that it was her own voice. "Ach, *Gott,* how could You let this happen?"

She felt Crist's arm around her, let him lead her gently to the bench at the table. The children pressed against her, wailing loudly, and she clasped them to her bosom, wishing that she also were too young to comprehend what had happened. Crist engulfed her and the children in his embrace, his sobs joining hers.

Images of the horrors her loved ones must have suffered rose before Barbara's eyes. She pressed her cheek against the tops of her children's heads, feeling that grief would cleave her in two.

When the worst of her anguish eased, she stiffened in alarm. "Have the Indians gone?"

"I think so—*ya.*" Johannes ran his fingers through his sweat-soaked hair.

"What if they come here?"

"They took off through Detweiler's field, probably to follow the Northkill up to the gap."

His voice rasped, and giving him a keen look, Crist grabbed the pitcher, filled a cup with cider, and handed it to him. Nodding his thanks, Johannes drained it.

"That's the closest way over the mountain. Now that it's daylight, they'll likely head back into French-controlled territory as quick as they can." Johannes set the cup back on the table and rubbed his bloodshot eyes.

Crist brushed away his tears and sank onto the bench beside Barbara. Gently he lifted Mary out of her arms.

"There's less chance they'll be spotted going that way. They'll be in the woods and only have to cross the edge of Kurtzes' plantation to get away from the settlement."

"Christli must be so scared. And Joseph and Daat too." Barbara shifted Mattie and Anna on her lap to free her apron and wiped her face with its edge. "Someone has to go after them! We've got to find them before they get too far."

Johannes's shoulders bowed. "By now they're likely too far off for anyone to get to them. When Indians are on the warpath, they travel real fast."

Barbara felt a chill go through her. "It'll be hard for Daat and the boys to keep up with them then. And if they kill them out there in the wilderness, we'll never know." Bending over, her arms tightening around her little daughters, she wept.

Some moments passed before Crist asked hesitantly, "How much . . . did you see?"

Johannes squatted down beside them and described what had happened as carefully as possible to avoid upsetting the children further. "The Kreutzer said they'd cover the bodies and send an alarm out to all the neighbors. Once we made certain there weren't any more Indians around, I took Katie and the children . . ."

He broke down again. With Crist gripping his shoulder hard, he wiped his eyes and concluded, "I hitched up the horses and drove them over to her folks."

"Did you see any other plantations that were attacked?" Crist ventured.

"*Nay*, but just after we got to Hertzlers, a neighbor came by and said there were other attacks a few miles from them. A soldier was killed and a man and some children were carried away. He didn't see any Indians anywhere around, though, so they must have taken off at daylight. He was going to spread the alarm to everybody in the area and alert the militia."

Barbara clutched Crist's arm. "Go warn your folks!"

Johannes stood up. "I stopped by Hans's house on the way here. He went right away to tell Jake and your Maam."

Barbara scooted Mattie and Anna off her lap and rose unsteadily with the children clinging to her legs. "Take me to . . . to Maam . . . and the others."

Johannes exchanged a sober glance with Crist.

"*Liebe, nay*. With the baby on the way, it isn't good for you to see them like . . . like that."

"They have to be washed and dressed. We'll need coffins—"

"Katie's folks are on their way here by now, and they were sending word to Buerkis," Johannes broke in. "The family should all be there soon, and they'll do whatever needs to be done. I know others from the church will come by to help out too."

Barbara wrung her hands. "What about Blancks? They're so close with Maam and Daat, and they'll want to know." Tears started again, and she dabbed them away with her apron.

"Dr. Blanck told me yesterday that they planned to leave Crist Mueller's place this afternoon. As soon as Hans gets here I'll send him over to tell them." Crist took her hand and drew her down beside him.

She sprang up again. "We'll have to have the funeral as soon as we can. As warm as it's been, we can't let it go for long."

Johannes picked up Mattie, who was quietly crying. "I already arranged things with Katie's Daat." As he gently rubbed the little girl's back, she burrowed her head against his neck and slipped her thumb in her mouth.

Barbara settled back onto the bench, her hand pressed to her throbbing head. With the baby on his lap and Anna cuddled in one arm, Crist encircled Barbara with his other.

"Maam can watch the children while you rest, *Liebe*. As soon as she gets here, Johannes and I will go and make sure everything's taken care of." He kissed her forehead. "You take care of yourself first of all."

Just then the door swung open, and Crist's brothers, Hans and Jake, and widowed mother hurried inside, shock and sorrow reflected on each face. Maudlin rushed over to Barbara, who rose to step into her loving embrace. Laying her head on her mother-in-law's shoulder, she gave way to grief, her tears mingling with the older woman's.

REPEATEDLY SLIPPING and sliding on loose rocks and soft dirt in their sharp descent from the ridge's heights, Jakob caught hold of a low-hanging limb to steady himself. Hastily he regained his balance and resumed his stride, at the same time glancing up through the treetops for a glimpse of the clear sky.

Even in the forest's dense shade, he was sweating profusely from exertion and the morning's unseasonable warmth. And it would be yet another couple of hours before the sun reached its zenith, he judged.

From the angle of its rays, after they passed over Northkill Gap their path had veered to the northwest, following the folds of the mountain's flank downward. They were traveling away from the Schuylkill River, which cut through the ridge a rapidly increasing distance to the east, and moving ever farther into territory he had no knowledge of.

They splashed through a shallow creek at a run. Within a short distance they reached the heavily forested valley floor and soon came to a larger stream. Here the warriors paused long enough for each of them to gulp as much water as he could swallow.

Jakob made sure his boys drank their fill before slaking his thirst. When he could drink no more, he soaked his raw hands in the cool water, then laved it over his heated face, grateful for this small mercy.

Their respite was brief. In moments they again moved forward, following the stream's course to the southwest. Earlier they had traveled in a comparatively compact body, but now Jakob noted that the lead warriors ranged ahead, vanishing from sight between the trees, while those at the rear lagged behind. Wherever the terrain made it possible, their captors broke into a run, clearly impatient to put as much distance as possible between them and the white settlements before nightfall.

Already Jakob's work-hardened muscles burned, and shafts of agony jolted through his body with every stride. His breath came in searing pants, while hunger clawed at his vitals, the need for nourishment making him lightheaded. He wondered how long could he and the boys could keep going without rest and food.

It was now abundantly clear why the Indians had killed Anna, Jake, and the baby, while taking him, Joseph, and Christian captive. The war party had spared only those able to travel with the rapidity they enforced. His and the boys' survival depended on their ability to endure the harsh trials of the journey.

Time and again he glanced anxiously behind him. But their guards kept them well apart from one another, blocking the boys from Jakob's view except for an occasional quick glimpse between the warriors' ranks. So far they had managed to keep up, but although he thanked God for this grace, he could not help questioning the Almighty's purposes.

His eyes stung from trickling sweat, and he repeatedly blinked and shook his head, fighting the overwhelming need to sprawl across the ground and surrender to sleep. That would be his death, he kept warning himself, and then his boys would face a fearful future all alone.

The farther they traveled, the more frequently they passed abandoned plantations with ruined buildings and crops trampled or burned in the fields. Occasionally Jakob caught glimpses of rawboned cattle straggling through the woods and lean hogs rooting for acorns beneath the oaks. These sights brought back vivid, agonizing images of his own home's devastation, and he wondered bleakly whether their owners had escaped or whether they, too, had been killed or carried away.

The sun rode high above the treetops when they came upon the advance party clustered around a tree on a well-beaten pathway that wound from the southeast to the northwest. The rear guard rejoined the main party shortly, and they waited for some moments, while the leading warriors talked and waved their arms in one direction or another. At length they turned together onto the path, heading northwest.

As he passed the tree where the warriors had gathered, Jakob saw that a ring of bark had been stripped from its trunk. A series of unintelligible symbols were freshly painted in red and black on the bare core.

The broad path they now followed, he suddenly realized, must be one of the Indians' ancient highways through the wilderness. He remembered hearing about the Tulpehocken Path, named after the Turtle clan of the Delaware. This path stretched from Colonel Weiser's home near Reading, through Bethel at the Blue Mountain's base several miles to the west of his Northkill community, and all the way to the old Indian town of Shamokin at the forks of the Susquehanna River.

His heart began to pound. Shamokin lay on the east bank of the Susquehanna where the river's eastern and western branches converged to flow south. The native inhabitants had abandoned the town the previous year when the British occupied the area. On its site the army had built Fort Augusta, a major stronghold in the line of forts that ran from north to south along the western frontier between British- and French-controlled territories.

If they were bound to the fort's vicinity, might they somehow attract the attention of its garrison?

He had neither time nor energy to ponder this possibility as they traversed the valley in a rush and began the rise onto Second Mountain. Mercifully it was an easier climb than the Blue Mountain ascent in spite of the shoulder-width gap they edged through, scraping against a cliff on one side to avoid the precipice on the other that fell sharply away to a creek some distance below.

In his physical extremity he knew he could not allow himself to think of what lay behind or what might lie ahead. He had strength only to focus on the need of moment—strength that was ebbing all too quickly.

Yet fearful images of his wife and children's merciless deaths tumbled before his eyes like the dry husks of leaves blown by the sere autumn wind, impossible to suppress. And on their heels the question of what unknown horrors still awaited sprang cruelly to his consciousness again and again.

As his jagged thoughts muted into an unbroken, wordless plea for God's protection and deliverance, he took a jarring step. And then another. And another. . . .

＊━━━＊

ON THE DESCENT into the second valley, Christian stumbled on a protruding rock and with a strangled cry sprawled headlong, the breath knocked out of him. Gasping desperately to fill his lungs, he looked up in mute appeal, tears and sweat stinging his eyes. He caught a glimpse of Joseph, several yards in advance, as he swung around to stare at him, a look of abject horror coming over his face.

The surrounding warriors continued on their course without slowing, casting only a narrowed glance at Christian and his guard as they passed, driving Joseph before them and out of sight. Sobbing, Christian rolled into a ball and pulled his knees to his chest as he awaited the blow that would end his life.

"Joseph! Daati!" he squealed, covering his head with his arms.

"*Yo-sef, Da-adi!*" his guarding mocked, bending over him, his eyes alight with savage glee.

Hot tears blurred Christian's sight. Panic caused his heart to pound so hard he felt consciousness fade as he cringed away from the man's fearsomely painted visage.

To his astonishment, the man swept him up in his arms and swung him onto his back as though he weighed no more than a feather. When he sprang forward, Christian's arms instinctively encircled the warrior's neck and his legs clenched around the man's waist.

They quickly passed the war party's rear guard and regained their former position. Several of the warriors scowled and shouted at them, but his guardian returned their jeers with a laughing retort and ran on as though unconcerned.

From his vantage Christian could see Joseph and Daat ahead of him, loping doggedly along where the trail leveled out, encircled by the racing warriors. As one, then the other, glanced back in his direction, he saw their expressions change from terror to amazement, and then to stunned relief.

Feeling the power in the taut, smoothly moving muscles beneath his captor's sweat-glossed skin, Christian squeezed his eyes shut and clung to him, a flood of intense gratitude washing away his fear. At last he gave in to exhaustion and let his head droop onto the warrior's shoulder, the steady, unceasing jolt and sway of his strides easing Christian into slumber

＋·······＋

THE BULK OF THE THIRD MOUNTAIN range loomed a distance ahead of them when the leading warriors suddenly raced back through the trees to rejoin the main party. With fierce gestures and low, vehement commands they directed everyone off the path into the underbrush and away from the creek they had been following, while the rear guard rushed up from behind.

"No speak," the warriors repeated to their captives in broken English, their gestures threatening. "Make sound and you die!"

His breath constricted, Joseph looked to Daat and Christian and saw that their expressions reflected his own anxiety. They stumbled blindly through the forest amid the circle of warriors, prodded forward at musket point, while the party's rear guard followed more slowly behind them, using the blankets they wore over their shoulders to sweep fallen leaves over their track.

After a short distance they came to a thicket of trees and brush. A low rocky outcrop lay within its cover, and Joseph's guard shoved him down into this shelter to find Daat already squatting there. In seconds Christian's guard swung the boy down from his shoulders and into Daat's outstretched arms.

While Joseph watched anxiously, a small guard dispersed to crouch behind trees around the outer perimeter of the rocky bank, muskets held ready. The rest of the warriors vanished soundlessly into the undergrowth.

It was the first time they had been close enough to touch or speak since being taken captive, and they clung to one another. Joseph could feel his brother shaking uncontrollably.

"Daat, what's going on?" he whispered.

Daat pressed his finger to his lips. His voice barely audible, he breathed, "Likely a patrol."

"We've got to get their attention!"

The muscles in Daat's jaw hardened, and he shook his head. "They'll kill us if we make a sound."

Joseph slumped back against the rocks, raging inwardly but knowing his father was right.

For an indeterminable period only by the sigh of the wind and the creak of branches overhead broke the silence. Suddenly feeling Daat jerk erect, Joseph straightened to follow his gaze to the line of warriors barely visible through the screening foliage.

Off to the north he could just make out the sound of hoof beats approaching and, as they drew closer, the faint jingle of bridles and spurs. When it seemed that the riders must be directly abreast of their hiding place, he caught the murmur of voices, quickly stilled. A faint rustle of movement through the brush followed, but whether it was the warriors or the outriders of a patrol, he couldn't tell.

Please, God, please let them find us! Joseph pled, while Christian buried his face against Daat's chest, tears coursing silently down his cheeks.

Against all hope, the sounds gradually faded away to the south, finally melting into the distance. Eyes closed, Joseph slowly released his breath and let his head droop against the rocks at his back, biting his lip hard to stifle a groan.

Chapter Sixteen

S HADOWS LAY LONG across the ground when Crist slowed the
team and turned the wagon past the last trees bordering the
track and into the barnyard. When he pulled to a halt, Barbara
clutched his arm, a low moan escaping her lips.

The charred ruins of her parents' home, still wreathed in
wisps of smoke, appeared almost ghostly in the fading light of
late afternoon. Stunned, she surveyed the burned-out barn and
outbuildings, the broken, blackened bake oven, the dead livestock sprawled across the blood-stained grass, already swollen in
the warm September sun. The odor of decaying blood and
singed flesh saturated the air, sickening her even through the
kerchief she held over her nose.

When Crist helped her down from the wagon, she spied a
familiar form nearby and knelt beside it. "Ach, Blitz," she
mourned, stroking the lifeless head. "Even you they killed
yet."

Crist drew her gently to her feet and held her until her tears
subsided, then indicated the smoke that hung in a heavy cloud
over the pasture. "The neighbors are burning the dead livestock.
With the weather so warm, they can't be left lying out in the
open, and burning goes faster than burying them."

She stared, speechless, at the men who were loading the remaining corpses into wagons. The destruction wrought by the attack was even worse than she had imagined. She breathed a silent prayer of gratitude that her mother-in-law had kept the children so they would not see it, and that her mother, brother, and little sister had been carried away to be washed and prepared for burial before she and Crist arrived.

He had been right. She could not have borne the sight of their broken bodies.

Renewed agony cut through her at thought of what they must have suffered. A grey veil obscured her vision and spots danced before her eyes. Feeling the baby turn in her womb, she bit her lip until she tasted blood, Crist's arm around her all that kept her from dropping to her knees.

When her stomach settled and her vision cleared, a small group clustered around them, each face reflecting love and sorrow. All day extended family, members of the church, and neighbors from the surrounding English and German community had stopped by their home to offer heartfelt condolences and practical help. Chores had been taken care of almost without their realizing it, and she knew that the same had happened at Johannes and Katie's place.

Now, one by one, still others took her hand and offered halting words of comfort. She felt entirely overwhelmed by the outpouring of kindness, and although gratitude filled her in equal measure, it was a relief when everyone except Crist, her aunts, and Katie and her mother finally drifted off.

"Your uncle got some of the men together to make the coffins," Aunt Katrina told her, clearly struggling to speak.

Katie drew Barbara into her embrace, tears streaming down her cheeks. "We took them over to our house. Since everything of theirs burned in the fire, we had to wrap them in linen sheets."

"We put Annali in your Maam's arms," murmured Aunt Mary.

Barbara felt as though a hole went clear through her heart. "*Danke.* Maam would want it that way."

Blinking back tears, Katherine Hertzler murmured in a choked voice, "Where do you want the . . . the graves?"

Barbara wiped her face with the edge of her apron. "Here. This is—was—their home."

Katherine tried to smile, but her round face furrowed with distress. "*Ya,* it's close to you and Johannes too. There's a nice level place over there between your Maam's garden and the orchard, where the trees give some shade."

The others looked in the direction she pointed and nodded their approval.

"*Guud,*" Barbara agreed. "It's the perfect place. Maam loved her garden and the orchard."

She leaned heavily on Crist's arm, feeling dazed, while she took in the activity around her. Wagons rumbled down the path to the pasture, while friends and neighbors collected the scattered debris in piles for disposal. Women bustled back and forth, setting dishes of food on the wagons beds and trestle tables arranged where the kitchen yard had been cleared.

The last thing Barbara wanted was food, but knowing she needed to eat for her own sake and that of her unborn baby, she didn't protest when Crist led her and the others to where the impromptu evening meal was being laid. As they approached the nearest table, Bishop Hertzler came to join them. She and Crist, with Johannes and Katie, had spent some time with the bishop and his wife early that afternoon, and the older couple's gentle kindness and wise counsel had done as much to ease their shock and sorrow as was possible.

While they stood quietly talking, Barbara heard Eva Kurtz's voice behind her. "And this wasn't the only attack."

Barbara threw a quick glance over her shoulder. Eva's flushed face reflected both fear and anger.

"Did you hear they killed a soldier and several from Michael Specht's family, then carried him off with two of his children, just like they did Jakob and the boys?" The older woman's voice rose. "If the British hadn't shut down our fort, this wouldn't have happened."

Barbara felt lightheaded. When she caught Crist's arm, he looked down at her in alarm, steadying her as she sank onto the bench next to the table.

As the others bent over her, she forced a reassuring smile and waved them off. "I'm all right."

She wasn't, however, and questions crowded her mind. How many more attacks would there be before the war ended? What if the French won? Was it foolish for their community to stay?

But if they all left . . . Involuntarily she lifted her gaze to where the long, hazy blue bulk of Blue Mountain sprawled across the western horizon, and her heart constricted. If Daat and the boys ever came home, how would they find her and Johannes?

When she turned back, she saw her brother and uncles approaching from the direction of Johannes's house, their gait heavy, shoulders bowed. Uncle Jakob reached out to Barbara, his eyes glistening with moisture, and she rose to step into his arms, while Aunt Mary patted her back.

"Why did God allow this? How could He let them die such a terrible death?"

Bishop Hertzler had followed Barbara's gaze to the narrow gap at the mountain's summit. He studied it for a long moment before turning to regard her with compassion.

"Even when we don't understand God's will, we have faith that His ways are right, and that He can bring good even out of this evil. We must forgive. We must not allow our hearts to become bitter."

Barbara pulled out of her uncle's arms. "And I will—in time, as God gives me strength. But right now I'm angry. I know Maam and Jake and Annali are with Jesus, but I want them here with me! I want Daat and my brothers to come home!"

As the women gathered around his sister, murmuring words of comfort and encouragement, Johannes turned to the men. "Maybe Colonel Weiser would be willing to send a detail out to see if they can find Daat and the boys and bring them back. He helped us when we were called to the fort—"

The bishop cut him off with a stern shake of his head. "*Nay*, we will not bring soldiers into this matter. If it's *Gott's* will to bring them home, then—"

Barbara rounded on them. "If we don't do something, we'll never see them again! We've all heard how the Indians treat their captives. Is it God's will for us to abandon them to torture and death when we might yet be able to rescue them?"

Johannes glanced uneasily at Katie, who chewed her lip while staring at her father. Further conversation was cut off when the Blancks' wagon pulled up among those crowded together at the end of the lane. Before her parents or siblings could step down, Anna jumped from the bed and raced to Barbara's arms, her face ashen.

"I didn't want to believe it! They said your Maam—and Jake and Annali—"

Sobs muffled the rest of her words. Finally taking a deep breath and drawing back, she directed a dazed glance at the destruction that surrounded them.

"We had such a good time here with all of them last night. And now everything's gone! How could this happen so quick?"

After greeting Anna's family, the bishop quietly excused himself. He and his wife went to speak to the men drifting back from the pasture.

Johannes had just turned to speak to the Blancks, when five buckskin-clad riders galloped into the lane. Pulling to a halt, they swung down from their saddles, the dust swirling around them.

Two of the men strode purposefully toward those gathered around the wagons, while the rest held the reins of the lathered horses. As they drew closer, Johannes recognized them as members of the local militia.

They stopped to speak to Hans Zug, who gestured toward where Johannes and the others stood. Immediately the two men came over to them. Pulling off their cocked hats, they bowed, then straightened and looked around them, their faces hardening.

The older man, who appeared to be in charge, fixed Johannes in a keen look. "*Sie sind Johannes Hochstetler?*"

"*Ya.*" Johannes crossed his arms and shifted his weight from one foot to the other.

"I'm Sergeant Hardt, and this is Corporal Geiger. We just got back from tracking the war party that attacked the Spechts and killed one of our men. We followed them north over the mountain on the old Tulpehocken Path, but they were too far ahead for us to catch up with them."

"We came right over when we got back," Geiger added, his look sympathetic.

"*Danke,*" Barbara whispered, wiping away fresh tears as she leaned against Crist's shoulder.

"Did any of you see what happened?" Hardt's tone was urgent.

Johannes looked down at Katie. She gave him a firm nod, and for several minutes he described in careful detail everything he and the Kreutzers had seen.

"My friend Hannes Mueller stopped by my place a little while ago, while we were building coffins for my Maam . . . and brother and sister . . . "

He stopped. Tears clouded his vision, and the words choked in his throat. Feeling Katie take his hand, he gratefully returned the pressure of her fingers.

Geiger gripped him by the shoulder, and Johannes sucked in a shaky breath. "His hand was all wrapped up. He said he was chopping wood early this morning up on the mountain, and a whole party of Indians came by and shot him."

Aware that Barbara and Crist stared at him, openmouthed, he forced himself to continue. "He says Daat was with them and yelled for him to run. I asked him about my brothers, but he didn't see them. Daat's head was all painted red like the Indians, he told me, and he had on Indian clothes."

"If he's still alive, then Joseph and Cristli must be too!" Barbara exclaimed.

Anna pressed her hand to her bosom, tears welling into her eyes. "Ach, think how scared they must be."

Barbara turned to the two soldiers. "If you went after them real quick, maybe you could find them. Every hour that goes by they're being carried farther and farther away."

Hardt exchanged a rueful glance with the corporal before saying, "By now they're too far ahead to make that possible, *Frau* Stutzman, and it's getting dark. But we'll ride out a ways to see if we can find anything." He turned back to Johannes. "You said they headed for Northkill Creek."

Johannes pointed toward the Detweiler plantation. "The Kreutzers told me they took off through the orchard in that direction. There's a place over by the spring where it looks like they stopped for a while. The creek is a little farther on, in Detweiler's field."

"We're familiar with it—been up to the gap a time or two," Geiger assured him.

"Once they cross over the mountain, they'll most likely head west to the Tuplpehocken Path and follow it to Shamokin. I'm afraid it'll be tomorrow before we can head up that way." Turning to Geiger, Hardt said in a low voice, "We ought to be able to get up to where Mueller was chopping wood before it gets too dark to see anything."

The two men took their leave and rejoined the rest of the patrol. Skirting the ruins of the house, they rode into the orchard and out of sight.

Crist blew out a breath. "At least they're going to go look for their tracks. I guess that's all they can do for now." He put his arm around Barbara's shoulders. "*Liebe,* you need some food and rest."

"If I try to get food down, it'll come up."

"I feel the same way, but we all need strength to go on." Johannes rubbed the back of his neck wearily. "Tonight while we sit up with the . . . with the bodies, we'll talk and try to figure out if there's anything else we can do."

The women had begun to serve the meal, and they turned around to find seats at the nearest table. Bishop Hertzler stood behind them, frowning, arms folded over his chest.

JAKOB SHIFTED HIS POSITION gingerly in an attempt to ease the chafe of the rawhide thongs binding him upright to a great chestnut tree. The bruising blows and vicious threats and taunts the warriors had subjected him to since making camp for the night had sharpened the day's already overwhelming terror. Time and again they had brought burning brands close to his face, mocking him when he shrank away. He had fought to make no sound, to show no fear, but several times a particularly savage blow had wrenched a guttural cry from his throat. Finally, when he thought he could endure no longer, his tormentors had appeared to grow bored with their sport and left him alone.

The worst torment was knowing that his boys had been forced to witness his abuse and humiliation. Their captors directed their vindictiveness only toward Jakob—to intimidate the three of them and ensure submission, he suspected—but Joseph and Christian had cowered together trembling, their faces averted, clearly distraught..

Darkness pressed in on hiim now. With nightfall, the air had turned sharply colder, and after the heat of the day the rising wind chilled him through. His arms, stretched awkwardly behind him around the tree trunk, were rapidly losing feeling, the blood flow cut off so that an agonizing prickle spread from his fingers to his wrenched shoulders.

In spite of his misery, the remembered sensation of his boys gathered in his arms hours earlier when they sheltered beneath the rock offered solace. It had been for much too brief a time, but he had been able to offer them a small measure of comfort and to draw the same from their nearness.

It was an effort to raise his head, yet he strained to see through the obscuring darkness to the blacker shadows where Christian and Joseph lay motionless on the dew-soaked ground, tethered by cords to their guards. He prayed they had given in to the healing sleep that his anxious thoughts and painful bonds denied him.

During the hours that followed the patrol's passing, while the sun descended behind the mountains and the light gradually faded from the sky, the war party had crept forward stealthily at a cautious walk, keeping well off the trail with their prisoners in their midst. They had crossed another broad, steep mountain range, the warriors on constant alert for the approach of an enemy from front or rear, their unrelieved tension erupting in repeated threats and blows that tormented Jakob and his sons as much as their former speed had.

The day's unseasonable heat had borne down on them with suffocating force, and although their captors allowed them to drink and splash water over themselves at each stream they crossed, by the time they reached a low gap between two more mountain ranges at sunset, all three were darkly flushed and dripping sweat red from the paint on their heads.

Along the trail they passed a number of unoccupied three-sided lean-tos with stick walls and slanting bark roofs but stopped at none of them. Instead they had taken cover for the night in another thick copse of trees a short hike off the path on the bank of a swift-flowing creek. There the warriors kindled a small, smokeless fire concealed by the surrounding trees and brush before sending out sentries.

Jakob pressed his back against the tree's rough bark in a vain attempt to find a more comfortable position. His stomach cramped with hunger. The warriors had shared pemmican, parched corn, and their stolen peaches generously among themselves shortly after they made camp, but offered only a sparse handful of parched corn to their prisoners.

To his relief, before being bound to the tree, Jakob had been grudgingly allowed to ration out a bruised peach to each of the boys and to choke one down himself. Watching his sons ravenously devour the fruit, he had longed to give them another from his store. Yet a sense that their supply might be needed in the days ahead had kept him from doing so.

His eyelids drooped, the need for sleep overwhelming him, and he sagged forward in his bonds. The jolt of agony that shot through his shoulders jerked him instantly back to consciousness, however, and groaning, he forced himself erect.

If he could gain no rest, how was he to endure the coming day? In silent anguish he cried out for succor, questioning why God had removed his hand of protection from him and his family.

The confrontation with Bishop Hertzler at Barbara's wedding years earlier haunted him now. Was it, after all, because of his pride? Was it his fault that God had turned away His face?

Unbidden, broken images of Anna in her nakedness scrambling to escape the clutches of their attackers and the prone, bloody bodies of Jake and Annali bloomed and receded before his eyes, each striking him with the force of a blow. Passages from *The Martyr's Mirror* describing the sufferings of those persecuted for their faith echoed in his memory.

Why, Gott? *Why? Why do you leave Your people to suffer and die?*

The only answer was the hiss of the wind in the treetops and the creak of branches overhead.

Yet by slow degrees the confusion and turmoil of his mind gave way to clarity. Had not Christ also been abused by his enemies, stripped naked, whipped, and humiliated? "*If they do this to*

Me, your Lord and Master," He had told His disciples, *"then they will treat you in the same way."*

Jesus had not shrunk from suffering. He had remained faithful to the end. Could Jakob do any less for the One who had died for him? No, for the sake of the gospel of Christ and as an example to his children he must endure whatever suffering lay in store.

As he squirmed to ease the painful constriction of his bonds and allow feeling to return to his arms and hands, a strange calm filtered through his veins, slowing his heartbeat and calming his breathing. Gott *will bring us home again.* With the thought came certainty. And guidance.

For some time he carefully reviewed everything that had happened that day, committing it to memory. If he and the boys somehow managed an escape, they would need to know the way back.

He determined to memorize every detail of their journey: each stream and valley and mountain they crossed, the direction and distance they traveled each day, every landmark they passed, whom they met—any information he could glean that might help them to find their way home. And he would pay close attention to everything their captors said. If they spoke in English or French, he might be able to make out enough of their conversation to help him. And if they did not, by their gestures and actions he might begin to understand their language.

He directed an assessing glance around the camp. Although he had paid little conscious attention over the course of the day, once the initial shock of the attack had dulled, the warriors' individual characteristics had gradually begun to impress themselves on his mind. From their clothing, the way they painted their bodies, and the ornaments they wore, it was apparent to him that the war party was comprised of a mixed band of the formerly peaceful Delaware and the fearsome Shawnee.

His own guard was one of the latter, a tall, muscular man noble in appearance and heavily tattooed, as were all the Shawnee he had encountered. During the raid they had gone naked, their well-formed bodies painted entirely black to make their appearance even more terrifying. They had donned breechcloths and leggings only after the Frenchmen appeared, while he and his boys were being shaved and painted. That detail, too, returned abruptly.

Although he could make out little of his surroundings in the deep shadows, he was fairly certain fifteen Indians made up the war party. On the morrow he would count them to be sure and would determine which tribe they belonged to.

No matter the exact number, however, they were a daunting force for him and his boys to reckon with. But before God they were powerless, and that assurance steadied him.

Finding the most comfortable position possible, Jakob propped his back against the tree and closed his eyes. At length darkness washed over him and consciousness mercifully faded.

❧━━━❧

"IF YOU ASK ME, it's pride that brought this on them."

The smug voice of an older woman from the church reached Barbara over the muted chant of mourning hymns from Johannes and Katie's *Stube,* bringing her up short. She knelt by the hearth to tidy Mattie's straggling curls back under her cap, while watching the small knot of gossipers from the corner of her eye.

The woman's husband shrugged. "You know what the Lord said about the man who built bigger barns and—"

"That house too!" his wife interrupted, keeping her voice low. She clucked her tongue and leaned closer to the others. "And warranting so much land yet. What did they need with all that?"

Barbara forced a smile and directed her oldest daughter back to her grandmother in the *Stube* with a kiss and a pat on the back. But hurt and resentment stabbed through her.

As if Daat and Maam were the only ones who built bigger houses and barns and warranted more land the last few years.

She looked up in time to see Bishop Hertzler step into the group. "The same must be true of all the attacks around here since the war began, then," he noted stiffly. "It seems there's been a considerable outbreak of pride in this community."

The woman reddened, while the others exchanged embarrassed glances. Her husband cleared his throat.

"We just meant that it's a sin all of us have to be on guard against."

The bishop gave him a curt nod. "*Ya,* I'll agree with that. I seem to remember that the Lord also said not to judge so we won't be judged."

Barbara watched as the couples hastened out the door, studiously avoiding her gaze.

Over the course of the evening, those who gathered to help that afternoon had taken their leave a few at a time, with many tears and expressions of love and condolence. But she had also overheard more than one comment among the church members that echoed the opinions of the couples who had just left.

Crist appeared at her elbow and helped her to her feet. When the bishop came to join them, she thanked the older man, gratitude welling up. His smile sympathetic, Bishop Hertzler waved his hand in a quick, dismissive gesture before ushering her and Crist into the *Stube*.

When they entered, the singers' voices trailed off, giving way to the halting murmur of sorrowful conversation. Only the Buerkis, Stutzmans, and Hertzlers remained, yet to Barbara the house felt crowded, the air heavy.

Chairs had been brought in to accommodate everyone. The two babies were already tucked away for the night, and the rest of the children slumbered in their aunts' or grandmother's arms.

Barbara's gaze was drawn to the two plain pine coffins, sitting side by side on trestles in the center of the room, their lids already nailed shut. She found it suddenly difficult to breathe, and waves of panic stole her breath at the thought that she could never have one last glimpse of Maam and Jake and little Annali.

With an effort she swallowed a sob, wishing it were all a dream, praying that she would awaken and they would be alive and in the midst of their gathering, and that Daat and her younger brothers would burst through the door, glad to have the evening milking done and eager for supper. Had it not been for the stark evidence before her eyes, she might have been able to pretend that their lives had not been shattered after all.

She pressed her fingers to her throbbing temples and glanced at the clock ticking quietly on its shelf, determined not to give way to tears again. There would be more than enough on the morrow when they lowered the coffins into the newly dug graves.

It was almost nine o'clock, past time for the children to be put to bed. The leftover food still had to be put away, the *Küche* set back to rights, and other common evening tasks attended to. Thankfully she and Crist had brought fresh clothing for the funeral and would stay overnight with Johannes and Katie rather than rousing the children for the ride home.

Johannes crossed the room to put his arms around her. Katie pressed close, and Crist enfolded them all. While they clung together, seeking strength from one another, Aunt Katrina started quietly upstairs, holding little Mattie's hand. Grandma Stutzman followed, tiny Anna's head bobbing sleepily over her shoulder, and, blinking back tears, Katie pulled away to shepherd her little brood into the downstairs *Kammer*.

✦ • • • ✦

THE THREE WOMEN soon returned and resumed their seats. Silence fell over the room. Barbara stared down at her lap and concentrated on pleating the edge of her apron between her fingers.

Bishop Hertzler cleared his throat, his kindly glance taking in her and Johannes. "At such a time as this, none of us can express the painful emotions that fill our hearts. Those from our own fellowship, our own family, have been taken away from us though violence, something none of us have experienced since we left the old country to come to this new land, seeking freedom to worship and serve *Gott* according to His calling.

"Grief can lead us at times to do what we would not otherwise. The Lord commanded us not to kill. This is why we do not serve in the military, nor must we seek the intervention of soldiers when we suffer wrong."

Barbara took her time answering. "Is it wrong to tell the truth when soldiers question us about those who have attacked not only our own family, but our neighbors as well?"

Johannes shifted in his seat and threw his sister a sidelong glance. Although her tone and look were meek, he sensed determination behind her words.

"These soldiers heard about the attack on Maam and Daat from others. They were pursuing the war party that attacked Spechts and needed information I could give them to find the ones who did this evil thing."

He had hardly finished speaking when Uncle Crist leaned forward, his hands clasped between his knees, the knuckles whitening. "The Bible says we're to be in submission to those who rule over us. The government employs these men to fight this war and protect all the people ruled by England's king, including those of us who don't believe in fighting and killing."

The bishop pursed his lips and regarded each of them with a thoughtful frown. "We must comply with the government's demands so long as they don't break *Gott's* laws. Just like when you men were called to the fort last fall, we will give to Caesar what is Caesar's, and to *Gott* what is *Gott's*. Whether they ask for taxes or information that will help another, we'll give it." He stopped, then added, "But we will not go to the soldiers and ask them to get involved in our affairs, nor petition the government to do so."

For a tense moment no one responded. Johannes noted that although the Stutzmans' expressions reflected the same grief and pain as the rest, they nodded their agreement with the bishop. His aunts and uncles, however, looked, stony faced, everywhere but at Katie's parents, while the same emotions etched Barbara's features that clenched his own gut.

Johannes gripped the chair seat with both hands, fighting to keep his voice level. "But they're already involved. Several of our English neighbors told me that besides the militia patrol that went out this morning, a message also went to Colonel Weiser. They said he'll most likely send out patrols from Fort Lebanon to go after the war party and probably bring more soldiers up from Reading too."

"If the soldiers or others in authority come around asking any more questions about the attack, then it's our obligation to answer as best we can. That's all we can or should do."

"I feel like we have to do something, not just stand around here while Daat and the boys are being taken farther and farther away from us!"

Barbara touched Johannes's arm lightly and turned a look of appeal on the Hertzlers. "Everybody talks about praying for them, and we're doing that. But I can't believe that God wants us to leave them to suffer—or be killed—if we can maybe find them and bring them home."

"Do you want to do this 'something' because you believe *Gott* is calling you do it . . . or because you think it'll make you feel better?" the bishop asked, eyes narrowed.

Uncle Jakob's face reflected frustration. "We're talking about our sister, Jakob, our brother-in-law, our nephews and niece!"

"Surely we have the right to decide what's best for our own family when something like this happens," Uncle Crist agreed forcefully.

Katie transferred her gaze from her mother to her father. "Daat, I know how I'd feel if it was my husband and children that were killed or taken captive."

Katherine reached to squeeze her daughter's hand. "We feel the same way all of you do, *Tochter.* It hurts us, too, that this happened, and we want Jakob and the boys back as much as you do. But we have to entrust those we love to *Gott,* even though it's the hardest thing we'll ever do."

"*Ya,* and it is hard," "Bishop Hertzler agreed. "We're believers, but we're also men, and we feel the sharp prick of grief and anger and fear and doubt—the things all people feel. And we ask why? Why did *Gott* allow this to happen to our loved ones?"

He indicated Johannes,his voice rising. "This is our son-in-law, the father of our grandchildren. He and his parents and brothers and sisters are precious to Katherine and me. We feel this loss deeply. Like all of you, we want to act, to do something to make things right. We don't want to sit here and feel like this is out of our control. But it *is* out of our control!"

He looked from one face to the other around the room. "If you chase after these Indians, you not only place yourself in danger, but also in the way of temptation. Would you take guns? If you have weapons and you're attacked, won't you be tempted to defend yourself and maybe kill somebody?"

Crist waved his words away impatiently. "We wouldn't take guns."

The bishop raised his eyebrows. "Then what if you ran into a war party—which most would likely happen on the other side of the mountain. They'd attack you too, kill you or take you captive. What good would that do your families?"

Johannes exchanged a rueful glance with his brother-in-law and slumped back in his chair. Several of those around him hunched forward, elbows propped on their knees, chins supported on their clasped hands, while others stared into space, tears trickling down their cheeks.

"*Nay,* the only thing we can do is to trust the lives our loved ones to the One who loves them even more than we ever can."

The bishop's gentle words eased the pain that held Johannes's chest in a vise, even as his mind refused to accept them. Unable to sit still, he sprang to his feet and took a quick turn around the room, rubbing the back of his neck with one hand.

"Why can't we petition the government to do something? That makes the most sense."

"Petition the government to do what? Send soldiers after the Indians to kill them—or be killed themselves? What else can happen if they overtake the Indians who took your Daat and the boys and try to get them away?"

Silence enveloped the room. Bishop Hertzler stared down at his folded hands for a long moment before continuing.

"We will submit to the government, but we will allow *Gott* to direct the authorities in carrying out His will as He pleases. We ourselves will not go after the Indians or petition the authorities to take this course or that, putting those who pursue in danger and tempting them to hurt or kill others."

His words held an air of finality. Taking his wife by the hand, he rose, deep lines of weariness creasing his face.

"With the funeral in the morning, Katherine and I had better head home and leave you to sit with the bodies and get rest as you can. Before we leave, let us have a time of prayer together to petition the Lord and seek His will."

The room filled with the sound of chairs scraping across the floor as everyone stood. They gathered around him, heads bowed, and for some time he led them in prayer, pleading for the Lord to bring comfort and healing to those who mourned, to keep the captives safe in the midst of their trials, and, if it was His will, to bring them home to the arms of their families and church.

"*Lieber Vater,* he concluded, "help us to trust You with our loved ones even when it doesn't look to us as if anything good can possibly come from this tragedy. Give us strength to forgive, to love even our enemies the way You love. And guide us in the days ahead that we may obey Your commandments and live as light in this world, to Your honor and glory. In Jesus' name."

Tears falling, each of them softly echoed his amen.

JOHANNES GLANCED QUICKLY at Katie then away. He noted that several of the others did the same.

Heat rose to Katie's face, and she sprang to her feet, fists on hips, eyes glistening with moisture. "Stop looking at me that way, all of you! I love my Daat, but I don't agree with him about everything, and I don't expect anybody else to. And I don't go running off to tell him and Maam everything that's said either."

Johannes put his arm around her waist, drew her to his side, and kissed the top of her head. "We know you don't, Katie. It's just that we don't want to say anything that might hurt your feelings."

Barbara gave her sister-in-law a hug. As the others gathered around, Johannes could feel the tension go out of the room.

Jake Stutzman ran his hand over his face and hung his head. "I can't argue with anything the bishop said. He just made too much sense."

"I don't want to admit it, but everything he said is right. It feels like we're backed into a corner with no way to go."

Uncle Jakob patted Barbara's shoulder. "I feel the same way, Barbli. It's easy to say we trust *Gott* when everything is going our way. But when evil happens to those we love and we have to put our faith into practice . . . well, we find out we really don't trust our Creator so much after all."

"*Ya,* it hurts our pride to find out we're not the ones in control."

Johannes winced and let out a short laugh. "Well, that sure hits me hard, Maudlin. It's weighing on my mind to go on over the mountain and try to find the war party's track regardless of what the bishop says. It sure beats sitting here hoping somebody else will do something."

A wave of grief swept over him suddenly with crushing force. Bending over the larger coffin, where his mother and baby sister lay, he laid his head on his folded arms and gave way to wrenching sobs, while the others wept with him.

At last he fought back to a measure of calmness. He straightened, pulled his kerchief out of his pocket, and mopped his eyes. When he turned around, the others were dabbing at their own tears.

"It's a waste of time to depend on others to try to find them. There've been so many attacks in the area that the soldiers are chasing their tails. " He blew his nose, his frustration building.

Crist shoved his fingers through his hair. "There aren't enough of them left out here to do any good even if we did ask for their help. Most of them have been pulled out to go fight somewhere else. And like the bishop said, if we're so foolish as to go after this war party, we couldn't get your Daat and the boys away from them without a fight. Most likely they'd end up taking us captive too—if they didn't kill us."

"Ach, *ya*. It just went through me when Daat said that."

The color draining from her face, Aunt Katrina rounded on Johannes and Crist. "You daren't go after them. If Barbara and Katie lost the two of you on top of your Maam and Daat, what would they and the children do?"

"There's no use in talking any more about it. The bishop said *nay*, and he's right. We just have to accept things the way they are and pray for *Gott's* will to be done."

Johannes regarded Maudlin soberly. He knew she spoke the truth.

Respect for the bishop and devotion to the church's long-held doctrine of nonresistance ran deep. But unaccustomed resentment knotted his gut. And he read the same mixed emotions on his sister's and uncles' faces.

+⸺⸺+

AFTER THE OTHER WOMEN went upstairs to lie down, Barbara and Crist joined Johannes and Katie in the kitchen, leaving the rest of the men to sit with the coffins. While they worked silently to clear away the food and wash the last of the dishes, Barbara suddenly stopped and buried her face in her hands.

When Crist tried to pull her into his arms, she pushed him away. "We're just going around in circles! We have to do what the bishop said, but I can't find any peace in that! All I can think about is what Daat and the boys must be going through—and what Maam and Jake and Annali suffered."

She wiped her flushed face and dabbed at her tear-swollen eyes. "I didn't see what you did, Johannes. Just hearing about it was bad enough. I know it's right to forgive even those who do such things, and if you're able to, then I'm glad for you. But I don't know if I ever can."

Chapter Seventeen

Wednesday, September 21, 1757

J AKOB HAD BEEN RIGHT. A careful count before they left the campsite had confirmed fifteen warriors in the party: seven Shawnee and eight Delaware.

An hour earlier he and the boys had been roughly shaken from exhausted slumber just as the first light of dawn was beginning to faintly illumine the forest. Released from their bonds, they had been allowed barely enough time to gulp down a peach and drink at the stream before they were again separated and driven across to the opposite bank.

A short walk had brought them back onto the path to resume their unwilling journey north, faint and weak from hunger, shivering in the early morning breeze. Their aching limbs trembled with a weariness the night's fitful sleep had done little to allay.

As before, several warriors ranged well ahead of them, with others lagging behind. The main party moved in close ranks, for the most part blocking Jakob's view of his sons.

He figured that they had covered little over twenty miles before nightfall the previous day. They moved more slowly now, every warrior appearing to be on high alert, and he estimated that they had gone barely three miles since leaving camp.

A short time earlier they had taken a wide berth around a sprawling windfall and entered a long, meadow bathed in dawn's rosy light, where path turned sharply west, edging the bank of a narrow river. Here the trail was uneven and partially overgrown in places, slowing their pace even more.

The terror and exhaustion of the previous day, intensified by the lack of food and the night's ordeal, made it difficult for Jakob to focus on his surroundings and memorize the landmarks they passed, as he had resolved to do. His eyes burned and stung, blurring his vision. The world seemed wrapped in a grey fog, and he repeatedly blinked and shook his head in an effort to clear his mind. How much harder must it be for Joseph and Christian?

From the direction of the rising sun's amber rays, he calculated that the path curved slightly toward the southwest as it hugged the stream's northern bank. Another mountain lay across their route several miles ahead, its long, forested bulk cast in a misty blue haze in the early morning light.

A number of times the evening before and again this morning he had heard the Indians use a word that sounded like *Sus-kwe-ha-na*. He was certain that they could not be farther than a couple of days' walk from the river—and Fort Augusta.

He held no illusions that their captors would risk passing very close to the British stronghold. Yet if they were to come within only a few miles of its walls, they might find opportunity to escape.

The tantalizing hope raised gooseflesh all over his body.

He cast a quick glance behind him and caught a glimpse of Christian. In spite of the early hour, the boy rode on his guard's back.

Jakob's elation instantly dissolved. All three of them were spent. Even if they came within sight of the fort's walls, he doubted that any of them would have the strength to elude their captors and reach it.

Absently he shifted his pouch from one aching shoulder to the other, silently thanking God for His provision and pleading for renewed strength to endure whatever the day might bring.

Was it possible that only a day had passed since this horror began? His thoughts turned to his two oldest children, who by now would likely be arranging the funeral. The dead had to be properly committed to God and their bodies laid to rest, perhaps yet today. That he and the boys would not be there for that final farewell hurt bitterly.

With an effort, he squared his shoulders and forced the tormenting thoughts to the back of his mind. Grief and fear would only hinder his efforts to keep himself and the boys alive and safe. Instead he focused on praying for Johannes, Barbara, and his brothers-in-law and their families.

His guard's angry shout jolted Jakob back to the present, and he saw that in his distraction he had wandered off the path. As he hastily stepped toward it, his foot slipped on a mud-slickened depression where the stream had washed away part of the bank, and he momentarily lost his balance.

His guard grabbed his arm and dragged him into line, screeching furiously and brandishing his tomahawk. Instinctively Jakob raised his arm to ward off the blow. In the same instant a staggering, visceral pent-up rage and grief seared through him with the force of a lightning bolt.

Teeth gritted, he stood nose to nose with the warrior, aching to wrench the tomahawk out of the man's hand and strike him. He thirsted to mete out to his enemies the same brutal violence he and his family had suffered at their hands, to take unsparing revenge for the horrors those he loved had endured and all that he had lost.

"But I say unto you, Love your enemies . . . "

Love them? his mind screamed. *How can I love these savages after what they did to my family?* Gott, *You ask too much!*

Unexpectedly he caught a glimpse of his own reflection in the warrior's dark, hate-filled eyes. Shocked by what it revealed, he cringed, a tide of shame and guilt flooding over him. He dropped his arm and bent his head, shoulders hunched, then swung away to plod down the path.

He felt his guard fall into step with him and forced his strides to match the warrior's. The laughter of those who surrounded them and his guard's jeering response rang in his ears.

It was God he was most angry at, he realized suddenly, and desperation reigned in his soul. *I don't understand! I kept Your commandment, Lord. Why did you not keep Your promise to protect those who obey You?*

Again he could discern no answer. Somehow his aching body kept moving forward against the sapping pull of exhaustion and the deep ache of muscles sore from the abuse suffered the night before.

At last he conceded grudgingly, *I'll submit to them. I have no choice. But,* Gott, *to love them is beyond my power.*

The previous day, as they were driven ever farther west and north, he had been too emotionally numbed to take much note of his surroundings. His greatest concern had been that he and his boys survive the day's trials. But now, deeply shaken, he became aware of the morning's flawless beauty.

Overhead, against the brightening azure sky, a hawk glided on the windstream on its ceaseless hunt for prey, a sharp, black silhouette that circled lazily over the misty forests cloaking the mountain ridges behind and before them. In the valley between, the meadowland they crossed was studded with autumn's last wildflowers and fairly throbbed with the rusty sound of grasshoppers and bees that droned through the drying grasses, while awakening robins and meadowlarks trilled their joyful songs to the heavens.

Gott *help me to love these men even as You love them,* he pled at last. *I cannot do it. I don't want to do it. . . .* With a groan he added, *But I am willing for You to change my heart if it is Your will.*

As he looked around him the seemingly unchanged beauty of the land he had taken joy in and praised his Creator for a lifetime ago wrenched his being as nothing yet had. For it served now only as a stark reminder of how profoundly his world—and he himself—had changed in the space of twenty-four hours.

And of how far he had yet to go.

HER VISION BLURRED, Barbara stared hard at the mounds of freshly dug earth on the far side of the narrow graves. Her uncles and Crist's brothers stood on opposite ends with shovels in hand, but she could not look at them, nor at the coffins being lowered into the ground.

Instead she let her gaze drift across the ruined garden to the orchard. Her heart contracted painfully as the fragrance of ripe peaches wafted around her on the cool morning breeze.

After a simple funeral they had walked from Johannes's house to the burial site, following the wagon that carried the coffins. Crist and Katie stood behind her and Johannes now, with the congregation gathered around, everyone dressed in unrelieved black, each face drawn with sorrow. The only sounds that broke the morning's stillness were muffled sobs and the occasional wail of an infant. Even the birds seemed to have lost their voices.

"It's so hard to think I'll never feel Maam's arms around me again, never kiss Jake and little Annali . . . " She let the murmured words trail off.

Johannes's only reply was to put his arm around her shoulders, his bleak expression reflecting her own emotions.

Without speaking, the men began to fill the graves, the shovelfuls of dirt sounding abnormally loud as they fell on the coffin lids. It took all of Barbara's willpower not to turn and run.

Johannes cleared his throat. "We can't see yet . . . what good the Lord may bring out of . . . out of even this."

Awkwardly he dropped his arm from Barbara's shoulders. Holding his hat in front of his chest, he clenched the brim with both hands.

Snatches of Bishop Hertzler's sermon returned to her, splintered like the sun's rays glimmering through the wind-blown leaves of the trees. Instead of the usual custom of one of the other ministers speaking first, he had preached alone. And to everyone's surprise, the scripture he had chosen was from *Das erste Buch Mose,* Genesis 50:20, Joseph's response to his brothers, who had sold him into slavery in Egypt many years earlier.

"But as for you, ye thought evil against me; but God meant it unto good, to bring to pass, as it is this day, to save much people alive."

His gentle words had seemed to Barbara to serve as both balm and goad.

"The One who cares for us from before our birth is still in control, even when such a great tragedy befalls us. His power is beyond anything we can do, and His wisdom is far above ours. He calls us to be patient and allow Him to work out His perfect will. Our part is to forgive those who have done this evil thing, as hard as that is, and to faithfully pray for the captives' safety and release if it is His will. But always for *Gott's* will to be done! For if we rush ahead with what we think right, then we may interfere with His great purpose, which is always to bring life to many."

For a long moment he had surveyed the congregation before concluding, "What Satan means for evil, the Almighty *Gott* will turn to good. It may take many years. Maybe we won't see it in our lifetimes. But our children and grandchildren and the generations that follow will see the day of blessing."

Barbara forced her gaze back to the graves. They were filled in now, the earth neatly mounded. She let out a trembling breath and dabbed away her tears with the edge of her kerchief.

Bishop Hertzler called them to silently pray the Lord's prayer and as they stood, heads bowed, every word of the prayer seemed to hit her like a hammer blow. She covered her face with her hands, tears trickling between her fingers, grateful for the strength of Crist's arm around her shoulders. It was a relief when the bishop finally pronounced the benediction.

She turned blindly and let Crist draw her into his arms, holding her until grief lessened its hold enough for her to breathe again. Then, hand in hand they followed the sorrowful procession back toward Johannes and Katie's house, where a meal awaited, carried in earlier by those attending the funeral.

Before they reached the lane, Anna Blanck intercepted them, eyes and nose red from weeping, cheeks stained with tears. As she and Barbara clung to each other, tears mingling, the words of the Lord's Prayer repeated over and over in Barbara's mind: *Vergib uns usere Schulden, wie wir unsern Schuldigern vergeben.* Forgive us our debts as we forgive our debtors.

But she thrust the words from her angrily, her anguish making any thought of forgiveness feel like a travesty, and the promise that good could come from such horror, an unspeakable delusion.

JOSEPH'S MUSCLES BURNED with fatigue, and his stomach protested painfully against the hunger that seemed to consume him. How much farther would the Indians force them to go? How much longer could he stay on his feet before he collapsed and a tomahawk's blow ended his life?

The party continued to travel more slowly than yesterday, skirting the slope of yet another mountain and pausing regularly at streams to drink and relieve themselves. When the sun had reached its zenith the warriors detoured to a secluded clearing well off the path to share a meager meal of parched corn and pemmican with their captives, to which Daat had added a single peach divided among the three of them.

Almost before swallowing their last mouthful of food, they had fallen asleep, curled together on a drift of dry leaves. For some reason, instead of immediately prodding them awake, the warriors had lingered. When he woke, Joseph estimated from the angle of the sun that about an hour had passed.

He was grateful for the rest but did not credit it to their captors. Resentment and bitter hatred for the savages ate like acid through his veins.

Since then they had loped down the path in a steady rhythm without pausing, the warriors occasionally calling out to one another or jabbering in their unintelligible language among themselves, while shadows gradually lengthened beneath the trees.

Until now Joseph had paid little attention to their conversation, which sounded like gibberish to him. But during the course of the day he had taken note that often when the others talked to his guard, they repeated the word *Shingas*. Now it occurred to him that this must be the man's name.

Watching his interactions with the other warriors, Joseph concluded that Shingas must be the leader of the war party. The respect the others paid him made it clear that he was a great warrior who held considerable power among his people.

And he controlled whether the three of them lived or died.

With the realization, jumbled, confusing emotions possessed Joseph, a wave of panic and grief so intense that he gasped for air, terrified he was going to suffocate. Instinctively he looked for Daat and caught a glimpse of his shaven, red-streaked head, bobbing with each step, at the front of the main body of warriors.

The sight brought immediate comfort and a measure of reassurance that he was not alone. He threw a quick glance over his shoulder, searching for Christian as well, let out a sigh of relief to see him still at the rear of the running warriors.

All day his little brother's guard had alternately led him by the hand or carried him on his back. For that Joseph was grateful, knowing that Christian would surely have given out and been killed long before without the man's help.

At the same time, the unfairness of the favor bestowed on his brother, while Joseph continued to suffer, fueled anger. More than once he had seen the two talking as if they were friends. He had heard Christian laugh. Although his little brother's voice sounded high and strained, even the pretense of cheerfulness seemed to Joseph an almost unforgiveable disloyalty.

Ever since their encounter with the patrol the previous day, thoughts of escape had crowded his consciousness. They had not yet traveled so far that finding their way home would be impossible—certainly not for Daat. The urgency of acting before the distance became too great continually nagged at him.

How to get away from their captors without being discovered was the puzzle. Every idea that occurred to him ran up against reality. Not only were the three of them too weak and weary to go very far or fast, but also their time together was rigorously limited, making it impossible to form a plan that might succeed.

At sunset they passed over another mountain by an easy grade. When they reached the valley floor beyond, to Joseph's intense relief the party turned off the path to a cluster of roomy lean-tos like the ones they frequently passed. In moments the advance and rear guards rejoined them.

Shingas threw his pack into a corner of one of the shelters and unceremoniously shoved Joseph inside. From the warrior's fierce commands and vehement gestures, Joseph inferred that he admonished him to stay there.

As soon as Shingas left, Joseph sat down cross-legged on the springy hemlock branches that covered the dirt floor. They were dried out and prickly but a comparative luxury after the previous night spent on the cold, rocky ground.

He leaned his back against the rear lean-to wall, his stomach burning with hunger, and watched small groups of warriors set up camp or head out to stand guard. Night had fallen, but he struggled to stay alert, the temptation to crawl stealthily out of the shelter and away into the darkness shortening his breath and causing his heart to pound. If only he could signal to Daat and Christian without alerting any of the warriors.

His eyes insisted on drifting closed, however, and his muscles refused to obey the insistent impulse of his mind. When Daat suddenly appeared in the shelter's opening, he jerked upright, clammy with sweat in spite of the cool air.

Daat held out a peach. "You're all right?"

Joseph nodded and took the fruit. He directed a meaningful glance at his father's guard, hovering behind his shoulder, then back to Daat.

Daat answered with a grimace and a slight, weary shake of his head. At a sharp command from his guard, he backed out of the shelter and followed the man out of sight. Hunger pains forgotten, Joseph stared after them, disappointment clogging his throat.

He focused on two warriors who were building a small, smokeless fire beneath a tree across from him, while their companions passed back and forth, laughing and talking boisterously. Christian was nowhere to be seen—probably in one of the other shelters, Joseph reasoned. There was no way to get to him or Daat without attracting notice.

After several minutes Shingas returned. He thrust a small piece of dried meat into Joseph's hand, then knotted a rawhide thong around his neck and securely tethered him to one of the lean-to's sturdy posts. Again he left Joseph alone.

Hunger forced Joseph to chew and swallow the food, but it seemed dry as dust in his mouth. It did little to relieve the pain that gripped his stomach and nothing to ease the despair that tore at his heart.

He finally lay down and with some effort adjusted the thong around his neck until he could rest in reasonable comfort. For the next hour he dozed intermittently but again jerked awake when Shingas returned.

The warrior wrapped himself in his blanket and lay down next to Joseph with his back to him. Joseph pushed tight against the stripped branches that formed the shelter's walls, putting as much distance between the two of them as was possible in the constricted space.

Several others soon crowded in with their packs. The lean-to, which had at first seemed generous, now felt cramped and the sour smell of sweat hung heavy on the air.

Silence descended over the camp. The night deepened, the darkness relieved only by the dying fire's faint flicker and the muted beams of moonlight filtering through the hazy eastern treetops. Gradually the damp wind turned keen.

Lacking any covering, Joseph was soon chilled by the cold air that seeped through the cracks in the walls. He began to shiver, at length reluctantly eased back against Shingas, seeking the heat of his guard's body. He froze when the warrior suddenly rolled over and spread his blanket over him.

For a long time Joseph lay motionless, vainly trying to fit this act of kindness into the memory of the warrior's cruelly driving his knife into Maam's breast. They were impossible to reconcile.

No sooner had he given up the attempt to understand what was incomprehensible than a host of other questions rushed into his thoughts. *Where are they taking us? How much longer before we get there? What's going to happen to us?*

He tried to swallow, but his mouth had gone dry. He had a feeling that he did not want to know the answers. The farther they were driven into territory controlled by the Indians, the smaller and more vulnerable he felt and the more intense his fear became.

He had watched his father be cowed and humiliated by the Indians. If Daat had been too weak to save his family from destruction and keep the three of them from being taken captive then, what could he do now when their captors held complete power?

And what of God? All his life Joseph had been told to trust the Almighty. But God had not shown up. He had not chosen to protect them in their hour of greatest need.

The devastating revelation struck Joseph hard: He and Christian had no protector in this hostile camp. Certainly they could never trust Shingas even if he acted kindly. At any time, for any reason, he might kill all three of them as mercilessly as he had Maam.

Everything Joseph had believed true had betrayed him. Curled under his guard's blanket, his knees hugged to his chest, he stared into the darkness.

He felt lost, abandoned all alone in a trackless wilderness.

Chapter Eighteen

Thursday, September 22, 1757

JOHANNES LEANED against the jamb of the open door, staring bleakly out at the misty rain puddling in the kitchen yard.

"Looks like Crist and I won't be helping his brothers cut corn today."

"I don't imagine." Katie sighed and looked up from the dough she was kneading on the *Küche* table. "It rained all night, and I expect it's going to rain for most of the day too. It almost feels like the whole world is crying."

Johannes glanced quickly back at her over his shoulder before returning his attention to the rain, absently tugging on his beard. He stopped abruptly, remembering that his father had often done the same. He swallowed hard and folded his arms over his chest.

"All this rain will set us back on harvesting the corn. And I have to do another cutting of hay yet if we're going to have enough to get two of our cows through the winter. I didn't plan on butchering more than one this fall."

"Winter's going to be here before we know it, and there's still so much to do, especially with all your Daat's crops gone . . . " Katie's voice trailed off.

The sound of young Jacob and John playing on the hearth seemed to echo in the silence. When Johannes turned around Jacob ran to clutch his leg.

He looked up, his brow furrowed. "Daati, are the Indians going to burn our house and kill us too?"

Johannes heard the sharp intake of Katie's breath and bent to lift his little son in his arms. Tenderly he brushed the hair back from the child's flushed face.

"*Gott* will take care of us, *ya?*"

Jacob clutched Johannes tightly. Burying his face against Johannes's neck, he whispered, "He didn't take care of *Grossmaami* and *Grossdaati*."

Johannes met Katie's gaze. "How do you explain such things to little ones?" Her voice was plaintive, and she gathered John against her petticoats.

Hearing the sound of approaching hoof beats, Johannes set Jacob down. "Everything's going to be all right." With a pat on the boy's bottom, he shooed him back to his younger brother.

He straightened and looked out the door. Several riders crossed the barnyard and pulled to a halt in front of the house, buckskins and horses darkly slick from the rain. When Johannes stepped outside, the lead rider touched his drooping hat brim in greeting, releasing a shower onto his shoulders.

"*Herr* Hochstetler?" It was Colonel Weiser.

As the soldiers dismounted, anxiety constricted Johannes's chest. "You bring word of my Daat and brothers?"

Weiser shook his head before gesturing to the young man at his side. "This is my son Samuel. May we speak to you for a moment?"

"*Ya,* please come inside. Your men are welcome to take the horses to the barn while we talk."

Weiser dismissed the men, then accompanied his son and Johannes into the house. Katie hurriedly covered the bowl of dough with a cloth and sent the children to play upstairs.

"Can I bring you some cider?" she asked, wiping her hands on her apron.

"*Danke, Frau* Hochstetler." Weiser gave her a weary smile. "We've been in the saddle since before dawn."

When the men were seated at the table with tankards of cider in front of them, Katie filled one for Johannes. He reached for it, then pushed it away, his hand shaking.

She bit her lip and whisked the tankard away. At their guests' questioning look, she faltered, "We made it at his Daat's place from their apples . . . the day before . . . before the attack."

Samuel's mouth tightened. "We were sorry to hear of it."

Weiser leaned back in his chair, his expression sober. "Early this morning we met with the patrol that stopped by here the evening of the attack. Sergeant Hardt said they rode up to the place where your friend *Herr* Mueller was shot and stopped to talk to him, too. He couldn't tell them much.

"Yesterday they rode over to Bethel and followed the Tulpehocken Path up through the gap over the mountain. They found where the war party came back onto the path. Hardt sent a detachment back to where they came down off the mountain, while he led the rest of his men farther up the Tulpehocken."

Johannes leaned forward, his eyes fixed on the colonel. "Did they find . . . anything?"

"If you mean bodies, no."

Johannes let out his breath and covered his face with his hands. "It's been in my mind that—"

"I understand."

"Hardt's party found one set of footprints on the other side of Broad Mountain that belonged to a child," Samuel said.

"Cristli!"

Samuel frowned. "We can't be sure of that, *Frau* Hochstetler. Two of the Specht children were also taken. They may have passed that way, too, though it's less likely."

Katie pulled out a chair and sat down across from him. "But if they found no bodies, that means they must all be alive yet, *ya?*"

"They made it at least as far as Sergeant Hardt went," Weiser agreed.

Staring down at the table, Johannes ran his fingers through his hair. "Where will they take them?"

"No way to tell. The Tulpehocken goes to Shamokin—Fort Augusta now. My guess is they'll follow the path as far as the Susquehanna. They won't go near the fort, so they'll probably cross the river at the ford, then head west to one of the French forts."

Thoughtfully Samuel stroked his chin. "They might go as far as Fort du Quesne over on the Ohio or maybe head north to Lake Erie."

Johannes felt chilled. He got to his feet and went to the hearth to stir up the fire.

"What'll happen when they get to wherever they're going?"

Samuel exchanged a glance with his father. "According to captives who've managed to escape, the French either divide the prisoners up among the tribes or send them up into Canada to be adopted by families there."

Katie gasped. "Canada! So far?"

"Sometimes. But it's most likely they'll give them to one of the local tribes."

Johannes stared into the fire without seeing it, his hand clenched over the poker. "Will they keep Daat and the boys together?"

"Captives are always separated," Weiser said. "That way they're less likely to try to escape. And if they're adopted into an Indian family, they'll get used to their new life more easily."

Johannes returned to his chair and sat, elbows propped on the table, his head in his hands. "Is there any way you can find them? We'd pay a ransom to get them back. I've heard of people doing that."

"The Indians aren't likely to negotiate the return of any captives while the war is still going on." Weiser's tone held sympathy—and a note of finality.

"It might be possible after the war," Samuel interjected.

Weiser glanced at his son and nodded. "If the French lose the war, you can petition the governor. While they're negotiating a treaty he'll be able to put pressure on the Indians to return their captives." He swallowed the last of his cider and set down his tankard. "Until then, you'll have to be patient—and pray that we win."

Lines of worry creased Katie's forehead. "Like everybody else, we're worried about staying here, but we don't know where we can go. We can't afford to just leave everything behind like some others have. Do you think the Indians are likely to attack here again?"

Weiser crossed his arms and rubbed his chin. "They probably won't come back for a while because everyone is on the alert now. I've increased the patrols as much as I can with the governor sending so many of my men up to Fort Augusta. But unless we get more troops out here, sooner or later there are going to be more attacks."

Shaking his head, he growled, "If you Amish won't defend yourselves—"

They all jumped when Johannes brought his fist down hard on the table. Standing up so abruptly that his chair almost toppled backward, he said fiercely, *"Nay!* We've always kept good relations with our Delaware neighbors. This attack happened not because we Amish keep the peace and refuse to be dragged into your fight. This attack happened because *die Englishe* insist on taking land the French claim, and the French incite the Indians to evil deeds to stop them." He jabbed his finger at his guests. "That's why *you* are at war—over land that belongs to the Indians!"

Weiser's jaw hardened and he stood, meeting Johannes's glare with a stern look. "I can't dispute what you say, *Herr* Hochstetler. But you and your people chose to come to this country and settle on land that is under contention. And as long as you stay here, you too will suffer the effects of this war."

❦ — ❦

DRENCHED THROUGH, Jakob shivered in the cold rain as he stared at the war party they had overtaken moments earlier.

There were eighteen of them, mainly Shawnee. With them were the three French scouts who had directed the attack against his plantation.

And three captives: a man and two young children.

They looked even more bedraggled, worn out, and terrified than Jakob felt. He saw that Joseph and Christian stared at them, too, openmouthed.

It was perhaps a couple of hours yet to sundown, but with the sky obscured by dark clouds and the steady drizzle, daylight was rapidly failing. Jakob weighed his pouch in his aching hands, thinking how much lighter it felt than three days earlier, when he and the boys had filled it with peaches.

These new captives had nothing with them. The children were hollow-eyed, their cheeks sunken. The man had obviously been beaten; his face, arms, and legs were bruised and scraped, his torn clothing streaked with blood.

Roughly they were prodded together in the combined party's center. The leaders moved a short distance off the path to confer in low tones with the French scouts.

Christian tugged at Jakob's hand and directed an imploring gaze up at him. "Daati, are they going to kill us now?" His voice quavered.

Jakob pulled the boy tight against him, and Joseph leaned into his other side. "What's going to happen to us, Daat?"

"Don't worry," Jakob murmured, his wary gaze on their guards. "*Gott* is yet with us." His words sounded hollow to his ears.

The other man drew closer, tightly gripping his children's hands. "Didn't I see you at Fort Northkill last year? You're one of the Amish."

Jakob studied him, frowning. "*Ya,* I remember. You were talking with another man."

"I'm Michael Specht, but my friends call me Hans. These are my *Kinder,* Franz and Hannah."

Jakob judged the children to be about six and eight years old. They stared blank-eyed at Christian and Joseph, their expressions unreadable.

What horrors have these little ones endured? Jakob's heart contracted painfully.

He introduced himself in turn, and he and Specht shared brief accounts of the attacks in which they had been taken, the family members they had lost. How many other families had been attacked on the same day? Jakob wondered, pleading silently, *Please, Gott, keep Johannes and Barbara and their families safe.*

Specht gazed vacantly down the path ahead of them. "I had a map of this area, and I speak enough of the Delaware tongue to understand most of what they're saying. We're close to the Susquehanna—maybe only a couple miles away."

"Fort Augusta's not far north." Shoulders drooping, Jakob added, "I doubt they'll take us anywhere close to it though."

They fell silent, both studying the warriors clustered around the scouts. Before they could speak again, the group broke apart. They were soon separated by their guards and moving rapidly down the path, the Frenchmen in the lead.

Jakob judged that they had traveled no farther than two more miles when he heard the rush of water ahead of them. Shortly they emerged from the forest onto the bank of a wide river. Here the water was shallow, broken by rocks and sandbars. They were quickly driven across to the far bank.

Another path hugged the riverbank, and they turned onto it to follow the river's course north for several miles. It was full dark when they finally left the path to make camp at the base of a rocky outcrop concealed by a dense stand of trees, and the clouds had blown away to the east, revealing diamond starpoints scattered in the black sky high overhead.

The captives were shoved together beneath a spreading oak, with guards stationed around them, muskets in hand. The rest of the warriors gathered around several large fires, drinking eagerly from the bottles the Frenchmen handed around. Soon they were dancing and shouting in fierce jubilance.

His heart pounding, Jakob huddled with the others, all of them keeping an uneasy eye on the carousing warriors. But other than throwing the usual share of pemmican and parched corn at their feet, their captors paid no further attention to them.

Jakob divided the food among them, noting that Specht and his children appeared even more famished than he and his boys. The meager allotment of food did little to revive any of them.

When Joseph and Christian looked hopefully at him after gulping down their portion, Jakob's heart sank. They could not eat the fruit and withhold it from the others. Ordinarily he would have been more than willing to share, but their supply was dwindling too quickly, and he had no idea how long a journey still lay before them.

The remaining fruit was growing soft, however. He reminded himself that the small store would not last much longer at any rate, and that it was on God they depended for provision. He opened the pouch.

As he handed out a peach to each of them, the children's eyes grew large. "*Danke,*" they whispered, accepting the fruit with wonder. They consumed their portion in moments as though it was the only food they had eaten in weeks.

While Jakob and his boys finished their peaches, Specht shared bites of his with his children. When it was all gone, Franz and Hannah licked their sticky fingers and eyed the pouch with longing.

"Thank you for sharing your peaches," Specht said humbly. "I'm sorry to take them from you, but we've had almost nothing to eat, and the children—"

Jakob dismissed his words with a quick wave of his hand. "We have to help each other if we're to survive."

Specht bent his head, tears leaving muddy tracks through the dirt that streaked his cheeks. "If we can only find opportunity to escape—"

"Impossible with the children. Too dangerous to try."

The sudden reappearance of their guards cut off Jakob's terse words, and he became aware that the drinking and dancing had died away. Several warriors wrenched the Spechts to their feet and led them out of sight. Dazed and numb, Jakob had no chance to bid his boys goodnight as they also were hurried away.

Jakob's guard tied him tightly to the oak's trunk before wrapping his blanket around him and curling up on a drift of leaves a short distance away. Within minutes the warrior was snoring.

Seated on the cold ground with his arms tied behind him, Jakob could find no comfortable position, and he suppressed a groan. In the cold wind his wet clothing clung to his body like an icy shroud, and he began to shiver uncontrollably. Despairing, he gazed up through the overhanging branches to the stars shimmering in the black night sky.

"*Danke, Vater,* that tonight I can sit instead of stand," he whispered, feeling as though his words fell to the ground instead of ascending to heavenly realms.

"*Danke* that the Indians have let me be," he said more firmly. "*Danke* for the ones you have brought alongside that we may help one another. Be with them and my boys that they may rest this night. *Danke* for Your provision for each day. *Danke* that You go before us."

With each word he fought back the hopelessness that sapped his courage. And by imperceptible degrees something akin to peace descended over him like a covering against cold and hunger and fear. At length he slept.

Chapter Nineteen

Friday, September 23, 1757

A DEAFENING CLAMOR greeted them as they approached the village. "They're calling it Shikellamy's Town," Specht muttered to Jakob on overhearing the warriors' conversation.

The Frenchmen strode ahead and disappeared into the crowd, while the warriors followed more slowly. Each one carried before him with great ceremony a long pole from which hung the scalps he had taken in the raids. Nauseated, Jakob averted his eyes, knowing that among them were those of his wife, son, and little daughter.

The warriors called out a warbling halloo for every scalp or prisoner they had taken, following the last with a series of shrieks that Jakob assumed expressed joy at their victory. In answer the villagers fired muskets into the air, shouting with equal glee as they raced to meet the approaching party.

Early that morning they had passed Fort Augusta, out of reach on the Susquehanna's eastern bank. The warriors kept to the forest's cover and enforced strict silence until the party was well beyond the rivers' confluence and moving rapidly up its western branch. Between the trees Jakob had only caught brief glimpses of the fort's palisade, the flash of red coats and glint of musket barrels atop its walls, a patrol leaving its gates and riding south.

They had passed by so heartbreakingly close, yet they might as well have been on the moon.

Jakob shrank from the crowd that pressed in on them and stared down the double file of townspeople beginning to form, snaking all the way from the village boundary to the large, bark-covered longhouse at its center. Elders and matrons, youths, even toddlers wielded clubs cut from tree limbs, switches of thorny brambles, rocks, handfuls of dirt—any weapon that fell to hand. With hostile gazes fixed on the filthy, footsore captives, they chanted and danced in frenzied anticipation, voices raised to a jubilant roar.

"The British call this running the gauntlet!" Specht shouted to him over the tumult, sweat pouring down his face in rivulets blood red from the fresh paint the warriors had applied to their heads early that morning. "They'll make us pass through their lines while they beat us. Those who get to their council house will be spared. Those who don't will be . . . " he gulped, then concluded, "beaten to death."

Emotions roiling, Jakob watched as two warriors grasped Specht's arms and propelled him toward the head of the line, while he vainly struggled to get to his terrified children. As he had innumerable times since they were carried away, Jakob glanced around for sight of his sons, panic surging through him with such force that his legs could hardly bear him up.

He doubted that Specht could make it to the longhouse, knew certainly that his two young children, now sobbing convulsively, would not. Jakob also was dangerously close to dropping in his tracks. Every muscle, joint, and bone ached from the forced march they had endured the past four days. Added to these rigors, the unaccustomed, unvarying diet of pemmican, parched corn, and peaches had given them all cramps, sapping the little reserves of strength they had left.

If I die, it's of little account, he thought. *All that matters now is that my boys live.*

But pressing against him, Joseph looked as exhausted and ragged as Jakob felt, while Christian huddled on his other side, gaunt and hollow eyed.

Of the three of them, the eleven-year-old had fared as well as could be expected. His guard carried him on his back when he could go no farther and attended to him almost as a father. Yet daily the boy grew noticeably more weak and wan.

Before they had left camp that morning, his guard had painted the boy's face in stripes of bright colors to match his own, then gathered his hair in a topknot into which he stuck feathers, all the while joking and making much of him. When he caught his reflection in the stream, Christian had looked in appeal to Jakob and cried, "Are we Indians now, Daati? Are we going to be Indians?"

Seeing the mixture of hope, fear, and confusion in his face, Jakob had come very close to weeping. The thought that there was nothing he could do to succor or protect his children tormented him, but he knew that if they were to live, they had to gain their captors' favor. "*Ya,* I guess we have to be Indians for a while," he had called back encouragingly, nodding and forcing a laugh.

Christian began to laugh, too, the sound high and strained. Although they didn't understand their captives' German language, this interplay had seemed to delight the warriors, who joined in their mirth while pointing from one to the other.

Only Joseph had not entered into their humor. His face stony, he had turned his back and stared off down the path.

By now the raucous crowd had pressed the captives into a tight circle. They were being thrust inexorably forward to the head of the long column. If they were going to live, one of them would have to do something, and quickly, Jakob realized.

Trying desperately to think, he shifted his pouch to a more comfortable position. As he did so, he caught sight of a tall, imposing man with an air of authority standing with the scouts a short distance away at the head of the gauntlet. From his ceremonial dress, Jakob guessed him to be the town's sachem, and the companions who surrounded him and the Frenchmen were also clearly leading men of the town.

Jakob clasped his boys by the shoulders. "Come, let us go talk to the sachem," he rasped, mouth dry. "It may be that *Gott* will give us favor before him."

Both boys nodded dumbly, clearly too frightened to protest, and Jakob summoned his waning courage. He placed them in front of him, encircled by his arms. At his urging, they dodged around their guards and wove their way through the crowd, moving as one, while ignoring the shouts, shoves, and threatening gestures directed at them.

They were drenched with sweat and smeared with dust by the time they broke through to where the sachem stood with his companions. Stiffening, the man glowered at them through dark, hostile eyes.

With his boys on either side, all three of them trembling, Jakob swung his pouch from his shoulder and set it gently on the dusty ground. Moving deliberately in hope of avoiding a blow, he squatted and opened it to expose the fruit inside, then rose with a ripe, fragrant peach in each hand.

He made a humble bow and extended the fruit to the sachem, motioning to him and his companions to take the pouch. "*Nchutièstuk,*" he said in Delaware, then in French, "*Pax, amis.* We make you this gift."

Behind them, the crowd had quieted. The sachem appeared startled, looking from the peaches to Jakob, then to Joseph and Christian in turn. At last his stance relaxed. Eyes still narrowed, he warily accepted one of the peaches.

He took a bite and juice ran down his chin and hand. A broad smile replaced his scowl. He turned to his companions and with a regal gesture motioned for them to take the fruit Jakob offered.

Each of the town's leaders accepted a peach and frowns quickly turned to nods of approval. The men clustered together, conferring in a guttural language Jakob could not understand.

Your will, O Lord, he breathed. *Your will, not mine. Only keep us in the shadow of Your wings no matter what befalls.*

After several moments the sachem gave an order. Jakob could not understand his words, but his companions began moving among the gathered villagers. Grudgingly they trickled off to their wigewas, some directing scowls toward the captives.

Jakob had no time to ponder this success. Their guards quickly surrounded him and the boys, while others shoved Specht and his children into the circle. They were led to the longhouse and thrust inside with a guard stationed at the door.

As soon as they were alone, Specht grabbed Jakob by the arm. "What courage! We'd all be dead if you hadn't acted so quickly."

Jakob stared at him, dazed. "*Gott* gave us favor."

"Then I thank God your party joined ours!" Squatting, Specht gathered his young son and daughter in his arms.

"He is good." Jakob blinked back sudden tears.

"If that's so, then why did He let this happen to us?" Joseph demanded, his voice shaking with anger. "How can you say He's good when He let Maam and Jake and Annali be killed? How are we supposed to believe He'll keep us safe when He didn't protect them?"

Jakob regarded him earnestly, reading his own pain and inability to understand in his son's face. "I don't know the answer, Joseph," he said finally. "I know only that *Gott* can bring good even out of evil when His people are faithful."

Joseph snorted and waved his arm at Christian. "Maybe that's so, but are we supposed to make friends with murderers—like Christli is?"

Christian hung his head. "He carries me when I'm tired and even shares some of his food with me."

"*Ya,* and I saw you give him some of your peach this morning, too, laughing and joking like he's your best friend."

"But he's nice to me, and if I'm mean back, he might . . . " Christian covered his face with his hands and began to wail, his shoulders shaking with sobs.

Jakob grabbed both boys and pulled them roughly to him, fighting his own tears. "*Nay,* do what you have to do to live! If we agree with them for now, we might gain their trust and kind treatment like today. And maybe, if it's *Gott's* will, a way of escape."

❖ • • • • ❖

"COLONEL WEISER DIDN'T SAY we should pull out, though?" Barbara threw an apprehensive glance from Johannes and Katie to Crist.

Johannes folded his arms. "He didn't think the Indians would attack here again as long as the militia is patrolling the area and everyone's on the alert."

"Winter's coming on too," Christian Beiler pointed out, his reedy voice hopeful. "Once the snows hit, it's not likely they'll travel this far."

Melchoir Detweiler leaned forward in his seat and grasped the back of Johannes's chair. "Then maybe we don't have to decide right away. It'll be hard to move out so close to winter. *Gott* willing, we'll have peace till next spring, then if there are more attacks, each family can decide what's best for them, *ya?*"

Beside him, Hans Gnaegi rubbed his forehead, his expression skeptical. "Most of you know that a couple of our young families are selling off their livestock and moving to Cumru Township to stay with friends for the winter. They're not sure if they'll come back or move down to Lancaster. I talked to a few others who are also thinking about moving out."

Bessie Kurtz's face flushed. "How long does Weiser mean to keep patrols out? Now that they pulled out of Fort Northkill, I wonder how serious he is about protecting us."

"He's low on men," Johannes explained. "The governor ordered him to send so many troops to Fort Augusta that those left are spread too thin to do much good."

Standing at the front of the church members gathered in his *Stube*, Bishop Hertzler held up his hand. "It's not on the power of men we depend for our protection, but on the power of *Gott*."

Barbara felt Crist take her hand in his, and clung to it, a veil of pain blurring her sight.

"We hear of many who take up weapons against their attackers, yet they and their families are killed anyway," the bishop continued. "So many of our people have endured serious testing. We can't expect that we won't. We're called to be faithful no matter what trials we face."

"Maam and Daat talked so often about how they knew *Gott* called them to this land as a witness to His faithfulness, and how they trusted him to protect them and us *Kinder*." Barbara stared down at her hands clenched in her lap. "Crist and I have wept and talked and beseeched the Lord for His guidance . . . " She stopped, unable to continue.

Crist's fingers tightened over hers. "We feel the Lord's leading to stay and trust that He'll watch over us and our children too."

"I can't bear the thought that Daat and the boys might yet get away and come back, and us not be here to welcome them home. I'm afraid for us and our children, *ya*. I can't believe that any good thing can ever come out of the evil that happened to Maam and Daat and my brothers and sister. But . . . I want to learn to trust Him more."

For some moments no one spoke. The only sounds in the room were sniffles and the clearing of a throat here and there.

Bishop Hertzler reached out to his wife. Although her expression reflected fear, she rose and placed her hand in his with a firm nod. He turned back to face the gathering.

"Katherine and I have talked and prayed over this, too, and we feel the Lord's calling to stay as long as any members of the church remain. We trust that He who led us to this place is able also to care for us according to His will and purpose."

Johannes had been listening with his arms propped on his knees, hands clasped between them, head bent. Now he straightened to look around the room and meet each eye, his expression earnest.

"Katie and I decided that we'll stay too. *Gott* planted us here, and until He leads us somewhere else, this is our home."

The tense atmosphere in the room eased. And one by one, the other couples who had gathered also made their commitment to stay in the place where God had called them.

◆———◆

FOR THE REST OF THAT DAY, Jakob, his boys, and the Spechts were treated with a friendly kindness, though their individual guards were never far from their sides. They sat with the townspeople at the evening meal, feasting on succulent corn, beans, and squash stewed with bear meat and turkey, and felt a measure of strength return.

Afterward they were allowed to linger and watch the nightly dances, and when the night wind turned chilly, they were given blankets to wrap around them in the fashion of the Indians. To Jakob's disappointment, however, they were still separated for the night.

As he and his guard sat together at a small fire outside the wigewa where they would sleep, he could no longer stifle the question that had haunted him since the attack. Gathering courage, he pointed to the east where they had come from. He pretended to shoot a gun, then gestured from himself to the warrior.

In a halting mixture of English and French he asked, "If we shoot, what you do?"

His dark eyes glittering, the warrior raised his hands horizontally in front of him, palms pressed together crosswise. In a quick, contemptuous motion, he swept his upper hand across the lower, away from him.

There was no need for words. Jakob bent his head, dull pain settling in his chest.

It was as he had feared. Firing on the war party would have incited their attackers to even greater violence.

And all of them would have been killed.

Chapter Twenty

T HE CAPTIVES WERE ROUSED at first light and herded together while the war party prepared to leave. While Jakob fumbled to secure his blanket around his shoulders as the warriors did, he noted that the Frenchmen were nowhere in sight. Had they gone to lead raids on more helpless victims? The thought oppressed him.

Now that he was no longer burdened with the peaches, the warriors from the second war party loaded him with a heavy bundle of plunder. Bowed beneath its weight, he shuffled over to where his guard waited, worry again clenching his chest.

Where are we bound now? How far have we to go—and how long can I endure under this burden? What will we do for food now that I gave all the peaches away?

He counted the days since the attack and realized with a shock that it was Sunday. Would the church gather this morning, or had the entire community been destroyed in the raid? He prayed that it had not, that today as for countless years his people would raise their voices in praise and thanksgiving in spite of the trials they suffered. The longing to join his friends and neighbors in worship weighed on him as heavily as the physical burden he carried.

He felt his guard's impatient prod and strode forward, head bowed, staring bleakly at the ground. They passed out of the village, skirting a refuse heap where growling dogs fought over scattered offal.

A handful of discarded peach pits lying amid the scraps caught Jakob's eye. For a suspended moment he stared at them, struck forcibly by the thought that these peaches had spared him, his sons, and their fellow captives a beating, perhaps even death. They were the last connection to home and to those he had lost.

While he hesitated, the leading warriors broke into a run. He knew that he dared not linger, and on impulse he bent and scooped up one of the pits as he passed. His guard eyed him through narrowed eyes but made no move to stop him, and Jakob hastily straightened and resumed his stride.

Clutched tightly in his hand, the pit's rough edges bit into his palm. He loped down the well-trodden path that lay before him, strangely comforted.

They left the scattered wigewas of Shickellamy's Town behind, moving rapidly north along the Susquehanna's western branch as they followed the sun's path inexorably toward the place of its setting.

❖┄┄┄❖

BARBARA POKED at the food on her plate with her fork, unable to choke down another bite. She threw a covert glance at the church members who crowded the *Küche* of Uncle Jakob's house to share in the simple meal that followed the Sunday morning service.

As she had been during worship, she was again struck by everyone's somber expression. Even the youngest children seemed subdued, and many clung to their parents.

Anna Blanck leaned close, her pretty face puckered with distress. "Daat says that Bishop Hertzler is right and we can't go asking the militia to do what we believe is wrong. But how can we just abandon them—not even try to find them until the end of the war? Who knows how long it's going to last yet or what your Daat and brothers are suffering!"

When Barbara looked down, blinking back tears, Anna bit her lip and gently touched Barbara's arm. "Ach, forgive me! I didn't mean to make it worse for you—"

"You couldn't. It's already as bad as it can be. I keep thinking the same as you, but I don't know what we—or the militia either—can do."

Barbara shared what Colonel Weiser had told Johannes and Katie several days earlier, adding, "By now they've got to be far into French territory. Unless the British win this war and force the Indians to turn over their captives, it looks like all we can do is pray and trust the Lord. Like the bishop said, that's much, though I admit it doesn't feel like it right now."

Anna pushed her plate back and rested her elbow on the table. "You aren't going to move away like some of the other families, are you?"

Barbara looked up as Crist took a seat on the bench beside her. Returning his smile, she patted his knee and said, "*Nay*. We had a meeting with the church and most of us feel like *Gott* is calling us to stay here."

She gave Anna an affectionate glance. "I'm so glad you and your family came to church with us today. Your Maam and Daat were so close to mine for so many years that . . . " She stopped and dabbed her eyes with her kerchief. "When we're together it seems like they're closer."

Anna gave her a quick hug, releasing her when Johannes and Katie came to sit with them. Johannes repeated Barbara's appreciation of the Blancks' presence and added, "I know you're concerned about Joseph. He never told us about his feelings, but we all saw how he looked at you . . . how he acted when you were around."

Katie reached to take Anna's hand. "He never could hide how much he cared for you."

Anna ducked her head, warmth rising to her cheeks as tears welled into her eyes. "Thank you," she whispered. "I felt it too, but I was afraid maybe I was wrong."

Barbara gave a soft laugh. "You weren't."

Across the room Anna's parents had been engaged in conversation with several others in front of the blazing hearth. Now they excused themselves and drifted over.

Dr. Blanck placed his hand on Johannes's shoulder and gave all of them a kindly look. "Anytime we can help you out, please let us know. We're not so far away than we can't come over, and we'll do anything we can."

"Your Maam was the best friend anybody could ever have," Mattie broke in, her lips trembling. "I'm going to miss her all my days."

Barbara rose to embrace the older woman, while the others gathered around. For some moments they clung together, unable to speak.

After they all sat down, Anna said, "Has anyone talked to others around here who've had people from their family carried away? Maybe they learned something that would give us an idea of where your Daat and the boys might be taken."

Johannes gave her a keen look. "I hadn't thought about doing that, but it's a good idea." He turned to Barbara and Crist. "Several of *die Englishe* who stopped by after the attack told us a little about what happened to their families."

"*Ya,* we had a couple come by the house too. We could tell they wanted to talk more, but—"

Catching Crist's gaze, Barbara said, "It felt like they didn't want to add to our burdens. And they had plenty of their own to carry for sure."

"The families around here might know others who've gone through the same thing," Katie pointed out. "And if I know Maam and Daat, they'll think it's good for us to reach out to others who are hurting. We're called to be good neighbors, and maybe we can find ways to help them and be a good witness."

Johannes glanced over his shoulder to scan the crowded room. "I'd sure feel a whole lot better if we can do something to help others instead of just sitting here. Let Katie and me talk to her folks, and then we'll get together and work out how to go about doing this."

When all of them eagerly agreed, Dr. Blanck pulled Mattie aside. They talked for several moments before taking seats on the bench on either side of their daughter.

"Anna, your Maam and I feel that you're not needed so much at home now that your brother and sisters are old enough to do more of the chores. Barbara and Katie going to need help with their Kinder, especially with new babies coming along—"

Anna clasped her hands, her face glowing. "Ach, *ya,* I'd be ever so glad to help out with the little ones!"

It took little discussion for everyone to agree to Barbara and Crist's suggestion that Anna come live with them and divide her time between their household and Johannes and Katie's as needed. It was by now growing late, and they had no sooner made the necessary arrangements than Katrina, Mary, and Maudlin joined them, bringing the children, already bundled against the chilly day.

Amid a bustle of movement and talk, families began to take their leave. Many again shared condolences, words of encouragement, and offers of practical help with Barbara and Johannes, which they gratefully received.

As Anna's parents prepared to leave, Barbara drew her aside. "You're so young yet, Anna, and I don't want you to get your hopes up. You know we may never find Daat and the boys."

She stopped, then continued firmly, "No matter how much you care about Joseph, you have to live your life. I know it's hard to think about it now, but don't tell yourself that you're going to wait forever."

Anna's expression softened, and she clasped Barbara by the shoulders. "I may be young, *ya,* but I've believed ever since I met Joseph that *Gott* meant us to be together. And unless He makes it plain that He has another plan for me, I'm going to keep on believing until the day he and Christli and your Daat come home. Deep in my heart, I feel they're going to."

Chapter Twenty-one

Monday, October 9, 1757

AT THE CREST OF THE RISE where the last trees fell away, Jakob came to an abrupt standstill. He stared at the fort atop a low bluff a quarter of a mile straight ahead, breath constricted. Instinct told him that their twenty-one days' journey had finally brought them to their destination, and his spirits sank.

The rest of the party had also stopped, the warriors squatting to pull brilliantly colored shirts, leggings, and silver ornaments from their packs. As was their custom before entering a town or fort, they arrayed themselves in their finest clothing and jewelry, painted their faces in bright colors, and dressed the top-knots of hair on their shaven skulls.

While they were thus occupied, Jakob wearily set down his burden and stretched in a vain effort to ease his aching back.

Specht took advantage of their guards' preoccupation to sidle over to him. "According to their talk, this fort's called *Presque Isle.* Means peninsula in French."

"There's one there, all right, Hans." Jakob surveyed the prospect that lay before them, his emotions as bleak as the windy, overcast day.

The stronghold overlooked the west bank of a creek that drained into a lake a few yards below it, where a wooded peninsula angled out to create a wide bay. Stout triangular bastions protruded at the four corners of a palisade higher and more imposing than those of the two forts their party had stopped the previous week. Judging by the soldiers who patrolled the ramparts and moved in and out of the gates, the garrison was also significantly larger.

Specht gestured toward the broad expanse of water visible outside the bay. "From the direction we've been traveling, that's got to be Lake Erie."

"How far you think we've come?"

Specht's gaunt, dirt-streaked face furrowed. "More'n 300 miles. A long way to make it back."

Jakob gave no response. A flutter of blue, red, and gold drew his eyes upward to where a white flag emblazoned with the ornate heraldic emblems of New France snapped in the wind above the fort's ramparts.

He transferred his gaze to the narrow, jutting arm that blocked the view of the lake. In the late-afternoon sunlight he could make out a haze of smoke from numerous campfires rising above the trees. The sight did nothing to encourage him.

Undoubtedly more soldiers stationed there, he thought. At the eastern entrance to the peninsula and on its western point, he glimpsed brick buildings that appeared to stand guard over the bay. *It'd be hard to escape from this place. No. Impossible.*

Unconsciously he scratched at the lice crawling in the folds of his ragged shirt, his attention turning to the Indian town on the creek's eastern bank, opposite the stockade. Arranged in no particular order, the hump-backed roofs of wigewas and long-houses shouldered up against ragged, dirty tents. The smoke of campfires drifted lazily upward from scattered fire circles.

Native men, women, and children in the varied dress of a multitude of tribes moved between the habitations, some entering or leaving the fort, others going down to canoes beached along the lakeshore or, newly arrived, striding up toward the town. On its outskirts he could see a cluster of white people in torn, dirty clothing huddled together under guard.

The sight made his heart hurt, and he hastily returned his scrutiny to the western bank. There squat log buildings large and small ranged along narrow lanes that radiated outward from the stockade. The broadest of these pathways led from the fort's gates up the rise to where he stood.

To his assessing eye many of the buildings appeared worn and ramshackle as though they had been hastily thrown up to provide temporary shelter and over time had become permanent. Here also people came and went on all sides: officers in white uniform coats and soldiers in blue; traders, trappers, and grizzled frontiersmen clad in buckskins; greasy-looking sutlers driving wagons or carrying loads. Moving among them he saw a couple of black-robed priests, a few women wearing fine gowns and others in coarse, dirty attire.

Specht's legs wobbled, and he sat down on Jakob's pack. "Beyond this water lies Canada. I reckon that's where these supplies come from. And where furs and other goods go from here."

Jakob followed the direction of his gaze to the canoes and bateaux drawn up along the lakeshore, some being loaded with bundles of goods, others swinging away into the current headed east. Yet more slipped through the narrow channel at the bay's entrance in a steady stream to find a landing place.

"From here they can portage supplies down to Fort Le Boeuf, then float them down French Creek and the Allegheny to Fort Du Quesne on the Ohio. You know that'll take them west all the way to the Mississippi."

Jakob gave Specht a sharp look. While rowing up French Creek from Fort Machault and during today's portage north from Fort Le Boeuf, they had encountered an even heavier traffic of Indians and French traders than before, many of the latter attended by native wives and children. Almost all the travelers carried bundles of furs, weapons, and other trading goods.

Jakob tugged at the neck of his shirt, hating the fetid stench of sweat and dirt embedded in the rotted fabric. His efforts to wash in the streams they crossed had done no more good than his prayers for an opportunity to escape.

"I heard some captives are taken all the way to Canada."

"Haven't heard them say anything about that." Specht leaned to catch the chatter of the warriors closest to them. "Sounds like this is where they've been bound all along. They're talking about who'll get us now . . . " He pressed his lips together in a thin line.

A heavy stone seemed to lodge in Jakob's chest. And he could tell by Specht's expression that he felt the same way.

THE LEAD WARRIORS finished their preening and began to move down the slope toward the fort. Specht hurried back to his place. Jakob sought his boys, held apart at the rear of the party with Specht's children, but caught only a brief glimpse of them before being prodded to move. He shouldered his pack and strode down the rise, pretending a confidence he was far from feeling.

Absently he ran his free hand over the lengthening growth on his head and jaw. Since leaving Shickellamy's Town, their captors had neglected to paint and shave their heads. It was a small change, but one that—with the exception of the unaccustomed growth on his upper lip—provided a surprising measure of comfort and normality amid this strange and hostile environment.

As he readjusted his burden with both hands, he pressed his elbow against the sash tied around his waist, reassured to feel the small lump where he had secreted the peach pit retrieved from the refuse heap. His gift of peaches to the sachem had resulted in better treatment not only for him and his boys, but for the Spechts as well. Except for a few of the fiercest members of the party who refused to be moved, the warriors had begun to accord them a grudging respect.

As long as they complied with their captors' commands, they had not been subjected to violent threats and mistreatment, and they traveled at an easier pace. They were still separated from one another while traveling and sleeping, but they were allowed to sit together while they ate, which did much to ease their anxiety.

The food rationed out to them had also improved significantly, making the rigors of the long journey easier to bear. At Indian towns along their route they had feasted on the natives' staple crops of corn, beans, and squash cooked with meat and greens. When they camped the party stopped early enough for the warriors to hunt, and they shared the roasted game equally with their prisoners.

These blessings had not included replacement of their badly worn garments, however. The Spechts' clothing had become so ragged and threadbare it hardly clung to their bodies. Jakob's shirt was badly stained, ripped here and there by thorns and brambles, while mud caked his leggings and moccasins, the soles of the latter worn through in places. And his boys were in as bad a state.

He longed for hot water and a bar of soap to wash the dirt and vermin from his skin and soothe the stinging insect bites on his arms and legs, but such things appeared to be foreign to the Indians. At least his blistered hands and feet had finally healed and the skin toughened, another blessing for which he was thankful.

North of Shickellamy's Town their path had veered away from the Susquehanna, curving to follow the river's course west, while remaining some miles south of it. After five days walk their path had again intersected the river at Great Island, an Indian town that occupied an island amid the stream.

There they had crossed at a ford to resume their journey along the river's northern bank, spending nights at Indian forts and French trading towns along their route until they reached the great trading center of Chinklacamoose. Quitting the Susquehanna, they had followed another long path that angled northwest into a flatter land of countless streams, low hills, and broad valleys. At last they reached a trading post called Wenango where French Creek flowed into a river Specht identified as the Allegheny.

A small French post called Fort Machault lay immediately above the town. At first Jakob concluded that they had reached their destination. But at daybreak the next morning they were loaded aboard several flat-bottomed boats the French called bateaux, along with the warriors and a small detachment of French soldiers.

He, Joseph, and Specht had been pressed to rowing and poling upstream with the other men. Keeping to the smoother, slower-moving water close to the river's bank, they passed low, rich bottomlands full of towering cypress trees and stretches of open woods by day, and at night camped along the creek's shore.

At the end of three days they had arrived at a second fort almost identical to the first. Fort Le Boeuf occupied commanding ground on the north side of a small branch of French Creek near a narrow, shallow lake. After spending the previous night there, early that morning they had left the bateaux behind and followed the portage to Presque Isle.

Each time exhaustion, fear, and the continual, nagging concern for his boys briefly eased, Jakob had thrilled to the vast breadth of the remarkable country they passed through. This wilderness, which seemed to stretch westward for endless miles beyond the far horizon, was rich and fertile, carved by unspoiled waterways from trickling creeks to roaring rivers and glimmering lakes, each overflowing with an abundance of fish.

Thick clouds of fowl in astounding variety often darkened the sky above them and filled the treetops, their melodious songs ringing in the crystal air. And below, the forests and sunny meadows were home to an equally staggering array of wildlife.

Several times they had skirted wide swaths of forest so densely overgrown with vegetation that sunlight could not penetrate to the ground. Specht had explained that these foreboding regions, commonly called swamps, were believed to be the habitation of evil spirits. Even the bravest warriors nervously avoided them, and more than once Jakob had felt a chill raise the hairs on his neck and arms while in their vicinity.

The source of his greatest astonishment, however, had been that the pathways that twined through what he had thought to be a trackless wilderness were, in reality, crowded highways along which travelers hurried to one destination or another. This stunningly beautiful land provided a wealth of resources that sheltered and sustained far more native inhabitants than he could ever have conceived. And even through a veil of grief and the fear of what the future held for him and his boys, he could not help seeing how desirable it was.

+———+

Joseph sat cross-legged on the ground in front of the rude wigewa, sullenly regarding the fort that loomed above the town's bark roofs. Although he could not make out the faces of the French soldiers who patrolled the ramparts, the setting sun's amber light glowed on their blue uniform coats and burnished their shouldered muskets. It was a foreboding scene that sent a shiver up his spine.

He had been greatly relieved that he, Christian, and the Specht children were not separated, but instead had been brought to this wigewa a short time after their arrival at the Indian town. He had watched anxiously as Daat and Specht were led off, all the while praying desperately that their separation would not be final.

Since then, they had been left in the charge of Franz and Hannah's guard, while the rest of the warriors hurried off to the fort. A steady stream of Indians staggered out of its gates carrying bottles, and Joseph watched as they broke into fights or collapsed to the ground in a drunken stupor. The sight caused his stomach to churn. He dreaded the warriors' return, especially for the sake of the younger children. There was no telling what they might do in such a state.

He scratched at a flea bite, his nose wrinkling at the dirt that crusted his skin and darkened his fingernails, the stench and coarse feel of his sweat-stiffened shirt, breechclout, and leggings. When Hannah climbed into his lap, he looked down, startled, then gathered her in his arms.

She turned her dirt-smudged face up to his. "Why do they have to get drunk?"

"I don't know, Hannah. I wish they wouldn't."

Franz crouched beside them, throwing a cautious glance at their guard, who lolled drowsily against the side of the wigewa. When the man paid them no attention, he sat down and leaned against Joseph's side.

"It makes them do bad things."

Joseph brushed back the matted, tangled hair from Hannah's forehead and gave Franz a reassuring pat. "Don't worry. I won't let them hurt you."

The words were no sooner out of his mouth than he wondered whether he would be able to keep that promise. He looked over at Christian, who sat apart from them on the opposite side of the fire circle, his blank gaze fixed on the ground. Noting how thin and wan his younger brother had become, Joseph bit his lip hard.

Christian's listlessness worried him. Ever since Shickellamy's Town, Christian had retreated into himself, only responding to his guard or to Daat, and then with little enthusiasm.

"When will Daati come back?"

"It shouldn't be long now," Joseph assured Franz cheerfully in spite of his fear to the contrary. "It's getting late, and we should get some food soon. We'll probably all eat together again like we have been."

Just then a group of white captives stumbled past, driven by a party of painted, armed warriors. Even from a few yards away he could smell the rum they had been drinking. Their angry shouts and the blows they laid on their prisoners made him cringe.

Hannah wrapped her arms around his neck. "I miss my Daati."

"*Ya,* I miss mine too." A wave of deep longing washed over Joseph.

Sobbing, Franz hid his face beneath Joseph's arm. "I want to go home!"

Joseph drew the children more tightly against him. The thought of being sent away from his father and brother and given, all alone, into the hands of savage, murderous strangers, terrified him. If the prospect affected him so strongly, what would it do to these younger ones? How would they and Christian survive, torn away from their fathers, the only family they had left?

Nor could he imagine losing any of them. He had come to depend on their presence, and he clung to them as much as they clung to him.

During the long days of their desperate journey, it had become clear to Joseph how numerous the Indians were and that this vast country belonged to them. Though French forts and trading posts dotted the wilderness, the Indians held power here. In this alien place he, his father and brother, and the Spechts were foreigners and outcasts whose welfare depended on the customs and whims of a strange and hostile people.

All thought of escape was now long past. That hope had died at Shickellamy's Town. It had been buried along their path as days had turned into more than a fortnight and countless miles separated them from all that had been known.

He started from his reverie when Hannah suddenly tightened her arms around his neck. He looked up to see several warriors from their party approaching.

Their loud voices and weaving steps warned him that they were drunk. Christian's guard was among them, and he beckoned to the boy as he slumped down against the wigewa's wall.

In spite of the man's slurred speech and bloodshot eyes, Christian became suddenly animated and went to him with apparent eagerness. The warrior dangled a trinket from his fingers, and the two were soon laughing together. Christian repeated some of his words as though trying to learn his language.

Balefully Joseph glared at the man. It felt as though he was stealing his brother away from him, as though Christian would soon be lost. And hatred and anger seethed in Joseph's heart, burning all the more intensely for the knowledge that he was powerless to stop it.

◆ ⋯⋯ ◆

JAKOB'S HEART ACHED. He had not spoken to Joseph and Christian since their departure from Fort Le Boeuf that morning, and then only briefly. His last glimpse of his boys had been when he and Specht were driven away to a separate cluster of wigewas.

The two of them had little to say as they sat at the fire circle, attempting to force down the oily, ill-smelling food set before them. Neither could swallow more than a mouthful.

At length Specht's guard rose with a grunt and motioned him to the next wigewa. They left Jakob alone with Shingas, who sprawled motionless on the other side of the fire, snoring, an empty rum bottle clenched in the crook of his arm.

For some time Jakob hunched by the fire, staring into the sputtering flames. He worried about how thin and pale Christian was becoming, about his emotional withdrawal and growing attachment to his guard.

Jakob had to admit that under the rigors of the journey he had become physically stronger. Joseph had too, although his seething anger worried Jakob as much as Christian's listlessness did.

The knowledge that he could do nothing for either of his boys or for the Spechts, who also continued to struggle, wore an endless circuit through his mind. Yet the dread certainty that all of them would soon be taken away from each other—perhaps even on the morrow—and concern for what would happen to his boys then oppressed him even more. And the despair he now fell into was deeper than the worst he had yet known.

The chill, windy night deepened and the flames died to sizzling embers. At last he withdrew into the small, bark-clad hut, where he fell blindly across the sleeping platform, his blanket clutched to him for the meager comfort it provided.

For an indefinite period he lay trembling in every limb, gripped by misery so intense he prayed that God would take his life. Then, clearly as though a voice spoke aloud, a verse from 1 Peter filtered into his mind.

"Ihr Lieben, lasset euch die Hitze, so euch begegnet, nicht befremden (die euch widerfährt, daß ihr versucht werdet) als widerführe euch etwas Seltsames; sondern freuet euch daß ihr Christo leidet . . . " Beloved, think it not strange concerning the fiery trial which is to try you, as though some strange thing had happened unto you: But rejoice, inasmuch as ye are partakers of Christ's sufferings . . .

It was a passage he had often pored over, praying for the bold faith of the martyrs if the time of trial should come upon him. Now it broke him.

I cannot bear this! Rejoice to have my wife and children killed, my home destroyed? Will you now take these boys—all I have left—from me as well? Ach, Jesus, spare us this! If we are to have nothing else, I accept it, Lord. Only leave us to one another!

Despite his pleas, the night remained as unyielding as iron. No soothing voice spoke from the wind that creaked the wigewa's stick walls and bark cladding. No tender, shielding presence comforted him.

During that seemingly endless night, unable to pray that God's will be done, he again mentally traced every foot of the path that had brought him to that place, as had become his habit each night before sleeping in order to hold despair at bay. Even the smallest details he committed firmly to memory in unyielding determination to someday escape, to somehow find a way to bring his boys home.

❖━━━━❖

CHRISTIAN WHIMPERED.

In the warmly lighted *Küche* Maami bent at the hearth, while the room filled with the tempting aroma of the stew bubbling over the fire. His mouth watering, he laughed at little Annali seated on the floor beside him, crowing and waving the wooden spoon Maami had given her to play with.

Blitz roused from sleep and trotted over to nuzzle his cheek, her fringed tail waving lazily side to side, and he buried his fingers in her luxuriant white coat. Suddenly Jake and Joseph burst into the house, red cheeked from the cold, windy night, elbowing each other playfully and giggling. Daati followed, carrying an overflowing pail of milk to Maami, who took it from him with the smile that always warmed Christian with the certainty of how much they loved each other.

He looked around him in delighted wonder. Johannes and Katie and their little ones were there too, and Barbara and her family as well. All of them were laughing and happy and safe.

The sharp crack of rifles rent the peaceful scene without warning. As suddenly, the fire on the hearth bloomed into an evil orange glare that exploded through the *Küche,* obliterating the others from his sight and leaving him all alone in a world of chaos and terror.

He jerked awake and threw off his blanket, shaking with wracking sobs, a deep void of loss crushing him. By slow degrees, consciousness returned, and he became aware that strong arms cradled him to a muscular chest, while gentle hands stroked his trembling limbs. When he opened his eyes, his guard was holding him securely.

The sight of the man's face brought the horrifying memory of the attack flooding back in full force, and Christian shrank from him, screaming for Maami and Daati.

His guard hushed him tenderly in a soothing voice, the soft syllables of his speech offering reassurance the boy so desperately needed. Yet Christian had watched this man and his companions kill mercilessly, and once more fear and confusion paralyzed him. As he did each time terror overwhelmed him, he repeated to himself his father's command to obey their captors.

He and Joseph and Daati were under these warriors' complete control. If he did not please them, they would kill the three of them. They would kill Hannah and Franz and their father. They might even go back and kill Johannes and Barbara and Christian's little nieces and nephews.

And he would be responsible.

Desperation seized him at the thought. Holding his breath, he forced a tremulous smile. As the warrior continued to rock and stroke him, Christian allowed his body to relax in the man's arms.

He soon became drowsy, and after a few minutes the warrior laid him back onto the sleeping platform. Covering Christian with his own blanket, he stretched out beside him. As Christian pressed against the warrior's body, with the man's heat warming him, terror receded, replaced by an unexpected sense of safety and protection.

For a reason unknown to him, this man who was stronger than his father and brother and who held the power of life and death over him, cared for him. In that lay safety for them all.

Relief flooded through Christian. He would do whatever was demanded of him without hesitation. By obedience, by offering respect and responding to the warrior's friendliness, he could save himself and the only ones he had left in the world.

And then maybe someday he would be allowed to return to them.

Chapter Twenty-two

Tuesday, October 10, 1757

HIS ARMS SHELTERING HIS BOYS, Jakob stared at the fort's commandant, feeling as though he was caught up in a nightmare that had no end. The tall, slender officer was clothed in a spotless white uniform trimmed in blue and gold. With unstudied ease he addressed the representatives of the tribes, both men and women, who crowded eagerly before the platform where he stood.

"Daati what are they saying?" Pressed against Jakob's side, Christian trembled uncontrollably.

Jakob shook his head. "Sounds like he's talking in the Indians' tongue."

He glanced at Joseph on his other side. The boy pressed his fist to his mouth, tears overflowing.

"They're going to take us away from each other."

Joseph's voice held finality, and Jakob tightened his arms around both boys' shoulders. *"Ya,"* he managed.

No reason to hold out hope when their future was clearly being decided, along with that of all the other white captives who huddled fearfully together, faces as pale and drawn as he knew his own must be. Even the youngest understood that none of them could stop what was happening, that neither protest nor resistance would make a difference and might earn a blow.

Jakob's stomach growled with hunger. He took in his surroundings, feeling dazed and weak, lightheaded from the long, sleepless night.

The walls of the large, square stockade were more than twelve feet high, with cannon ports cut into them at regular intervals, interspersed by smaller loopholes for muskets. Stout buildings of log or stone lined the central parade ground, and others occupied the interior of the triangular bastions projecting from each corner. It was an intimidating sight meant to arouse the bleak hopelessness that overwhelmed Jakob.

Early that morning all the captives had been driven into the fort, where representatives from the tribes had already gathered. Specht and his children had been carried out of Jakob's sight in the commotion, but by fierce effort he had managed to keep Joseph and Christian at his side.

At first wails of grief and despair had risen from the women and children, while the men clutched their loved ones in silent anguish. But after waiting for more than an hour without food or water, while the sun rose and soldiers came and went, they at last settled to stand hushed and motionless, numbly anticipating the moment when the last treasure left to them on earth would be rent from their arms.

Both boys pressed into Jakob, making no effort to conceal their fear, while rage and terror twisted in his gut in equal measure. There were perhaps fifty white prisoners, he estimated. How many others had passed through this fort since the war's beginning? And what had become of them?

Now he and his boys would join those invisible ranks. And Johannes and Barbara and the rest of their family would never know where they had been taken or whether they still lived.

A few moments earlier a low moan had greeted the commandant as he took his place on the platform to hear the petitions of the tribes. Their representatives spoke in turn, different factions clearly debating what was to be done with individual captives, often waving an arm toward one or another, who cowered from the dark glances directed toward them.

Suddenly and simply it was over, and a ripple of motion passed through the crowd like a sigh. The French commander made a short final address, smiling broadly. Then he gave a signal, and warriors from each tribe petitioning for its share of the prisoners strode to the captives to unceremoniously tear children from the arms of their parents and wives from their husbands.

As anguished cries rose from their ranks, Jakob pulled Joseph and Christian around to face him, speaking as calmly as he could manage. "If they take you so far away and keep you so long that you forget our language, never forget the Lord's Prayer. Do you hear?"

Both boys nodded dumbly, blinking back tears.

"Say it with me now," he commanded, and then, his voice quavering, he led them in reciting the familiar, cherished words: *"Unser Vater in dem Himmel! Dein Name werde geheiligt."* Our Father Which art in heaven, hallowed be thy name.

Tearfully Christian struggled to repeat the words, catching his breath in a convulsive sob between each one.

"*Dein Reich komme. Dein Wille geschehe auf Erden wie im Himmel.*" Thy kingdom come. Thy will be done in earth, as it is in heaven.

Turning his head away, Joseph stared hard at the far side of the fort. *Is this God's will?* he demanded bitterly.

"*Unser täglich Brot gib uns heute. Und vergib uns unsere Schulden, wie wir unsern Schuldigern vergeben.*" Give us this day our daily bread. And forgive us our debts, as we forgive our debtors.

Forgive? Anger constricted Joseph's chest. *How can I ever forgive what these murderers have done—what they're doing to us now?*

They were enveloped in tumult as all around them mothers screamed and children fought to tear out of their captors' arms. Through the milling crowd, Joseph saw one of the men resist, only to be viciously clubbed to the ground.

As though he were oblivious of the chaotic scene around them, Daat continued: "*Und führe uns nicht in Versuchung, sondern erlöse uns von dem Uebel . . .* " And lead us not into temptation, but deliver us from evil . . .

Deliver us from evil? The words choked in Joseph's throat, and he wrenched out of his father's embrace as Daat concluded in a rush, "*Denn dein ist das Reich und die Kraft und die Herrlichkeit in Ewigkeit. Amen.*" For Thine is the kingdom, and the power, and the glory, forever. . . .

A storm of grief, anguish, terror, and confusion raged inside Joseph. Like a flame, the image of Jake's limp body sprawled on the ground, his skull bared by the scalping knife, burned in his memory. This God they prayed to had allowed Jake—his closest confidante, his hero, his unfailing advocate and defense against their father's unbending sternness—to be violently ripped away from him.

Where had God been when Daat refused to allow them to defend themselves while there was yet hope they could do so? Where was He when they were trapped in the cellar with the house burning down over their heads and when the Indians fell upon them in brutal slaughter?

Where was this supposed God now when Christli and Daat were being torn away from him too?

Sobs convulsed him. Shaking off Daat's hand, he pulled away.

What purpose could God have in any of this? Was there even a God at all? Had he and Maam and Daat and their whole family built their lives on a lie?

If Daat really loved us, he would at least have allowed the rest of us to defend ourselves! Joseph's mind cried out. *This is all his fault! If he'd only given a little ground, none of this would have happened!*

Through his tears he focused on Christian's ashen, drawn face, and his heart went out to his little brother. Why had he ever resented Christian and pushed him away? How could he not have loved him as he had loved Jake? Now he yearned to clasp him to his bosom before it was too late and share the comforting words Daat ought to have said and hadn't.

"Christli—" Joseph began. He broke off as Christian's guard stepped to the boy's side and took him by the hand.

"Wait!" Joseph shouted, heat rushing to his face. "Let me talk to my brother!"

The warrior responded with a scowl and a guttural snarl. Snatching Christian up in his arms, he started to walk away.

Everything around Christian blurred into a black void. "Daati! Daati!" he screamed in panic, reaching desperately for his father as he tried to fight out of the arms that held him fast. "Don't let them take me away! Please let me stay with you, Daati! I promise I'll be good! Joseph, don't go—don't leave me alone!"

"No! Give us just a minute together! Just one—"

Daat's imploring cry was followed by the sound of a blow, and his words abruptly choked off. Swinging around in horror, Joseph caught a glimpse of Daat's face, blood dripping from his mouth. Their eyes met for a brief instant, then one of the fiercest warriors from a tribe Joseph did not recognize wrenched his father toward a small clutch of captives held under guard near the fort's gates.

A stern command broke into Joseph's consciousness. When a rough hand clamped over his shoulder, without thinking he thrust off the painful grip and fought to break through to Daat, and then to Christian, each being carried off in a different direction.

Although his heart cried out to them, his throat was too tight to allow speech. And quickly he was surrounded by a circle of warriors who blocked them from his sight.

+ - - - - +

THE LAST SIGHT OF HIS SONS as they vanished into the churning crowd of captives and warriors burned into Jakob's memory: Christian reaching out to him in terrified appeal. Joseph's desperate, accusing gaze.

O Gott, *be merciful to them! Keep them faithful to You. Keep them alive.*

Instinctively he bowed his head and hunched his shoulders against the glancing blows that drove him and his fellow captives through the fort's massive gates. But he felt nothing.

The company made its way along the narrow lanes between wigewas and tents to the town's outskirts. In dull surprise he became aware that Specht walked beside him, shaking with sobs so wrenching that he repeatedly stumbled.

"They took my children!" he cried, inconsolable. "They were all I had left, Jake, and those French devils sold them to the savages who killed their Maam!"

Fighting down tears as they turned onto a path angling to the southeast, Jakob blindly caressed the small lump the peach pit made under his threadbare sash. This time, instead of the comfort it had always provided, the feel of it brought an ache so intense it was all he could to keep from crying aloud.

Beside him, Specht slipped on uneven ground and lost his balance. Had Jakob not caught him, he would have sprawled headlong.

Immediately the nearest warrior drew his tomahawk, his face contorting in a fierce frown as he stepped menacingly toward them. Jakob grabbed Specht under the arms and straightened, jerking him to his feet in terrified haste, and all but dragged him along the path. On either side, their fellow captives glanced at them, then quickly away as though fearing a blow, their faces reflecting Jakob's own anguish.

Specht pulled out of his grip and staggered forward, weeping, his hand pressed over his face. "I'll never see my little ones again. I'll never know whether they live or die!"

Each word tore at Jakob's heart. *I didn't tell Joseph and Christli I love them,* he thought numbly. *How could I have let my boys go without telling them that?*

In the midst of that sorrowful company, his vision so blurred he could hardly make out the ground beneath his feet, he stumbled on, his heart bleeding slowly out, drop by drop, with every painful step.

Coming soon!

The Return

Book 2 of the Northkill Amish Series

IN THIS DEEPLY MOVING and inspiring conclusion to the Northkill Amish Series, Jakob and his sons struggle to adapt to new lives among the tribes to which they were given. Joseph and Christian are adopted into separate Delaware clans and families and gradually reconcile to their new lives. Meanwhile, held among the Seneca, Jakob never gives up hope of finding his boys and bringing them home.

In May 1758, Jakob makes a daring escape. Enduring a harrowing journey over rugged terrain and long miles while evading recapture, he finally reaches home to discover that Barbara, Johannes, and Anna Blanck have never given up hope of finding him and the boys.

Together, while the war grinds to its close, they repeatedly petition the government for aid to find Joseph and Christian and negotiate their release. Jakob travels to conferences between the British and the Indians hoping to find his sons, each time suffering another bitter disappointment.

Undeterred by frustrated hopes, false promises, dead ends, and discouragement, Jakob, his older children, and Anna cling to faith that God's perfect plan will one day be accomplished and that the day of blessing, promised through all the years of sorrow, will at last find a joyous fulfillment.

Glossary

Colonial Terms

palisade: stockade; the walls of a fort constructed with pointed logs set upright in a trench

plantation: common colonial term for farm

shift: a women's long undergarment, also worn as nightwear

French Words and Phrases

ami, (pl.) amis: friend, friends

bateau, (pl.) bateaux: a flat-bottomed,shallow-draft boat used for transporting goods

bon: good

paix: peace

German Words and Phrases

Apfelschnitzen: a gathering to cut and prepare ripe apples for drying and cooking

bleib still: stay quiet

Blitz: lightning

Daat, Daati: dad; daddy

danke: thank you

die: (pronounced dee), the

English, (pl.) Englishe: the English; non-Germans

Frau: woman, Mrs.

Geh vek: go away

Gott: God

Grossdaati: grandfather

Grossmaami: grandmother

guud: good

Halsduch: women's neck cloth or cape

Halt, halten: halt, stop

Haube, (pl.) Hauben: cap, women's head covering

Haus: house

Herr: Mr., Lord

Hochzeit: wedding

iss: is

iverzwarich: crosswise, at odds

Kammer, (pl.) Kammern: bedchamber, bedchambers

Kind, (pl.) Kinder: child; children

kom: come

Küche: kitchen

Liebe: love, beloved, dear one

Maami, Maam: mommy; mom

nay: no

nieder: down

schnell: quick, quickly

der Schweiz: Switzerland

Sprüche: Proverbs

Stube: parlor

Täuferlehrer: Anabaptist minister

Tochter: daughter

Vas is des? What is this?

Vas iss los?: What's going on? What's the matter?

Vater: father

ya: yes

weltlich: worldly

Indian Words

nchutièstuk: friend

wigewa: a domed dwelling for one family, common among Eastern
Woodland Indians, framed with poles and overlaid with bark,
woven mats, or animal hides

Appendix

IN WRITING A WORK of historical fiction, the author's goal is to interpret a long-ago period to modern-day readers for education, inspiration, and entertainment. As we developed *Northkill,* we carefully researched the period and what is known about our ancestors so we could make the story as accurate and authentic as possible. Unfortunately, the historical record always includes problematic gaps, and it inevitably becomes necessary to make educated or imaginative guesses to fill them in. The following is an explanation of the most important decisions we made in writing this fictional account of our ancestors' lives in the Northkill Amish-Mennonite community in eighteenth-century Pennsylvania.

Names

When we began planning *Northkill,* we had a ready-made cast of characters, including Jacob, his wife, their children, and the members of their community. But we had a huge problem. The names of our maternal ancestor, Jacob's wife, and the baby who was killed in the Indian attack don't appear in any historical accounts. We couldn't write the story without naming them, so we had to make the best decisions we could.

Virgil Miller's suggestion in an article in the December 2000 issue of the *JHFA Family Newsletter* that Jacob's wife might have been named Anna "because it is the only female name used in all the families of the immigrant Jacob's children," held a great deal of weight. Also, in the March 2001 issue, Daniel Hochstetler speculated that she may have been the sister of Christian Berkey, who settled in Berks County in 1737. *Early Amish Land Grants in Berks County, Pennsylvania,* also lists a Jacob Berkey, whose land adjoined Christian's as possibly being Christian's older brother.

Thus in *Northkill* Jacob's wife is named Anna, and Jakob and Christian Buerki (using the German spelling) appear as her brothers. And since Jacob and Anna's first daughter was named Barbara, it seemed plausible that the second daughter, who was killed in the attack, could plausibly have been named after her mother. Accordingly, we chose the diminutive form, Annali, as her name.

There were a number of other choices we had to make regarding first names. Many of the German names were given in their English form in the records of the time. In addition, in the Amish and Mennonite culture, you encounter many repeated names that result from common patterns of naming. Our family members and many others in the Northkill community shared the same names. To help distinguish between them, we settled on varying the spellings of names according to whether the character was born in this country or not.

In *Northkill,* when the English spelling of a name is different from the German spelling, the original German spelling is used for those born in Europe, and the anglicized form is used for those born in this country. Thus Jacob becomes Jakob, Jacob Jr. is shortened to Jake, and other younger members of the community with the same name are designated as Jacob. There were multitudes of Hans (John), so our John became Johannes, and other Johns became Hans or Hannes. There were lots of Christians, so we decided that because he is a main character our Christian would remain Christian in narrative passages, but during his childhood his family members would call him by the diminutive form Christli. Christian Stutzman and Christian Buerki share the nickname Crist.

Characters' Ages and Birth Order

Since we don't know the birth dates and exact ages of most of our characters, it was necessary for us to go with what seems most likely considering the facts we do know, such as the year of marriage and/or the first child's birth, where known.

Tradition holds that John was around 3 years old when he came to this country with his parents. There was possibly another child with them, Barbara being the most likely. Since family tradition has proved to be remarkably accurate, we chose to go with John being around 3 years of age when our ancestors immigrated in 1738. If he was 3 when they arrived in November of that year, he would have been born in 1735. However, it's also possible that he was 3 when the family embarked on their journey and 4 by the time he arrived in November 1738.

The next issue we had to resolve was whether Barbara was the older or younger of the two. No documentation has been found to resolve this dispute, and the estimates we found split fairly evenly between placing her birth date a couple of years before or after John's. Obviously we have no way of knowing which is correct. If she was older, John married and had a child before she did, which is not as likely.

In our story we made her the younger, with John being born in 1734 and Barbara a little more than a year later in the fall of 1735. That would make her 3 when the family arrived in Philadelphia. In *Northkill* she has just turned 17 when the story begins in September 1752.

We felt Jacob, Jr. was most likely born within a year of the family's arrival in this country. Considering the documented hardships of a journey in a crowded, primitive sailing ship across 3,000 miles of ocean, it's highly unlikely that the mother of the family became pregnant while aboard due to crowded conditions, lack of privacy, sea sickness, and other illnesses. If she was pregnant when the journey began, she would almost certainly have lost the baby en route. And if they brought an infant with them, it's doubtful it could have survived the journey. Wrenching contemporary accounts document numerous deaths of immigrants' small children and infants aboard these ships.

Some accounts place Jacob Jr.'s birth in 1740, and it's reasonable to assume that he was born about a year after the family settled in the Northkill community, after the hardships of their emigration were over. If true, that would make him 17 at time of the attack.

For the ages of Joseph and Christian, we followed Beth Hostetler Mark's account in *Our Flesh and Blood* and Jonathan J. Hostetler's chronological account in "Jacob Hochstetler and Descendents." They place their birth dates in 1742 and 1746 respectively, thus Joseph would have been 15 at the time of the attack, and Christian 11. This is in line with the information Jacob gave when he petitioned the governor to have his captured sons returned to him.

The age of the young daughter who was killed was another question that can't be answered. Some accounts make her older than Christian. We felt that was unlikely for several reasons. For one, there is no family tradition about her. If she had had several years of shared history with the family, some things about her would surely have been remembered and passed down in oral tradition.

The fact that her story is completely blank argues to us that she was an infant. Another strong argument for her being very young is that the Indians killed her. Because of the brutal pace the Indians set when they carried captives away, those who couldn't keep up because they were wounded, as Jacob, Jr. was; unfit for the journey and of no value to them, as Jacob, Sr.'s middle-aged wife was; or too young to travel, as an infant would be, were killed.

If this daughter had been older than Christian, or even a few years younger, she would more likely have been a valuable captive, who would be taken, as many young chldren captured in frontier raids were. But she was not, and it seems the most plausible to set her age at around a year.

Another puzzling issue was the gap in Anna's childbearing between Christian and the baby who was killed. It was very common during this period for parents to lose children at an early age. More than likely Anna suffered one or more miscarriages, stillbirths, or had a baby who died not long ssafter birth. If the legend is true that the Indians killed the mother of the family in such a violent manner because of her hostility toward them, such a loss could account for her being overly emotional and protective of her children. The confrontation with the Indians at the beginning of *Northkill* portrays this, foreshadowing the attack and the manner of Anna's death.

Dress

Contrary to what you might think, Amish clothing has changed quite a bit over the centuries. There aren't many resources that give descriptions of eighteenth-century Amish dress; however, *Mennonite Attire through Four Centuries* by Melvin Gingerich was very helpful although it doesn't include much specific information about the 1750s. During that period, however, Amish dress would have been similar to Mennonite dress, but plainer, so we made some educated guesses.

In colonial times Amish men would most likely have worn a long shirt that also served as nightwear, a waistcoat, and knee breeches, with long hose and plain shoes without buckles. A dress jacket was added for formal occasions such as attendance at church. Amish women would have worn a plain mid-calf-length petticoat with a separate bodice pinned together in the front. For underwear, a voluminous shift did double duty as a nightgown. Over this and under their bodice, colonial women wore stays to support the bosom, but we have no way of knowing whether Amish women did so. A white linen cap, a neck cloth that covered the neck and bosom, an apron, hose and shoes completed their attire.

Outdoors both men and women wore black beaver-felt hats with a low crown in cooler weather. In the summer women wore wide-brimmed straw hats with low crowns. These were called scoops because of the shape that resulted when they passed a ribbon or cord over the crown and tied it under the chin, pulling the brim down on both sides of the head.

Anna Blanck

We know that Joseph married Anna sometime after he returned from captivity among the Indians. Because they were with the Indians for so long, both he and Christian found it very difficult to re-assimilate into the Amish culture. It was through their marriages that they became reconciled to their return.

Although there is no definitive proof that Joseph and Anna knew each other before his capture, there is some evidence that their parents knew each other in the Alsace. That makes it plausible that they had at least met. By giving them a prior relationship, we're able to make Anna a strong ally in Barbara's quest to find her father and brothers and bring them home, and also to strengthen the bonds that enabled Joseph to finally readjust to his family and community.

Map

Our story wouldn't be complete without a map showing the probable route Jakob and his sons were taken on when the Indians carried them away. The map included at the beginning of this book is based on one drawn in 1756, just a year before the attack. At that time, Pennsylvania had not been completely surveyed. Clearly the mapmaker made some guesses about the colony's western regions, which were under the control of the French at the time. The Western Branch of the Susquehanna River, for example, isn't correctly laid out, and distances between various points aren't exact. But we chose to keep these quirks because the American colonists were familiar with this and similar maps, which would have informed their understanding of their environment.

Just as we do today, the Indians traveled along established "highways" rather than wandering through unfamiliar wilderness. These paths were established by the native peoples in ancient times for travel between towns, trade, and warfare. The Hochstetler plantation lay about two miles from the base of the Blue Mountain, and it is most likely that after the attack the war party took our ancestors over this ridge via the Northkill Gap in order to avoid encountering settlers and militia patrols. From there they would have headed west to the closest Indian path, the Tulpehocken-Shamokin Path that led to the old Indian town of Shamokin at the confluence of the eastern and western branches of the Susquehanna.

Shamokin was abandoned the previous year when the British occupied the area and built a major stronghold, Fort Augusta, there. According to the deposition Jakob gave the British after his escape the following spring, they forded the river twenty miles below the fort and traveled along the west branch of the Susquehanna. This route places them on the Great Island Path, several miles south of the river but bearing along its course to Great Island, the shortest and most direct route to their eventual destination.

At Great Island they would have crossed the river to follow the Great Shamokin Path to Chinklakamoose. There they would turn onto the Venango Path, heading north to Fort Machault, the first of the French forts Jakob mentions in his deposition. After a three-day journey aboard large canoes the French called bateaux, they reached the second fort he described, Fort Le Boeuf. And from there, after a one-day portage, they reached Fort Presque Isle.

In all, their journey took them approximately 370 miles in 17 days. It is a testimony to their fortitude and endurance that they made it there. That Jakob managed to escape and make his way home over such a distance in spite of daunting obstacles is astonishing. That he found his boys and eventually brought them home as well is even more so. In Book 2, *The Return,* our map will show the route he took to come home.

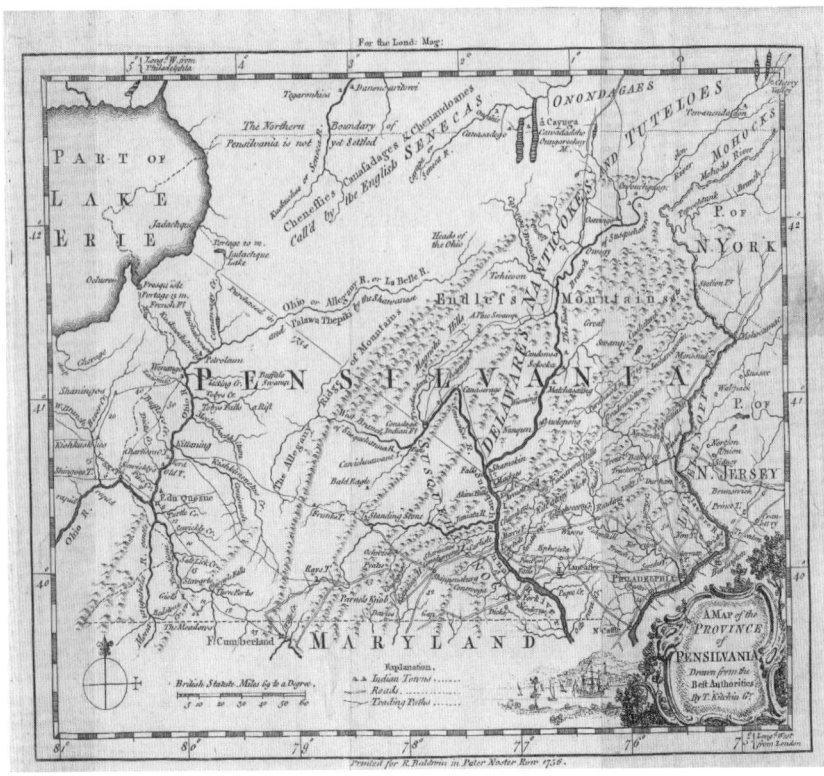

The original 1756 map used as the basis for the one that appears on pages 10 and 11. For a larger image, go to http://northkill.blogspot.com/2013/10/mapping-captives-journey.html.